Beneath the Waves

Shannon Carse

*For anyone searching to figure out who you are or where you belong.
I see you. Open your eyes and take a deep breath. You're already exactly
where you're meant to be.*

And for Betty

Playlist

Secondhand Smoke — Kelsea Ballerini

Growing Sideways — Noah Kahan

Modern Girl — Bleachers

I'm Not A Cynic — Alec Benjamin

Caught in the Middle — Paramore

Mind Is A Prison — Alec Benjamin

Landslide — Fleetwood Mac

Blame Brett — The Beaches

Changes — David Bowie

Backwards Traveller — Wings

Treacherous (Taylor's Version) — Taylor Swift

Chicken — Your Neighbors

Falls — ODESZA ft. Sasha Alex Sloan

Electric Touch (Taylor's Version) — Taylor Swift ft. Fall Out Boy

How Long — Suffs
This Is Me Trying — Taylor Swift
Paper Crown — Alec Benjamin
The Reason — Hoobastank
Mirrorball — Taylor Swift
I Found — Amber Run
Ease My Mind — Ben Platt
Hurt — Johnny Cash
Keep Marching — Suffs
And So It Goes — Billy Joel
Half of Forever — Henrik
Flesh and Bone — CJ Starnes
The Scientist — Coldplay
Francesca — Hozier
You're My Home — Billy Joel
Timeless (Taylor's Version) — Taylor Swift
Forever — Dropkick Murphys
Thank You Aimee — Taylor Swift

"Fearless is not the absence of fear. It's not being completely unafraid. To me, fearless is having fears. Fearless is having doubts. Lots of them. To me, fearless is living in spite of those things that scare you to death."

—*TAYLOR SWIFT*

"We're all traveling through time together, every day of our lives.
All we can do is do our best to relish this remarkable ride."

—ABOUT TIME

Prologue

SECONDHAND SMOKE BY KELSEA BALLERINI

There's a carousel in Boston Common that I've been coming to since I was a child. Every Saturday morning when I was little, without fail, my father would bring me there. He'd watch me hop on and pick the same horse every time. She was hand carved, with a white mane, blue eyes, and a golden saddle. Inspired by the mother in *The Aristocats*, I named her Duchess.

Riding Duchess, I was a knight on a mission, galloping off to save the kingdom. I always lived in these daydreams as a child. I'd build entire worlds in my head and make my home inside them.

The first time we came, I wasn't old enough to ride alone yet, so he would hop on with me. He'd pick the horse next to mine and we would laugh together as our horses ran up and down on a joint mission to save the kingdom. We came every Saturday, right after breakfast, while dew still kissed the grass.

When I was four, I was old enough to ride alone. Dad would pay for three rides and send me on my way while he waited on a bench, the same one every weekend. He'd sit there, reading the newspaper, glancing up every so often. That bench became part of the tradition, too. Just me, my horse, and him.

Then, one Saturday, everything changed.

I remember it was April. The mild spring air was chilly. I whizzed around in circles, pretending my horse was outrunning a dragon. Even in my imaginary world, I could sense something was different. I remember my father's face every time the carousel rotated past him. He was watching me, making sure his kid still had ten fingers and ten toes, but in his eyes was a far off look. Like he was there, but not really *there*. He didn't look happy, or even sad. Just empty. I knew something was going on, even at such a young and innocent age. He was silent the entire walk to the park. It felt like he needed to tell me something, but couldn't figure out how.

When I got off the carousel, I ran over to the bench to get money for a few more rides.

"No, three rides are enough. Sit down, sweetpea. We need to talk," he said as he gently patted the spot next to him on the bench.

I climbed on to the bench next to him, my little legs in small yellow Wellington boots dangling off the seat.

Dad looked at me and took a deep breath. His eyes that moments ago seemed somewhere else, now seem locked in and serious.

"Alice," he said, voice tight, "you know I love you very much. That will never change, honey. But it's just going to be the two of us from now on, okay?"

I didn't understand. "Mommy?"

He sighed and looked around like the answer might be hiding somewhere in the park. As a child, I couldn't name the look on his face, but now I know—it was the expression of a man trying to explain something he barely understood himself. He glanced wistfully over at the carousel I was just riding. I was mindlessly happy, and didn't realize my life was about to change. His face filled with guilt, as if he realized he was about to shatter the glass dome around my perfect world.

"Well, you know how some people love the carousel and can ride it dozens of times in a row and not get dizzy? And other people can't ride it at all without getting sick?"

I nodded, still confused.

"Well... Mommy doesn't like the carousel like you and I do. Mommy gets dizzy with the spinning. She had to get off the carousel, honey."

At four years old, I couldn't comprehend what he was trying to explain to me. I cried a little and then just accepted it, as children tend to do. I didn't realize that "from now on" didn't mean till dinner time, it meant *forever*.

We continued to come to the park, and to the carousel, every Saturday morning after that. It was our little tradition, but it became less magical, less innocent. He would pay for three rides and sit on the bench with his newspaper or a case file. I would play and then we would sit together for a while.

I kept riding until I got older and the horses lost their charm. Eventually, our tradition became just the bench. We'd sit and talk—about school, sports, politics. But never, ever, about *her*.

When I was in college and home for school breaks, we picked the tradition back up. We would talk about my courses and professors. He would read my papers and offer his opinions or praise. He'd show me plans for his latest home renovation projects. Most of our outings consisted of the routine of everyday conversation - not boring, but comfortable. We kept our conversations at a surface level, avoiding anything deep or emotional.

Then, during grad school, he asked me to sit down again.

Same bench. Different news.

He told me he was sick and I instantly felt like a child again, unable to fully comprehend what he meant. I kept asking if it was a cold. Something easy that I could fix. I think I always knew what he meant, but I needed him to say the word. The big one. *Cancer.*

That's impossible. He's too young. Has time truly been this harsh on him? Hasn't he been through enough? Haven't we both?

I remember feeling, once again, like I'd been blindsided. I thought back to that first time, many years ago, and how my legs swung off the bench as he talked. This time my legs touched the ground, and yet I felt no more grown up or prepared.

At that point, I realized that our tradition was more than just carousel rides and casual conversation. Mixed amongst the pleasant outings we shared here were moments of loss and pain. He would use my place of joy and escape to deliver the worst news to me throughout my life. I believe he thought he was softening the blow, or perhaps he didn't even realize he was doing it at all. But internally, it meant that I couldn't trust anything, even a good thing. Maybe *especially* a good thing. Something will always pull the rug out from underneath me. Even a safe place can become haunted.

Life is a lot like a carousel. Round and round we go, circling to nowhere in particular. The horses go up and down, like the way life moves through peaks and valleys. We can rise to the top, but something will certainly always bring you back down.

There's no way to get off. No matter what, the world keeps moving. We love people; we lose people, but the carousel continues to turn. It never stops.

Chapter One

"Ali. Hey? Are you still with me?"

My senses quickly come back to me as a warm voice snaps me out of the rabbit hole of thoughts swirling through my head. I can taste the slight bit of salt in the corner of my mouth that's been rolling down my cheek. My body is burrowed in the corner of the sofa, knees bent and held up to my chest. I grip my legs tightly with my arms. My knuckles are almost white from holding myself into a tight ball.

I look like I'm playing defense. And maybe I am. It's like that popcorn game kids play on a trampoline where you jump and try to break the others open. Only this time, I'm an adult and it's my therapist, Dr. Julia Kassen, trying to break me open.

I've been seeing Dr. Kassen for the last year. Long enough for her to have me figured out. I'm desperate not to repeat my parents' mistakes, but if I'm being honest, I'm terrified that I already have. I can't help myself from sabotaging my chance of happiness. I want things, but I don't know how to let myself have them, or enjoy them, or even be worthy of them.

I quickly try to recover composure, readjusting in my seat to appear more present. I straighten out my back and clear my throat quietly, brushing away invisible dirt from my jeans. My mind traveled somewhere and I don't want her to follow the trail. I don't even remember what we were talking about before I drifted off to that memory.

"I'm sorry," I murmur. "What was the question again?"

Her eyes narrow on me as she peers over the glasses sitting on the end of her nose. She's writing something in her notepad. I'm curious about what she writes, but I'm also afraid to know. I imagine it's something like, *emotionally avoidant* or *classic abandonment issues*. What's even scarier than someone being wrong about you is them being right. Especially when it's a truth you already know about yourself. But having someone hold the mirror up for you to face it head on is even more daunting. It's easier to take the worst parts of you and shove them into a corner to avoid them.

"Well, I asked how your personal life has been going lately," she says, voice even. "But, after that look on your face, I'd like to know where your brain went just now."

"It's nothing," I lie. I quickly try to shut down where this is going. I know it's relevant, but I don't want to talk about it. I'd almost rather talk about my lack of a personal life or pathetic attempts at dating than get into the traumatic shit from my childhood, even though I know, broken as I am, that those two things are directly related.

Dr. Kassen doesn't flinch. "Well, it's not nothing. Judging by how cagey you're being, I'd say it's probably the answer to everything." She sets down her notepad, her tone becoming softer, more serious. "Ali, come on. What were you thinking about?"

I sigh, tilting my head back and forth, debating whether to offer any crumb of information. I know I need to open up, but I'm also hesitant to see where this leads. I cave in a little.

"My mom," I say nonchalantly, hoping the casual tone will make her think there's nothing to see here. It's like I'm tossing a pebble into the water and hoping it doesn't ripple.

"What specifically about her?"

"Nothing. Let's move on." I tighten the hold I have on my legs, wishing I could burrow into the sofa and disappear. Why did I decide therapy was a good idea? I knew I'd have to open up about this stuff, yet when the time comes, I don't want to. I want Dr. Kassen's help, but I don't know how to just let her do her job. I want to heal, but I'm terrified of ripping off the bandage and exposing my wounds to the open air.

Dr. Kassen refuses to move on. "No, Ali. This means something. Come on, open up. I know it's hard, but you won't heal without bleeding a little first." She isn't letting me out of this one.

"I was thinking about the day she abandoned me," I say matter-of-factly. Maybe if I say it like it means nothing, it will.

"What do you remember?"

I sigh, annoyed. "I was four. I remember it was April. My bedroom window was cracked open, and the air felt cool. I know it was a Saturday morning because I remember watching cartoons. Dad had run out to get coffee. Mom put me in the den to watch television and shut the French doors behind her when she left, and she never did that. She never shut the doors. I remember feeling like it was to distract me from something, but I wasn't sure what."

"And then what?" Dr. Kassen presses.

"I remember the sounds. I heard her run up the stairs, and it sounded like she was moving something heavy. The front door opened and all the movement upstairs abruptly stopped. Everything went still. After a few moments, I could hear her and Dad's voices in the upstairs hallway. Not the words, but the panic in their voices. I heard rushed footsteps coming down the stairs. I peeked through an opening in the curtain on the door and saw a yellow leather suitcase in the hallway."

I take a breath, letting the memory settle. "Once they were outside, I could hear my dad pleading, 'Katherine, what about Alice?' Mom said, 'I'm sorry.' Her voice sounded sad, but firm. His hand was around her wrist, and she pulled away from him. I moved over to the bay window and watched her walk out the door with her suitcase and get into a taxi. She didn't even look back."

Dr. Kassen sighs and tilts her head. "Ali, I didn't realize you saw it happen."

"Yeah." I shrug. "I sat there for a while. I wasn't sure if I should come out, and I knew eavesdropping was naughty. I could hear Dad pacing back and forth in the hallway. Eventually he came in, put my shoes on, and said we were going to the park."

"And that's when he told you what happened?"

"Yep. Well... sort of. He said nothing the entire way there, just held my hand as we walked in silence. He let me ride the carousel like usual and then sat me down on the bench to drop the bomb on me. He gave me some metaphorical bullshit about carousels and how she had to get off." I sigh and shake my head. "The long and short of it, I came to realize eventually, was that she just didn't want to be a wife and mother, so she just got up and abandoned us."

"And there it is." Dr. Kassen sounds like she's just had an epiphany. The imaginary light bulb shining brightly over her head. The realization of: *oh, this is why Alice is so fucked up*.

"There what is?"

"Ali, you've used the term abandoned twice now. You haven't said your parents split, or your mother left. You've chosen to use the term abandoned. Why do you think that is?"

"Because that's what she did." The words come out sharper than I intended. A spade is a spade. Why would I call it anything other than what it is? "She dumped me in the den like I was just a plant that needed watering later."

"But have you ever considered this could be why you struggle with relationships? Maybe why you don't trust people or let your guard down for them?"

"What are you talking about?" I stare across her office, fixing my gaze on a vase of flowers on her desk. It's easier than looking her in the eye while I pretend my mother has had no influence on me.

Dr. Kassen leans forward and presses again. "Ali, your mother left you. This wasn't just a typical divorce and split up of the family after years of struggle or unhappiness. You've said your childhood until that point was idyllic, that you didn't see it coming. She left your father, giving almost no reason, and left you behind. That *has* to affect you."

"Nope, not at all." I sit in my indignation. I dig my heels in, though I know I have no standing. I don't think my childhood before her leaving was idyllic. It was never a Hallmark movie. I just think as a child I was blind to all the red flags and didn't realize I was living in a lie.

Even at only four years old, I wasn't particularly close with my mother. She wasn't doting or hands on, we just sort of existed in the same space. There were moments where she seemed to display affection toward me, but they were scarce. Between my workaholic father and my distant mother, I learned to be self sufficient at a very early age. Her leaving me wasn't an emotional gut punch until years later, when the development of my brain could catch up and unpack it all. It wasn't until those moments growing up when you truly need your mother that I understood the impact of it. Like when I was a teenager and my body changed, or when the first boy broke my heart. Dad did his best to fumble through the embarrassing topics, but we never really discussed her again.

"Stop it," Dr. Kassen says, seeing straight through my facade. "You know it has. It's okay to admit that."

Fine. Let's dig up this grave then, shall we?

The anger that's been building inside me bubbles to the surface. I slap my right hand down onto my open palm. "It's not fucking fair! She just left me. She put me in that room and just walked out the door. She didn't say goodbye. She barely gave me a thought. Who fucking does that to a child? She didn't want me and she sure as shit has made no effort to know me my entire life. She shouldn't get some power now to be the reason for how I've turned out or what problems I have. She doesn't even deserve the honor of being a terrible mother. She wasn't a mother at all." I am breathless, and I can feel my cheeks burning as my hands shake. "Whatever, I don't need her. I had Dad, that was enough. I did just fine on my own."

Dr. Kassen's eyes are sympathetic as she pushes her glasses back up the bridge of her nose. She's clearly gotten the spark she wanted from me. She shifts in her chair to redirect the conversation.

"Ali, did you just hear yourself? You said even though you had your father, you did just fine on your own. You've been isolating yourself. You keep everyone at an arm's length, pushing away any connection."

I feel myself getting angrier and defensive. "Yeah, well, they can't hurt me or leave me if they never get close enough." I cross my arms, as if my obvious attachment issues are some kind of battle wound to be proud of.

"Look, Ali. You have endured unfathomable loss in your life, and I know how much pain it has caused you. You've been so occupied trying to protect child Ali that you've neglected to take care of adult Ali. You are resilient. But in that resilience, you have built walls around yourself. And those walls don't just keep danger out, they also deflect love, joy, and happiness. You deserve those things, Ali."

"I don't know how to have them," I admit, voice small.

"That's why we're doing the work here. Because one day, you're going to meet someone worth bringing down your walls for and taking that risk."

If you say so, Doc. I don't know why I get so defensive with Dr. Kassen when I'm the one seeking her help. Truthfully, I do want these things. I don't want to be alone, but I've dug myself into a hole so deep I just can't see a way to climb out. I just don't know how to let myself be happy without the crippling fear of life pulling the rug from under me. I know I've put walls up, and those walls are crushing me.

Dr. Kassen puts her notebook down on the end table beside her.

"That's enough for today. We'll pick this up again next time."

It astounds me how Dr. Kassen can get a rise from me, and then just halt the conversation and send me on my way. I know I'll stew and gnaw on this revelation all week like a dog with a bone. I grab my jacket and bag sitting on the sofa beside me, huffing in annoyance to myself.

She gets up from her seat and strides over to her desk as I reach the door.

"Oh, and Ali? Do try to have some fun this week. Maybe step outside your comfort zone a bit?"

I roll my eyes and laugh, with my hand grasping the door frame. "We'll see about that."

Chapter Two

MODERN GIRL BY BLEACHERS

My alarm goes off at 5:30 a.m., but it doesn't startle me. I've been awake for hours, lying in the dark and replaying last night's session with Dr. Kassen over and over in my head.

I stare at the ceiling, rubbing my eyes and stretching my arms above my head, pondering whether I really need to get up and go to work. I didn't sleep much overnight and now find myself exhausted and wishing to stay right here, buried in the warmth of my blankets. I roll myself out of bed and feel around in the dark for the light switch, tripping over the boots I lazily kicked off last night. I flick on the light in the bathroom and check myself in the mirror.

Oh, these bags under my eyes are just gorgeous.

I pull my chestnut brown hair into a loose ponytail and start a hot shower. The steam snaps me halfway awake until the coffee can finish the job. After drying off and letting my soft waves fall naturally past my shoulders, I queue up my morning playlist. "Modern Girl" by Bleachers blasts through my nightstand speaker as I dance into my closet, slipping into black pants, a scalloped white tank top, and my favorite royal blue blazer.

The old hardwood floors creak underneath me as I bop around my closet to the music. It's as if they are audibly groaning at my dancing. One floorboard in particular has been loosening by the year, and I keep reminding myself to fix it, but I never do.

The one lucky thing about living alone is that there's no one here to see me make an idiot of myself, dancing around the house in the morning. I return to my bathroom vanity and put on a light layer of makeup, just some moisturizer, concealer, and mascara to brighten up my jade green eyes. I tap my foot on the floor to the music, which makes it difficult to avoid stabbing myself with the mascara wand.

I live in a three-story Federal-style brick row house in Beacon Hill, one of Boston's oldest neighborhoods. It's more than a house. It's home. There's still notches in the door frame in the kitchen that my father made to mark my growth. Most of my childhood it was just the two of us. My mother had planned to leave without even talking to Dad. She even had a letter written, but he caught her before she could make an Irish exit from being a wife and mother.

He tried to shield me from as much of it as possible, but I remember his face as he read her letter. It was as if something in him died with her words. A few years ago, I found the letter amongst his belongings after he passed. She wrote that she wasn't living the life she imagined for herself, that she never wanted to be a wife or mother, and that she had tried for a long time to ignore those feelings. She asked him not to follow her, and to my knowledge, he never did.

They met when my father was just establishing himself in his career. They met by chance at a party with mutual friends, and he was smitten straight away. Working to become a partner at his firm kept him incredibly busy, affording my mother, who was a free spirited artist, plenty of the independence and alone time she craved. They traveled, attended parties and galas, and had little structure in their lives beyond their social calendar. Perhaps she thought things would always remain that easy and carefree. And perhaps they would have if it hadn't been for my arrival. Mom was upfront with Dad that she didn't want children, an idea he agreed with at the time, though maybe out of love for her. Imagine their surprise when a stomachache ended up being me. Her parents pressured them to marry, and Dad, ever the traditionalist, agreed. I think she felt trapped. The more her parents got their hooks in him, the more they convinced him to expect my mom to just comply and be a mother. His love for her became blurred by the heavy weight of expectation from those around them. He genuinely believed that once she held me or saw me, she would change her mind and love me.

I think perhaps she genuinely tried to love me, to love us, and our family, but you shouldn't really have to *try* to love someone. My parents were probably two people that never should have been married to each other or had a child together. Mom liked life how it was. She enjoyed having independence and living spontaneously. She was always upfront that she didn't want to settle or become some kind of unrecognizable soccer mom. Dad knew all of that and he pursued her, anyway. I think as much as he may have loved her; he loved the idea of her even more. He loved the version of her he saw, the version of her he hoped she would be.

She let Dad name me, though she criticized his choices. He named me Alice Kelly Murphy. My middle name, Kelly, was the maiden name of his great-grandmother. Mom argued that the name Alice sounded too old-fashioned and stiff. She even likened it to an old yellowed lace tablecloth. I can only imagine her insulting such a personal choice must have upset Dad quite a bit. She suggested some artsy bohemian names like Fiona and Hazel. I'm glad Dad won that one, though I can't imagine she put up much of a fight.

Dad always told me he chose the name Alice because of a famed Boston suffragette named Alice Carney. He would tell me stories about Carney's writing in the Boston Suffragette Weekly magazine, and how influential she was to the movement in the area. I've always hated the idea of being named for someone you've never met. What kind of narcissism does a parent have to set a standard so high for their child? 'Here, we named you for this incredible woman. Hope you're worthy of it.' I've insisted on being called Ali ever since I was a child, hoping to avoid the weight of expectation and the disappointment if I don't measure up.

Dad picked up the pieces as best as he could after she left. He essentially became my friend, but he gave me a fun childhood. He never missed my soccer games. He showed up for every school event. We had Boston Bruins season tickets, which I still have today. But he didn't know how to be what I needed him to be, and I didn't even fully understand at the time what I needed from him, either. We went on adventures together and I never wanted for anything material, but we didn't talk about the important things. I had everything I could want, but nothing I needed. He was emotionally closed off, and I grew up learning to be the same.

I had no one I could talk to, to understand why she left, and why she didn't want me. Dad was a lawyer and threw himself into his work, taking on bigger and bigger cases. He became well known around Boston as a no nonsense ace of a district attorney. But I was a child without any kind of outlet or support, so I threw myself into taking care of him. I taught myself to cook so we could at least eat together at night. I spent all my free time reading historical books and case studies just so he would at least talk to me about *something*. A child shouldn't have to do that. A child should not have to stand near a feast and hope for scraps.

We got by, but I think we were both kicking so hard to stay above water. We were just surviving. In retrospect, I realize that while I needed him to explain it all to me, he couldn't because he didn't understand it himself. He was grieving too, and possibly by shielding me from his pain, he thought he was protecting me. Though I think maybe if we had shared our pain with each other, it would have been a little more tolerable to bear.

There was only ever one time that we even got close to talking about her. I was preparing to move away to college, and I was so worried about leaving him alone for the first time. That's something a teenager really shouldn't be worried about at such a time of excitement and transition. I asked him about getting out there and maybe dating, finding some kind of company to fill the hole left in his heart, and he showed no interest. I was always proud of him for his achievements, but I worried that he didn't leave space for anything else in his life. It's a tragic flaw I seem to have inherited as well. I asked him if he ever regretted marrying my mother, considering all the hurt that came after. He said 'Of course not, kiddo. It got me you.' And that was the one and only time we acknowledged her in any way. It wasn't enough, but it was something.

My four years of undergrad were uneventful. I traveled home as much as I could, and as graduation loomed closer, I applied for the master's program at Chisholm. I had been away from home long enough and couldn't bear to be away from Dad and Boston anymore. Dad got sick just as I was finishing my degree. As I had done all my life, I moved heaven and earth to take care of him. But it wasn't enough. He faded quickly and passed away when I was twenty-four. As his only child, I inherited the money and the house, which has been in his family for over a hundred years.

Despite all the pain and loss that has transpired here, I love this home and I cherish the memories we created in it. I don't even feel like she was ever here. It feels like it was just his and mine. When I was a teenager, he gave me the master suite, which I still use today. I converted one of the other bedrooms into a home office. One is still my childhood nursery, and the other two are guest rooms. A five-bedroom brownstone in Boston is astronomically expensive, especially in Beacon Hill. I could never afford it on my salary or even my salary ten times over. I admit it is quite a large house for just one person, but I'm grateful my father left it to me when he passed away because I can't imagine anyone else living here. It has original hardwood floors and woodwork, with dark gumwood molding and stained glass paned windows. Many of the homes in the area have been gutted and modernized into sleek and sterile magazine ready homes where every paint color is something bland and ridiculous like honey butter beige or stargazer cream gray. They're devoid of any life or character. My father retired early and spent the last few years of his life restoring the home, even finishing off the basement and converting it into his own wood shop. I think he poured himself into fixing the house because it was the one thing he could control. He retro-fitted it with all the modern amenities, but left the integrity of the original craftsmanship. Every inch feels warm and cozy, like a worn in flannel blanket. The kind you curl into and just watch the rain wash away your plans.

I love everything about this city. There is no shortage of history to absorb here. The city skyscrapers reside alongside Revolutionary war era landmarks. The juxtaposition is something I find so fascinating. It's as if two entirely different universes exist parallel to each other in time. I could never leave this city, which is why I'm grateful for the opportunity to work at a nearby university. When my father left the law firm at the end of his career, he kept busy between home improvement projects by teaching law classes at Chisholm. He forged connections there that helped me become the youngest historian in my department. I know nepotism got me in the door, but I'd like to think I've worked my ass off to prove myself and stay there. I did have some pull on my own, having gotten my masters there, but I know Dad pulled some strings and reached out to every colleague possible before he passed to ensure I was taken care of. He also left me a sizable inheritance. Between his own finances and old family money, I don't have to work if I don't want to.

But I want to continue to learn and absorb history, and hopefully ignite that same passion in someone else. I was willing to pay my dues. I didn't expect any handouts or special treatment from Chisholm just because I was Sam Murphy's kid. Alongside my research projects, I pitch in and teach a few classes each semester. Many of the established professors prefer to teach the upper level advanced courses. Most of the staff in the department are wonderful and welcoming. Others, however, are essentially coasting toward retirement, cashing a paycheck but have mentally checked out. Professor Scott Black, for example, teaches World History, which I find ironic considering his idea of world history is a walk through Epcot. As the lowest in seniority, I've been tasked with teaching large lecture courses like American History 101 and 102. I enjoy rolling up my sleeves and getting into the classroom. Our profession will die if we don't inspire more historians and teachers. I've also been using my research to help create the curriculum for a new course being offered next year, the History of Women in Modern America.

I grab my bag and throw on my favorite pair of pointed toe flats and head out the door. I stand on the front stoop, just breathing in the crisp October air. There is a slight autumn chill and the trees are vivid hues of red and orange. I love October, and like Anne Shirley, I'm happy to live in a world in which it exists. I get a childlike joy from crunching the falling leaves under my feet.

Once the weather shifts to winter, I tend to drive to campus, but when it's nice out, I like to take advantage and walk. My commute to work by foot is a twenty-minute walk when the weather cooperates, thirty minutes when I get distracted and veer off into the local coffee shop. This is most definitely a coffee morning.

The coffee shop, Holy Grounds, is tucked into a narrow red brick building on Commonwealth Avenue, alongside other quintessential artsy boutiques, pubs, and general stores. String lights adorn the outside awning and patio. Inside is a mixture of mismatched tables and chairs. Comfy armchairs create reading nooks in the corners. On the walls are scattered works of local artists. I approach the counter and order the usual. A black coffee for myself and a white chocolate mocha latte for Ben, my best friend and colleague. Ben Turner works down the hall from me at Chisholm University. We are both historians, but specialize in different areas. I focus on American history and Women's History, but I've dedicated much of my recent research to the Titanic disaster, whereas Ben is primarily a military historian. I've always had a fascination with the Titanic, both in its opulence and in its tragedy. I never thought my career path would bring me to pouring over ship manifests and blueprints instead of the newspaper with my morning coffee, but it is a curiosity that has brought me to one of the most prestigious universities in the country.

It's still early enough in the morning that campus isn't bustling with people yet. It's an easy walk over to Abbott Hall, the history building. It's situated in a corner of campus across from Whitmer Hall, the English building, with a grassy quad between them. Ben and I usually opt to sit in the quad for lunch instead of the staff break room inside. It's a change of scenery and fresh air. Neither of us care for the water cooler gossip that some of the professors partake in. I swear, sometimes they're worse than the students with childish antics and talking shit.

I put my back against the door of Abbott Hall to swing it open, juggling both coffees, but taking great care not to spill them or burn myself. When I walk into the main lobby, our department intern Rebecca is sorting and dispersing mail.

"Good Morning Miss Murphy! You're here early." Rebecca pushes her glasses back up her nose and nervously tucks her straight blonde hair back behind her ears.

"Rebecca, we go through this every morning. You can call me Ali. Drop the Miss Murphy business. You're an intern, not a servant," I remind her, taking my mail with a smile.

I know some professors and historians in the building make her nervous, when they're even acknowledging her at all. They send her on coffee runs and odd jobs not included in her internship program. Professor Black even sent her on a shopping trip to find a birthday present for his teenage daughter. She does it with a smile because she knows their letters of recommendation will carry a lot of weight in her future endeavors. I don't use her beyond the occasional run to the library or making copies of exams for me.

I smile warmly at her as I hit the elevator button to the fourth floor, pausing as I step in. "Hey Rebecca, have a good day, alright?"

She blushes and nods. "You too, Ali."

As I step off on the fourth floor, Ben is standing there, leaning up against the wall with his head in his phone. He glances up when he hears the doors open and looks at me, and then immediately down to two coffees in my hands, one outstretched toward him.

"Al, you're an angel, truly," he says gratefully as he takes his coffee from me and playfully taps his heart. Ben usually arrives on campus just minutes before me, but his morning routine never leaves him enough time for coffee, so I end up grabbing it for both of us.

"What would you ever do without me?" I tease as I take a sip of my coffee.

"Fuck if I know." Ben laughs as we walk down the hall together to our offices. "You catch the Bruins game last night?"

"Yeah, Ullmark was a beast, stood on his head most of the night." I ramble on for a good five minutes about the Bruins game up in Buffalo. I love hockey almost as much as I love history.

"Are you going to the game tonight?"

"No, they're in Toronto tonight." I remind him of their road trip. "I don't think they play at home again till Tuesday." I really hope they win tonight. I fucking hate the Leafs.

At thirty-two, Ben is almost four years older than me. It's a fact he likes to point out often. He often acts like an older brother and tries to take care of me, which is not something I'm used to, especially considering he's the one I think that needs to be taken care of. Ben is over six feet tall and muscular. It's obvious he grew up on a beach and spent his childhood surfing. His blonde hair is swept to the side, letting his piercing blue eyes steal the show.

We met when we started here at Chisholm last fall. We both started on the same day. It was my first job as a historian and he had just transferred from a university out in California. Neither of us knew anyone, and being the two youngest members of the department, we felt a heavy weight of expectation and judgment from more senior staff. We spent the entire exhausting day painstakingly trying to prove ourselves to our colleagues and justify the positions we now held.

By the end of the day, we collapsed on opposite ends of the sofa in his office, passing a flask back and forth while exchanging stories of our lives. I told him about growing up as an only child in Boston and how it was just my dad and I for the longest time until he passed. He told me about growing up with three brothers in Newport Beach. I wondered to myself how the California boy with sun kissed skin and a jawline that even 90s Brad Pitt would envy would handle a harsh New England winter.

He told me he moved from California after a breakup with his long-time boyfriend, Ryan. We bonded over our mutual relationship issues. He's at least been in one in the last few years. I close myself off from relationships. In my head, you can't hurt me or leave me if I don't let you get close enough.

After sharing way too much whiskey, we both joked that we now felt trauma bonded. We've been inseparable ever since. We do almost everything together, from shopping and dining to traveling.

As we sip our coffees, I listen to the recap of Ben's date from last night. I live vicariously through his social life. Ben met Andrew on a dating app and they've gone out a couple times.

"Yeah, so we went to this new sushi place." I immediately crinkle my nose in disgust. Ben notices and smirks. "It was good! You need to give things a try, Ali."

"When do I get to meet him?"

"Oh, I don't think I'll be seeing him again," Ben says, shaking his head. "Andrew was a nice guy, but I don't see it going anywhere."

And there he is, right on schedule. I like to joke that he's "three date Ben." He always has a date, but nothing ever lasts past the third one. He's had no one with any staying power since Ryan, and that was a while ago now. At least he's getting out there. It's more than I can say for myself. Although that's not for lack of effort on Ben's part, he's tried setting me up with just about every straight male friend he has.

After tossing our empty coffees into the garbage near the elevator, we head down the hall toward our respective offices. I have a Titanic sized rabbit hole to jump down and he's been knee deep in World War I weapons and tactics. I swear I'll go crazy if I have to hear him droll on about the invention of mustard gas and its impact on modern warfare any longer.

My office is the smallest on the floor, which goes without question when being the lowest of seniority. But I actually quite like it. It's like my personal cave, my little hideaway. It gets wicked cold in here sometimes, so I often have to kick the heater in the corner to wake it up. There's two windows behind my desk that overlook the courtyard outside. The window ledges have a few framed photos displayed, one of Dad and me when I graduated college, one of us in the park when I was a child, and one of Ben and I at the Cape over the summer.

Across from my desk is a sofa and table for when I need a change of scenery with my research or when a student is in my office. Teaching the large lecture courses means I typically have students who are taking the course as an easy elective. But I'm also one of the more approachable members of staff, so I signed up to be an advisor. I think my demeanor and age make it easier for students to accept guidance from me rather than an old man covered in tweed and elbow patches. The sofa is also where Ben likes to spread out, pretending that I'm his personal therapist. That seems like the blind leading the blind, if you ask me. Although I will say I'm much better at giving advice to others than handling my own business.

Above the sofa, I have one of my favorite possessions displayed. It's a framed original copy of the Boston Suffragette Weekly, a women's rights pamphlet that circulated in the years prior to the ratification of the nineteenth amendment. A group of women in Boston published poems and essays to stoke the flame of the movement for the right to vote. This issue, published in 1911, has cover art that I've always found quite beautiful. It shows a woman at the head of a table of men, her arms outstretched as if she is leading the discussion. Underneath her is the phrase: *We just want a seat at the table.* The author, Alice Carney, wrote a beautifully moving essay on the expectations put upon women and how they contradict the potential women have. Her words are often the most powerful and impassioned, and I look toward them when I need comfort or inspiration. It's a reminder to myself anytime I feel small or unseen that I have a power within me to be brave, that my voice is louder than I realize.

My father gave me the pamphlet when I was a child. He told me he named me after Alice Carney because he wanted me to have similar ideals of self worth and bravery to grow up with. It hung in my childhood bedroom for years, before making its home in my office.

The most fascinating thing about Alice Carney is the fact that no one knows who she is. There is no census record of her existing in Boston during the time of publication. Most historians believe she was an alias used by one, or multiple, suffragettes to publish their strong, and at the time controversial, opinions. It's become a focus of mine, a pet project essentially, to uncover who the real Alice Carney was. Maybe it's not just professional interest. Maybe I think if I find her, I'll find a missing part of myself.

Ben stands in the doorway of my office, leaning up against the door frame with his arms crossed, as I toss my bag onto the armchair and hang up my coat. His eyes scan the room, noticing the stack of books and articles strewn about the table. I think he's deducing that my pet project of finding Alice Carney has slowly become my focus.

He tips his head toward all the paperwork. "Oh boy. Another Carney day, huh?" His voice sounds playful on the surface, but I sense a tone of concern underneath. He has chastised me before for being so focused on this project. He thinks it has caused me to develop tunnel vision.

I lean over the desk to turn on my diffuser so my office doesn't smell like old wet books like the rest of Abbott Hall.

"I just feel like there's something obvious I'm not seeing. I feel so close."

"Close to what?"

"I don't know. Just *something*." His eyes narrow on me, shifting into a doubtful, concerned expression. "What? What's that face for?"

Ben shrugs his shoulders. "I just worry about you, Al."

I turn to look out the window into the quad, my back facing Ben as I answer. "Why?"

"I worry that you're hiding in your work," Ben says nervously, as if he's afraid to broach the subject with me.

"From what?" I turn around and casually sit down at my desk. I'm trying to appear as nonchalant as possible, as if his concern and worry are entirely misplaced.

"Truth?"

I nod. "Truth."

Ben studies me for a beat, then exhales. "I think you're lonely. And I think you're unhappy." I lean forward in my chair, ready to defend myself, before Ben continues. "I don't think you're depressed or anything like that, or that you feel unfulfilled. But I think you feel like you want more, and you're afraid to have it. You're afraid to admit you want something, or that you lack something, because you think it makes you look weak, like you can't handle things on your own. And you're afraid that if you had that something more, it would just leave you. So why bother trying? Why bother wanting it at all? And I think you detach from those feelings by hiding in these rabbit holes. If you can solve the world's mysteries and problems, it will distract you from your own. You think you thrive on being alone, when all you really do is survive."

"Hmm." I quickly nod as I assess his diagnosis.

"Did I say too much?" Ben's face fills with worry, as if he said something too honest and crossed a line with me.

I lean back in my chair and laugh. "No, I'm just wondering why I pay Dr. Kassen so much money to analyze me when you hit me pretty good for free."

Relief seeps into Ben's face as he realizes that I'm amused, not angry. "I'm sorry if I upset you, Ali. I just want the best for you."

"I know, Ben. We're good, I promise. I've gotta get to work. The quad at one good for lunch?"

"Perfect. It's my turn to grab it today. I'll catch you in a bit." Ben leaves and heads down toward his office.

Luckily, I don't have any classes to teach today, so I can just dive straight into research, though I do need to get some grading done at some point. I usually stop and grade papers or tests when I've hit a mental roadblock with my research. It feels as though only minutes have gone by when suddenly there's a knock at my door. I look down at my watch and realize that it's almost twelve forty-five and four hours have passed by. I look up and see Rebecca peering nervously into my office, fumbling with something in her hands.

My eyes drop back down to the article I've been reading, not wanting to lose my place. "What is it, Rebecca?"

"Hi, uh, Miss... sorry. Ali," she corrects herself before continuing. "I have a note from Dr. Conrad for you."

Okay, well, that has my attention.

I look back up at her, confused. Did I hear her correctly?

"What? Dr. Conrad?"

Like theoretical physicist Dr. Conrad? Ben's godfather, Dr. Conrad?

"Yes. His secretary came to the front desk and told me to give you this." She hands me a sealed envelope. I can see the curiosity in her face just eating at her. She seems just as dumbfounded as I am. "She was very adamant that I give it directly to you."

I cautiously take the envelope, examining it with suspicion.

"Uh, thanks Rebecca." I am beyond confused as to why he has sent me anything. I'm dying to know what's inside, but I wait for the eager intern to depart first. I don't know what this is or why it was sent to me, but the nature of its arrival makes me think it's quite important and should be kept confidential.

Rebecca leaves the office and the door latches shut. I wait until I hear her footsteps walking down the hall before opening the envelope. I pull out a piece of carefully folded paper. I can see Dr. Conrad's office stationary and his handwriting.

Come to my office at 8pm.
Bring Ben.

Destroy this.

Tell no one.

What the fuck?

Chapter Three

I'M NOT A CYNIC BY ALEC BENJAMIN

I swing open the building doors and scan the quad for Ben. He's sitting at our usual table in the courtyard near the fountain. It's slightly secluded so we can talk but public enough that it's still great for people watching. It was his turn to grab our lunch today. I see him sitting and waiting with his usual, a Cobb salad and iced tea and my usual, a chicken bacon ranch wrap and lemonade.

He's calmly bobbing his head to music, lost in whatever playlist he's curated this week. I march over and yank out his left AirPod.

"Ben, what the hell does your godfather want with us?" I demand.

Startled, he blinks up at me. "What the hell are you talking about, Al?"

I attempt to discreetly slip him the note, but it ends up just looking awkward as I check over each shoulder behind me multiple times.

Very smooth, Ali.

Ben reads the note and his brow immediately furrows.

"Wait, what?" He examines the note for authenticity, wondering if this is all an elaborate joke. "Ali, what is this? What does it mean?"

"I don't know! Rebecca came to my office and said his secretary personally dropped it off. It's his stationary and his handwriting though." I stop myself when I realize I'm practically pacing in the quad.

"Well, I'm intrigued. But I'm also confused about why I didn't get one." Ben scoffs, as if offended he didn't receive his own personalized secret note.

"Come on, Benj. You'd lose it. This says to destroy it. You're a security risk."

"Hey!" He motions as he laughs, feigning being offended. "That's *so* not true!" He knows it's for the best. He's never been the most organized. Ben would lose himself if it was possible.

I settle into my seat further, holding onto the sides. I'm going to start overthinking this. Anchoring myself down, I lean in toward him and whisper. "Honestly, what do you think this is?"

"Is it a golden ticket? Did we win a tour of Wonka's factory?" Ben is so casual about this. He's easygoing and goes where the wind takes him, while I think of every possible outcome and prepare for the worst one. It drives me insane when he does this.

"Ben," I sigh, shooting him a look.

"Okay, okay. Is he sending us to the moon?" He's just toying with me now. He's literally sitting there casually eating his salad. How can he eat at a time like this?

"Benjamin." I tilt my head and break out his full name, so he knows I'm getting annoyed.

"Oh. I've got it! He wants to do lab experiments on us!" Ben has way too much fun getting me riled up. "Maybe you're going to be the next Captain America!"

"I hate you," I say as I roll my eyes with a smile, trying to stifle a laugh. Ben knows I need him to be serious, but I also know he needs me to lighten up a bit.

"Wow, Al. You're really stressed about this."

"I am! Join me, won't you?" Just once I wish he'd meet my level of anxiety, so I feel less unstable.

Ben finally relents on the playful antics. "Honestly, Al. I don't know what he wants from us." He shakes his head as he continues to stare at the note, probably trying to think of more outlandish theories to set me off with.

"Should I go home and change? Is this professional enough?" I'm suddenly self conscious that I'm dressed inappropriately for this secret meeting. I'm well aware that I'm grasping at any excuse to worry.

"Al, we got summoned to a secret rendezvous in the moonlight and you're worried you're not in the right outfit for it? What is the right outfit for this occasion?" He's mocking my tendency to worry and over-analyze everything. I plan for everything, and this meeting is going against all that.

"I know…I just…" I stop myself before I get too worked up thinking about every situation and outcome awaiting us. "This isn't how I operate. I like information. And plans."

Walking into something blind? That's how people end up in documentaries.

"I know," he says gently. "I'm confused too. But hey, mystery and the unknown can be fun. Loosen up, Al."

Loosen up. A hysterical notion for me. And he knows that. He says it like it's easy. As if it's a switch I can just flip. Like I'll just worry about this later when the time comes, and I won't stew on the possibilities for the rest of the day.

I try to eat my chicken wrap and ask Ben questions about his date to distract him from the fact that I am deep in my head thinking about this mystery meeting.

Chapter Four

CAUGHT IN THE MIDDLE BY PARAMORE

It's 5:30 p.m., and Ben and I are making our way to The Railway, a cozy pub just off campus. We both figured a drink would calm the nerves and pass the time before the big unveiling in Dr. Conrad's office later. We also didn't want to just mill around campus long after work hours were over. And truthfully, right now I need a distraction.

The pub is a favorite neighborhood haunt for university students and staff alike. It's dimly lit with a mix of high and low top tables and plush blue velvet seating. Bookcases and large televisions replaying sports highlights cover the brick walls.

Ben gets his usual Old Fashioned and stands in the bar casually leaning up against the dark wood pillars attached to the exposed overhead beams. He honestly looks like a model doing a whiskey ad standing like that, and

I can see his eyes scanning the room to see if he's been noticed. I order my usual, whatever local IPA is on tap, and start pacing in circles around him.

"Al. Stop circling. I haven't had that much to drink and you're making me dizzy."

"Sorry." I try to force my brain and my body to connect and stop spiraling.

He takes a sip of his drink, then shoots me a grin. "I really don't know how you drink that hoppy beer, Al. It's so bitter."

I laugh and shrug my shoulders. "Bitter like me, I guess."

"Well, I'm not even going to argue with that." He knows and loves my self deprecating humor, even though he sometimes can't tell if I'm serious or not.

We couldn't talk about the meeting too much in the bar as it's a typical hangout for students and staff and we couldn't risk anyone overhearing that a meeting even existed. I zoned out, half-watching hockey highlights on the television while Ben caught up with our normal bartender, Jenny. We have two drinks each and begin our walk back over to campus.

As we approach Dr. Conrad's office building, Ben turns toward me, walking backwards.

"Alright! Any last guesses?" he asks, way too casual for my liking. He views every obstacle and challenge as a new adventure. His fearlessness is something I love about him. But at this moment, I need him to come back down to earth and worry with me.

"Not at all," I say. "What does a theoretical physicist want with two historians?" I'm not interested in placing bets on what this could be. My mind will run away from me if I let that train leave the station.

Dr. Conrad's secretary, Caroline Thayer, is waiting in the lobby to welcome us into the building. Caroline is in her mid forties with thick curly black hair. She's sharply dressed in a gray pantsuit and black heels. I envy the ease with which she walks in heels. She glides, whereas I look like a baby giraffe taking its first steps.

We wait for the elevator to take us to the ninth floor where Dr. Conrad's office is. Caroline taps her foot on the floor while we wait, and it's making me even more anxious. The silence is tangible. We all know each other and have spoken before on numerous occasions, yet this time she's not even attempting any polite small talk to fill the awkward space between us.

I've been to this building once or twice before today. Ben brought me here for a staff mixer to meet his godfather just after we started at Chisholm. Dr. Conrad has always been welcoming to me, which I appreciated being in a new job. He and Ben's father were roommates in college and have remained quite close, hence why he was named godfather to Ben. He was so involved in his research he never married or had children, so he sees Ben and his brothers as his nephews. When Ben moved from California, he called Dr. Conrad, who helped him secure a position at Chisholm.

His office building is more sleek and modern than ours. Our building feels almost like an extension of the campus library, with warm color tones and bookshelves throughout, with small pockets of space to burrow in. Dr. Conrad's building is white and sterile. I'm half expecting a robotic butler to come out and take my coat. I take this as a reflection of the amount of funding his flashy profession gets compared to ours. He's innovating for the future while we're stuck in the past. As expensive and high tech as all the furnishings and decor is in this building, I find it to barely have the personality of an Apple store at the mall. It feels like I've stepped into an episode of *The Jetsons*.

As we step out of the elevator, Caroline motions for us to follow her down the hallway. We pass the main conference room, which is glass paneled on all four sides. I always find that room to be odd, like a cage on display. I expected to be meeting there, but she continues on to Dr. Conrad's personal office, where he has a separate smaller conference room attached. As she opens the door, I can see Dr. Conrad at the head of the rectangular table speaking in hushed tones with a man who I know to be his research partner, Dr. Malcolm McCoy.

Dr. McCoy and Dr. Conrad could not be more different physically. Dr. McCoy is at least six feet tall and is lean with salt and peppered black hair. He's in his late fifties, clean shaven and well dressed in a tan suit. His green tie pops against his dark brown skin. He looks hilarious juxtaposed against Dr. Conrad, who sometimes looks like he's just been startled awake. Dr. Conrad is at least six inches shorter than Dr. McCoy and about ten years older than him. He has thick-rimmed glasses that are attached around his neck. He's heavier in the belly and his flannel shirt sticks out the bottom of his sweater vest.

"You're here!" Dr. Conrad's eyes brighten with excitement as his gaze lands upon us. He stretches out his arm to Ben first. "Dr. Turner! You need a shave, kid," he says with a warm laugh deep from his belly.

His eyes turn toward me, taking my hand in both of his. His hands are warm and inviting, like him. "Alice, it's so good to see you again."

"Dr. Conrad, it's —" I intended to remind him I prefer to be called Ali, but he interrupts me.

"James. You're welcome to call me James, you know that. Though I suppose, given the nature of this meeting, we should stick to the formalities for now."

Ben jumps in before I get the chance. "Right. About that. Why are we here?" He looks around the room for any clue leading to why we have been summoned here.

"I promise it will make sense soon. Be patient and wait until everyone is here," Dr. Conrad replies.

Everyone? Who else are we waiting for?

Dr. McCoy walks over to join us and shakes Ben's hand. Dr. Conrad steps in to introduce me. "Malc, this is Alice Murphy. Alice, this is my research partner, Dr. Malcolm McCoy."

Dr. McCoy reaches out to shake my hand. "I've heard a lot about you, Alice. That's a name you don't hear often anymore. It's lovely."

"Thanks." His hand grips mine in a firm shake. "I prefer Ali, though. It's nice to meet you." Although I attended the mixer here with Ben, I didn't get a chance to meet Dr. McCoy.

After a few moments, two more people enter the room that I'm not familiar with. They must be who we have been waiting for. The woman is tall, she's a good six inches taller than me, and I'm 5'3". Her sleek blonde hair is pulled off her face with a red headband. She's wearing a red and gray plaid shift dress and Mary Jane's. She looks to be around Ben's age and she sits down to the right of Dr. McCoy. Behind her is a tall male, around six feet, with ash brown hair slicked back. He's wearing black dress pants and a gray shirt and black tie. He quickly takes the empty seat next to her and nods at us as he sits down.

"Alright everyone!" Dr. Conrad bellows from the head of the table to get our attention. "Now that you're all here, I have one last thing before we get started."

Caroline re-enters the room with a cart and begins handing out bottles of water and large manila envelopes. I carefully open my envelope while Ben excitedly rips his open beside me like it's a Christmas present.

I pull out a stapled packet of paperwork. At the top of the first page, I see the phrase *Non-Disclosure Agreement.*

Ben's eyebrows immediately shoot up. "An NDA? What the hell is this?"

Dr. McCoy clears his throat and begins to stand before Dr. Conrad taps him on the shoulder and interjects, "Ben, I promise to tell you everything, but I need you all to sign this first. We have to protect our research."

Ben frowns. "From who?"

"Everyone," Dr. Conrad quietly replies.

"But mainly the United States government," Dr. McCoy deadpans.

I don't even know if that's a joke or if he's serious.

Ben and I turn and lock eyes and exchange a look we both know the meaning of.

What the hell is going on here?

I flip to the last page and quickly sign mine. I don't read the terms and conditions. I don't read them when I set up a new iPhone, I'm not going to read this either. I respect Dr. Conrad immensely, so if he asks for this favor of secrecy, I'm happy to oblige. I also just want to keep this show moving forward and I'm dying to understand why we're here. Plus, the only person I'd care to tell is sitting next to me, anyway.

Once Ben looks over and sees that I've signed mine and am quietly twirling the pen between my fingers, he signs his and pushes it forward to signal he is done as well. Our mystery companions follow suit, and we all stare at each other.

Dr. Conrad stands up to join Dr. McCoy and he motions for Caroline that we are ready to begin. She shuts and locks the door and I can feel a knot in my stomach beginning to form. Dr. Conrad's attached conference room has no windows and only one door. I'm realizing now that this room must have been chosen with ultimate secrecy in mind.

Ben leans close to my ear while keeping his eyes on Dr. Conrad. "They definitely want to run tests on us," he whispers with a soft laugh.

"First things first. Introductions," Dr. Conrad interrupts. He motions toward our mystery companions across the table. "This is Sarah Henderson and Eric Rivers. They are members of our research team. Sarah, Eric...this is Dr. Ben Turner and Alice Murphy. They are historians here at Chisholm." Dr. Conrad gestures in our direction.

We all nod nervously at each other. I awkwardly wave across the table and immediately feel any merit I hold as a historian becomes laughable in a room full of scientists. Sarah's eyes narrow on me and it feels like she hates me already, like she's pegged me as the weak link in the room.

Dr. Conrad and Dr. McCoy join each other standing at the center of the room. They both take a deep breath and exchange a look. The room is silent, but filled with thick anticipation.

"We did it," Dr. Conrad excitedly blurts out, almost breathless.

Ben leans in, more confused than ever. "Did what?"

Is this an announcement or a confession?

"Time travel. We cracked it." Dr. Conrad wipes sweat from his brow, almost in disbelief himself. I can see the pride in his face over the achievement and the immediate fear scanning our faces for a reaction.

Ben's jaw practically hits the table. "I'm sorry...what?!"

Dr. McCoy takes over explaining. He seems to be the more organized and structured of the two, whereas Dr. Conrad is often untidy and intense. He's able to explain things in layman's terms instead of hard to understand scientific jargon.

"I know it's hard to believe, but we've done it. We've run small tests, going back a day or a week, that have been successful. We're ready for a real major test," he explains.

Ben asks a thousand questions to understand how they did it, but both doctors are adamant that information cannot be shared for security purposes. Sarah and Eric clearly had a prior understanding of the subject of the meeting, as their faces made almost no change during this revelation, except to seem annoyed at Ben's questioning.

I tap my pen on the table, swirling in my own thoughts as I listen to them explain everything to Ben. I'm stuck in a daze, half listening to Dr. McCoy's explanation, and half wondering how the hell I got here today.

Finally, I drop my pen, and all the formalities, and bluntly ask, "Okay, but why the hell are Ben and I here?"

Sarah looks annoyed, as if I personally offended her by interrupting her heroes, but Dr. Conrad smiles and chuckles. This already feels like a sharks versus jets, scientists versus historians rivalry.

"Well, I was wondering when you were going to snap and ask that, Alice. You're right on time, as always. I need you both to bear with me while I explain this, ok?"

Ben and I look at each other and nod back at Dr. Conrad.

"Alright. We've been working on this theory of time travel for a long time. Once we started making serious headway, we stopped and asked ourselves a very simple question: why are we doing this? If successful, what purpose could this serve? How can we use this gift for good? We quickly decided that our history is riddled with tragedies and mysteries. Events we wish we could understand, but time and records have muddled the truth. We created a plan that, if this worked, we could travel to events in history to better understand what happened and how we could preserve the accurate story for posterity. This is where you both come in." He takes a deep breath. "We want to begin our first real mission. Titanic."

Did he just say... Titanic?

I'm staring into space, hardly realizing that I haven't exhaled yet. Ben pats me on the back and laughs. "Take a breath, Al."

I don't know what I expected him to say, but time traveling to the Titanic was certainly not it.

Ben then looks back at Dr. McCoy and Dr. Conrad. "Alright, so let me guess here? You're going to send these two on a potential suicide mission to a doomed ship and you want us to be consultants? Make sure they know the ins and outs of the history of the time?"

My brain followed the same thought process as Ben. I assume now that our purpose here is to prepare these two to cover all the historical bases.

"No. We want you to go to Titanic with them," Dr. Conrad says flatly.

Is this actually happening? He actually said that, right?

The pit that has been knotting itself up in my stomach is quickly making its way to my throat. I couldn't form words to answer, even if I wanted to. My mouth feels wired shut. I'm desperate for air, water, and someone to snap me awake from whatever this is.

Before either of us can say anything, Dr. McCoy takes the reins. "We want to send a team back to the Titanic to understand what happened. There have been so many theories over the years, you know that, Alice. Eyewitness testimony can be skewed by many things, emotion and even financial gain or notoriety."

I have to admit he isn't wrong. There have been constantly changing theories about what happened. Whether there was a flaw in the blueprints and shipbuilding to whether it could have been avoided by simply going through the iceberg instead of trying to go around it to simply outlandish conspiracies about whether the Titanic was swapped with her sister ship the Olympic prior to sailing. I know that the idea of being able to watch history unfold in person is fascinating, and the opportunity of a lifetime.

"Our plan," Dr. McCoy continued, "is to send the four of you back in time to Southampton, where you will board the Titanic's doomed maiden voyage. We will send you there with the necessary materials to collect data to bring back for study. We've even worked with a design team to create items with hidden cameras for you to use. You would have everything accurate to the time, all the latest fashions and accessories."

"How is this safe?" I finally ask. As usual, my brain goes right to the worst-case scenario. We die. Time travel doesn't work properly. We all turn to dust. No re-entry.

Dr. Conrad steps forward and rests his hands down on the table. "Look, I know what we're asking of you guys. And I know how crazy this sounds. But please consider it. There are, of course, risks with anything. We've had several successful trials of sending people back days and weeks in the past. I can't tell you anything else until you agree. We can't risk this information getting out. We'll give you a few minutes to make a decision before we go deeper into the details, but this offer has a half life of about ten minutes."

Dr. Conrad and Dr. McCoy exit the room. The room is silent. We all stare at each other, waiting for someone to make the first move and break the awkward silence.

Ben finally breaks open the silence and laughs. "See, I told you they wanted to run tests on us." I suppose in a way he was spot on with that hypothesis, they are essentially asking us to be guinea pigs in an elaborate experiment.

He looks at me expectantly, as I'm always the first to cave in and laugh at him. Surprisingly, Sarah and Eric follow and we're all chuckling over the madness that we were presented with. Sarah and Eric obviously knew of the plan before we did, but I think hearing it all laid out, even they could see how utterly insane it is.

Ben scoots up in his chair to a more professional posture, clasping his hands together as if he's leading a board meeting. "Alright. So I guess we should discuss this, huh?"

"Well, Eric and I have both already signed on, so it's down to the two of you to discuss," Sarah answers, confirming my suspicion that they knew about everything prior to this meeting.

Ben shifts sideways in his chair, now speaking only to me, and props his head into his hand. "Alright, Al. What do you want to do?"

"I don't know. This is crazy." I shake my head in disbelief. "They know this is crazy, right?" I'm still completely floored that this is what this meeting was about. This was not on my bingo card for today.

"Well, I'm going," Ben says confidently. "This sounds like an adventure." There's an air of excitement in his voice.

"You've got to be kidding, right? You'll go, just like that? It's that easy for you?"

I am astonished that he is willing to dive headfirst without any semblance of thought. It's like he's blindly jumping off a diving board, and hasn't even bothered to check if the pool below is full of water or cement. He's always been the fearless one, jumping from airplanes, swimming with sharks, even going on blind dates. Everything that terrifies me excites him. I don't understand it, and yet I envy it too.

"Absolutely, Al. Come on, come with me. Take a risk. For once in your life, take a goddamn risk." He's smiling at me, but his eyes and the tone of his voice are pleading. Before I can even play devil's advocate and explain everything that could go wrong or why this is such a terrible idea, Ben continues asking me to go with him. "Look, I get it. It's scary. And maybe it's insane. But what's the point of a life if you don't live it? Stop going through your life alive but not living. You'll regret this if you don't go, Ali. Jump with me. Your life is happening without you. Do something crazy, something wild, something stupid. Just live, Al."

I sit back in the office chair, close my eyes, and begin swiveling back and forth, mulling over my options.

I could go. Literally travel back in time. Can I handle that? Can I travel to one of the worst disasters the world has ever seen and just be a tourist? Just stand there and watch it unfold like a movie when I know how the film ends? I can't stop it. I can't help anyone. I have to interact with people, get to know them, all with the knowledge of knowing they might die and I possess the ability to prevent it. I know the consequences of altering history. I know it could cause catastrophic changes to the world and potentially eliminate generations.

On the other hand, I could just stay here. Politely decline and leave this room and this opportunity behind me. Move on with my life as if this offer never happened. Continue my research. Maybe make a tremendous impact in my field. But maybe not. Maybe I'll just continue life as I always have. Safe, but surviving. Just keeping my head above water.

I am cautious, maybe even to a fault. I've always lived my life afraid of choosing the wrong path. The reality in front of me now is that I've actually been afraid of choosing *anything*. Afraid to jump, afraid to hope, afraid to fall, afraid to live, really. Maybe the thing to be afraid of isn't stepping out of line, it's not stepping at all. At least if I've made a mistake, I've made *something*. This fear inside me is a paralyzing force. I think the thing I'm afraid of most of all is wasting my life. Getting to the end of my days and realizing they've all been half full. I mean, what do I have to show for myself right now? Sure, I've been through a lot over the years. Life has beaten me up and down with loss, but I've also experienced great triumph. I have a great job, a career I genuinely enjoy being a part of. They say the definition of insanity is doing the same thing over and over and expecting different results. If that's true, then how would one define doing nothing at all? It might be safe, but it's not fulfilling. Is that what I want my life to be? Predictable? Just keeping my head above the water? It's exhausting, kicking and kicking, just to stay afloat. Years from now, could I live with myself for passing up the chance to not only view history but preserve it? Could I stand by while someone else takes this opportunity instead of me? And what about the person who does take that opportunity? Would they have honorable intentions?

I finally open my eyes, stare at the ceiling for a moment, and sit up straight in my chair. I look over at Ben, who is still facing me with his hands clasped together. I take one last deep breath.

"I'm in."

Chapter Five

MIND IS A PRISON BY ALEC BENJAMIN

Dr. Conrad re-enters the room with fresh paperwork and waivers for us all to sign. I'm not really sure what the waivers are good for. I can't sue anyone if I die time traveling to the Titanic, but I sign it anyway.

I'm in a daze over what I've agreed to do. Everything is moving in a whirlwind.

Did I seriously just say I'd go?

 Holy shit, I did.

I know I've made the right decision, but I still can't believe I actually agreed to it. It's like I've been swept into a whirlwind too strong to avoid. This is risky, maybe even morally gray. But I can't let this chance fall into the hands of anyone who wouldn't honor and respect it. What if someone else attempted to alter history for their own personal gain? At least I just want to listen and learn.

He starts by laying out a schedule for us. We'll spend the next month preparing and studying before we travel. Dr. Conrad has created an Edwardian 101 curriculum to prepare us. He gives us a schedule of times we need to meet. We will learn all we can to fit into 1912 customs smoothly and without suspicion.

Ben minored in theater while at university, so I have a feeling he will adapt easily. I know the history of the period well. But the idea of performing like a proper lady terrifies me.

There are four cardboard boxes neatly stacked on a table. Dr. Conrad distributes them to the four of us as Dr. McCoy begins instruction.

"Take these home with you and begin studying," he says. "In the box you'll find books and newspaper articles on national and global events in 1912. There are books on proper etiquette and language of the time and popular culture. Sarah and Alice, there is additional information in your boxes on the fashion of the period and the responsibilities and interests of women."

Once we all have our boxes in hand, Dr. Conrad motions to dismiss us. "Okay team, as you can see on your schedules, we're going to be meeting daily. I know this is a lot to learn in a short amount of time, but I know you can do it. I must emphasize the importance of keeping this information confidential."

As we turn to leave the room, Dr. Conrad calls back to us, "Oh, and guys? Thank you again, truly. We are so grateful to all of you. See you tomorrow."

My hands clutch the box's corners. I hold it close to my chest. Ben uses his to hit the elevator button. Sarah and Eric go back down the hall to their offices, giving Ben and I the chance to speak privately on our way out.

As we stand in the elevator, Ben finally breaks the silence between us. "So, that was wild, huh? *Titanic*! Can you fucking believe it?" His blue eyes are alive with excitement.

"Stop." I shoot him a sharp look and point around the elevator. "Cameras. Wait till we're outside." I don't know who is watching, and I don't want to take any risks.

He nods, sobered.

We make our way out into the lobby and through the front doors. The courtyard around Dr. Conrad's building is still. The only sound is the light tapping of water in the fountain. In the distance, I can see the fluorescent lights of the Glasner Student Union building. I'm glad we're walking in the dark. In the daylight, two employees with cardboard boxes would look like they've just been sacked. Instead, we're just hiding secret materials for a time travel expedition to the Titanic. *Totally normal.*

Ben and I walk toward the Union. It is on our route to the walking path off campus toward my house. It's 9:30 p.m. on a Friday night, and the center of campus is wide awake. As we pass the Union and several residential dorms, I can hear the sounds of students laughing and the low steady bass beat of loud music. No doubt they're all getting ready to go out. This place will be a zoo soon as they all convene outside to go to the neighborhood bars and clubs. I don't miss those days at all. I'm already in bed by the time the students are just beginning to go out.

We step off campus and onto Commonwealth Avenue. This is normally where Ben and I split on our commutes home in the afternoon, but he stops and grabs my arm.

"You're not walking alone. It's dark," he says.

I raise an eyebrow. Ben knows I'm used to the walk back to my house; it's only a few streets away. I can walk it in twenty minutes if I really rush it, though I never actually walk home in the dark. If I'm on campus late, I know ahead of time and drive myself to work or call an Uber home. He's protective, as always, but I have a feeling he wants to talk about the events of the evening. And truthfully, I do too. I'm not too proud or independent to admit that walking alone in the dark back to my house makes me uncomfortable.

"You know, I think I've got a bottle of wine at home calling our names," I say with a smile. "Do you want to just stay over tonight?"

Ben sleeps at my place more often than he sleeps in his own apartment. We joke that he's my ghost roommate with how often he's here and how much of his stuff he leaves behind. Ben lives across the Charles River in a modern high-rise loft in Cambridge. His apartment is concrete and minimalist, not by choice. He doesn't spend enough time there to decorate it. I tell him all the time he could save so much money on rent if he just moved into my house. I've got plenty of room, and it feels like he lives there already. It's become less of a joke and more of an inevitability, especially with his lease ending soon. It just makes no sense for him to keep the apartment. He stays at my place multiple times a week, especially after Bruins games.

"Oh, I thought you'd never ask," he quickly says with a cheeky smile.

As protective as he can be, I know his offer to walk me home was because he wanted to talk. I can see it in his face when he needs more than he's saying he does. It is easier to recognize in others than it is in me.

I wrestle my phone out of my coat pocket. "I'll order Ray's so it's there when we get home." Ray's is local to my neighborhood and, in my opinion, the best pizza in Boston.

Ben and I stay up all night talking about what we've agreed to. Neither of us can fully believe what has transpired, and talking about it almost feels like a fantastical hypothetical situation. I walk him through a history of the ship, from the route of the voyage to a rough timeline of events during the sinking. I am curled up in my armchair with my legs hanging off the side while Ben sprawls out on my sofa. I admit I enjoy getting to show off how much I know, especially given the number of speeches he's given me about minute-by-minute details of every war known to man.

Ben gets up and heads toward the kitchen. As he opens our third bottle of Merlot, he finally asks the question I've been waiting for all night.

"Al, I've gotta ask. Why did you agree to this? This is an enormous leap of faith into the unknown." He grips the corkscrew firmly and twists it with ease. "It's so unlike you."

Ben walks over and pours more wine into my glass. Then, he stumbles back to his spot on the sofa, placing the bottle on the coffee table between us. I'm curious if he purposely asked this question after some alcohol, hoping I would be more honest with a little liquid help.

"You answered your own question," I reply, swirling my wine. "It's so unlike me. I hate that phrase. All of this is unlike me. I don't take risks; I do what's safe and expected. I don't want to do that anymore. I've done the safe thing all my life, and where has it gotten me? Alone."

Ben leans forward on the sofa, eyes serious. "You have me though, Ali. You'll always have me."

"I know." I meet his gaze. "And I love you for that. But you know what I mean."

Ben smiles faintly and sips his wine.

He knows what he means to me, but I could do better at expressing it. I've spent a long time with my head down, focused on school, and

Dad, then work. I've never made time for anything else. I've dated, sure. Tried to at least. But nothing concrete. Nothing that ever made me feel like more than just myself. I want more. I want someone that makes me feel like *more.* Being alone started as a choice. I wanted to focus on my career. But I've dug myself into that hole so deep it's hard to pull myself out. The walls around me are just too high to climb. I've used so much energy trying to be strong that I haven't left room for anything else.

The most stable relationship I've ever had is my friendship with Ben. He sees me, flaws and all, and want to change me. He's the one person I never feel like I disappoint. I begin to wonder why someone as incredible as him is alone, too.

"Ben, can I ask you a question?"

"Yeah, of course."

"Why do you never talk about Ryan?"

He flinches, just a beat. "Well, why do you never talk about your mom?"

Touché.

"Hmm. Fair enough." He's got me on that one. "I guess I find it difficult to acknowledge the pain."

"I get it." His expression softens. "What did you want to ask?"

"You speak about him so fondly. And I know you've dated a lot here in Boston, but nothing with any permanence. I guess I'm just curious why you guys split?"

Every time the subject comes up, Ben goes quiet. He says it just didn't work out, or that they wanted different things. I don't know if he's protecting Ryan or himself. But I have to imagine that whatever happened between them causes his lack of commitment now. He goes on dates, but never more than three with the same person.

Ben exhales deeply. I think the alcohol is making him feel more honest, too.

"Ryan's a couple of years older than me, which was fine for a while. But eventually it became pretty clear to me that we were on different paths. He wanted to settle down, get married, start a family, that whole deal. I thought I wanted those things too, but he was just a few steps ahead of me. I was just starting on my doctorate. I asked to table the discussion until I finished. He waited patiently and asked again, and I kept pushing it off. I really wanted to establish myself in a steady position first. Ryan got frustrated and, in hindsight, I don't blame him. I was just stalling. He wanted things I wasn't ready for. We had this big argument about it. He gave me a hard deadline, a 'get your shit together or I'm out' kind of ultimatum. And that's when I realized why I'd been pushing things off."

"Why?"

Ben sighs. "I don't want kids. I blurted it out in an argument, at first out of anger, but once the words left my body, I felt fifty pounds lighter. Like the truth had been weighing me down. Deep down, I always knew that I didn't want children, but I felt ashamed to admit it. I mean, who doesn't want kids?" I look at him and smirk with a raised eyebrow, clearly reminding him of my mother. "I thought maybe, over time, I'd change my mind, you know? But I kept finding any reason to push off the discussion again. And eventually I realized it wasn't fair to keep making him wait. I didn't want to steal any more time from him. I couldn't ask him to sacrifice more than he had or keep waiting for a life I didn't even want. So, I made the tough decision to end things."

I reach over and place my hand on his. "Oh, Ben. I can't imagine how hard that was for you."

"It really was. I love Ryan, and I think a part of me always will. But he shouldn't have to give up his dreams just because I don't share them. And neither should I. My dreams are different, but they're just as important as his. In the end, I loved him enough to let him go."

"And that's why you moved to Boston?"

"Yeah, I felt like I needed a clean break. Distance. I knew if I stayed near him in California, I'd cave in just to keep him, and that's not doing any service to either of us or to a child. I can handle breaking my own heart, but I'd never forgive myself for breaking a child. So I decided to get as far away as possible and start over. Plus, my mom didn't take the breakup well, and I needed to get away from all the fallout."

"Oh?"

"She's never cared that I liked men; in fact, she's always accepted me and advocated for me. And she loved Ryan; they got along great. But I know she wanted grandkids, and I think she assumed that even though my partner would differ from that of my brothers, that my life would evolve in the same way. She belongs to that generation that believes you go to college, get married, and have kids in that order or else you're doing life wrong. My brothers both got married and had kids and followed that perfect step-by-step program. And then there's Ben, still doing things differently. I always felt like I failed her."

"But there's no singular way to get through life perfectly," I say gently. "There is no step-by-step program."

"How do you figure that?"

"Well, you know how we met up at the Sox game over the summer?"

"Wait, what?" Ben shakes his head, confused.

"No, no. Stick with me on this. You live in Cambridge. I live in Beacon Hill. We took different routes, but we both ended up at Fenway. Do you get me now?"

Ben chuckles. "Leave it to you to use a ridiculous sports metaphor to comfort me, Al."

"Hey! Don't knock my metaphors. They always work!" I laugh. "What I mean is, just because your path is different doesn't mean it's the wrong one."

"I just feel so selfish for choosing myself."

"Ben, I come from a mother who didn't want me. I know what it's like to be an accident, an inconvenience. It is not selfish to decide you don't want children and to stick to that. In fact, I actually find it *selfless.*" Ben looks at me with a surprised expression. "No, really. I think it is selfless to make that choice, to know you don't want children, or can't give them what they need. I think it's brave."

I know I'm projecting my trauma here, and I don't regret my existence at all, but I can't help but wonder how things would have been different for my parents if my mother had been allowed to make her own choices.

"Alright," Ben pivots the conversation. "Well, while we're at this, I have a question, too."

"Oh boy," I groan. It's my turn in the hot seat now. "Shoot."

"Since we're talking about relationships, I've been wondering. Why don't you ever date? I've tried setting you up so many times; you either find a reason not to go at all or you scare them off on the date. I don't get it. You're smart, kind, funny, incredibly beautiful..."

"Oh, stop." I blush. I pretend to fan myself. Deflective humor is often a coping mechanism for me. I hate receiving compliments. I never know how to accept them.

"No, you are! Come on, even I can see that. I can appreciate beauty; I just don't want to hop into bed with you." Ben laughs. "Hell, I'd marry you for your carbonara alone. But Ali, seriously, you're a catch. And it seems so weird to me how indifferent you are to even the idea of a relationship."

"I'm not indifferent," I say softly.

"Ali..." Ben tilts his head, as if he doesn't believe me.

"I'm not." I exhale. "It's just hard. It's my fault, and believe me, I know that. I've spent a long time toughening up to protect myself, but all I've really done is push people away. I have two simultaneous and contradictory fears: letting people in and being alone."

"Do you know why?"

"That's the million-dollar question, isn't it?" I laugh. "I pay my therapist a lot of money to explain that one to me. I guess I'm afraid of getting hurt again. If I let someone in, they could leave me. I want love, but I can't quite figure out how to accept it."

I wasn't expecting to be so honest tonight. But I'm sure the wine has helped those feelings bubble up. It is true, though; I don't want to be alone. I want to find someone I could share my life with. Life is about who you tell your stories to. In the darkest, coldest night, who keeps your flame going?

Ben lies on the sofa, staring at the ceiling. "You know what, Al? One day you'll meet someone worth letting your guard down for."

I chuckle. "If you say so."

"I promise you, you will. Probably when you least expect it."

"How will I know?" Maybe that's a silly or naive question, but I'm curious. I've never been in such a situation before; I don't know if I would recognize it.

He smiles, eyes heavy with sleep. "It's hard to explain. But when you look at them, like *really* look at them, time just stops. Nothing else matters besides you and them, and being with them, or even just being near them. Your head hands over the reins to your heart. Every part of you that didn't make sense before will suddenly seem balanced."

"Christ, Ben. You make it sound transformative."

"It is."

"And was that Ryan? For you?"

"It was."

"Doesn't that make you sad, though? That it's over?"

"No." His voice softens.

"Why not?"

"I've got hope left that it will happen again someday."

I smile to myself. "I think it will, too."

"You know what, Al?" His voice is veering into slurs, the wine finally making him drowsy. "I know you'll find it, what you're looking for." Ben closes his eyes and settles himself further into the sofa.

I turn my head and watch him drift to sleep. I look at the ceiling for a while. I count the details in the pattern before finally letting myself fall asleep.

Chapter Six

CHANGES BY DAVID BOWIE

"Ali! Wake up!"

Ben's voice cuts through the fog as he gently shakes my shoulder. I crack open one eye and am met with a shock of warm sunlight. Through the glare, Ben's face comes into focus, staring down at me. Sleeping on the sofa all night has tousled his blonde hair. He's wearing dark blue jeans and a white T-shirt, from the collection of items he constantly leaves at my house.

I stretch out, groaning as I unfold myself from the crumpled ball I apparently slept in. My mouth is dry and sticky, my head pounding with a maddening rhythm. I stare around the room, trying to figure out how we got here. I look at the kitchen counter and see the three empty wine bottles. *Oh, shit. That's how.*

Ben hands me a bottle of water like it's medicine, and I gulp it down like it might save my life.

"Come on," he says with a wry smile. "We've got Titanic practice in an hour."

Oh, right. That.

So last night wasn't a dream.

I stumble toward the bathroom, pausing for a moment to allow the room to stop moving. In the mirror, my reflection is exactly what I expected: hair matted to one side, the pattern of the blanket pressed into my cheeks, and the dark circles under my eyes that only too much wine gives me.

I quickly tame my hair into a ponytail, wash my face until my skin feels more alive, and swipe on enough concealer to make me look less like a haunted Victorian widow. I squeeze some toothpaste on my brush before plunging it into my mouth and dashing to the closet. I grab the quickest outfit I can throw together, jeans and a gray crew neck I got in Cape Cod last summer with Ben and some friends. Cozy and forgiving, the sweater is my official hangover uniform.

I run back to the bathroom and spit out the toothpaste. It's funny how a fresh mouth makes you feel ten times cleaner and more awake.

I take one last look in the mirror. Not bad. I actually look half human.

On the outside, I look put together, but inside I'm churning. And I can't tell if it's the lingering effects of the alcohol or the nerves.

Back in the living room, Ben's pulling on his shoes, now dressed in a light blue V-neck sweater. He looks up and grins.

"Ah, the hangover sweater returns," he says.

"You ready to go?" I ask, grabbing my keys.

He nods and we head out the door to what Ben jokingly calls Titanic practice. Dr. Conrad calls it Edwardian 101. I'm still calling it completely fucking crazy.

It's eleven thirty in the morning as we make our way to campus, and "class" starts at noon. I check my watch as we walk and turn toward Ben. "We've got time for coffee." It's going to be a necessity today. I think Dr. Conrad would rather we be late than deal with a hungover and caffeine deprived Ali.

We veer off into the coffee shop and order our usual. Ben pays this time and flashes a wink at the barista, Peter. Peter smiles back like Ben just made his entire morning. I am eternally amazed at Ben's ability to be magnetic and command attention everywhere he goes. He casually tosses a few dollars into the tip jar before we head back out into the crisp fall air.

Once back on the sidewalk, I glance sideways at Ben.

"You know Peter?"

"I go there a lot," he says, too casually.

"Why? You live across the city, Ben." He lives in a completely different area of Boston. This is my neighborhood spot, not his. He only ever comes in here when he's staying over at my place, or so I thought.

Ben shrugs, smile widening. "I just like looking at him."

I can't blame him. Peter is about as tall as Ben, but he has striking jet black hair and blue eyes.

I laugh. "Just looking?"

"Alright, alright." He raises his hands in surrender. "We talk whenever I'm there. And maybe, sometimes, I go out of my way to find a reason to go there?"

"Just to see him?"

"Maybe."

"Have you thought about asking him out?"

He sighs. "Yeah, of course I have. But come on, you say it all the time, I'm three-date Ben, remember? What's the point?"

I nod. "Why do you think it never goes beyond three dates?"

"Oh, that one's easy. Usually by date three, you know whether you really like the person, whether there's any staying power. That's typically when the harder questions come up, like what you want out of life in terms of marriage and kids. I like to dip out before I disappoint someone with that one or get too attached."

I want to tell him that avoiding disappointment guarantees it. That he can't assume what lies beyond date three without ever going there. But it would be hypocritical of me, and I know that. I've built my own walls too carefully to start poking in his. I let it pass, for now at least.

As we head down Commonwealth Avenue, we step onto an empty campus. It is 11:45 a.m. Everyone is still sleeping off last night's fun. I envy them. I wish I were still asleep, too.

We swipe into the building with our keycards and head to the basement level—Dr. Conrad's carefully chosen meeting place. No windows. No cameras. One locked door. Maximum secrecy.

As we step off the elevator, Eric greets us enthusiastically. "Good morning, travelers!"

He's much friendlier than Sarah is. Eric tries to make small talk about the Bruins game with us. Sarah hovers beside him like a reluctant shadow. She seems annoyed that Eric is so friendly to us, whereas she looks at us like we don't deserve to be a part of this project. I sip my coffee and continue to talk about the hockey game, hoping I don't slip up and make a sarcastic comment and make things more awkward than they already are.

Dr. McCoy swings open the door of the meeting area. "Come in!"

Upon entering, I see a whole slew of people waiting for us. I recognize Dr. McCoy and Dr. Conrad, but everyone else is a stranger, many of them even to Sarah and Eric.

Dr. Conrad waves us over to where he is standing at the front of the room.

"Good morning, everyone," Dr. Conrad says. "Thank you so much for coming. And please, let me thank you again for agreeing to this. We're going to get started in a moment. First, I'm going to divide you up for a bit. Ben, Eric, go find Dr. McCoy. Sarah, Ali, you'll stay with me for now."

I shoot Ben a dramatic "don't leave me" stare, but he disappears with Eric. Once Dr. Conrad has us alone, he waves over two older women and continues speaking.

"Okay ladies, this is Sheila and Jane. They are specialists in art and fashion design. They're going to measure you both to create your attire for the journey. We will outfit you with all the high fashions of the time."

Sheila and Jane could not have been more kind, but it is uncomfortable for a woman to be poked, measured, and spun around like a mannequin.

"I guess we should get used to this, being nothing but a display," Sarah mutters, with a subtle eye roll.

Her first attempt at a joke, or even conversation at all. I offer a small smile in return. It's not much, but it's at least a small crack in the wall between us.

We both know we're going back to a period that was restrictive to women. Honestly, I'm grateful to be going through this with another woman. We may not agree on much or have anything in common, but at least I'll have a female to confide in.

After finishing our measuring, we convene back at the head table with the boys, who were also being measured for attire.

"Alright, here's the plan," Dr. McCoy says, clearing his throat. ""Here's the plan: we're sending you back to the Titanic with First-Class tickets. Ali and Ben, you're siblings. Sarah, you're the maid. Eric, the valet. This setup will ensure you stay together and give you access to both upper-class guests and crew."

"Wait," Ben interrupts, raising an eyebrow. "Who's going to believe Ali and I are siblings?"

He makes a good point. I don't know much about biology, but I'm not sure where genetics would allow a mother to have one child with blonde hair and blue eyes and another with brown hair and green eyes.

"One step ahead of you," Dr. Conrad responds. "It's quite easy; you're a few years older than Ali. It's reasonable to think you have different mothers. Given the period and medical treatments of the time, let's say she got sick, and your father remarried."

"You *killed* off my fake mother?!" Ben puts his hand to his forehead and pretends to faint from shock. He's going to enjoy this play-acting way too much. My performance will be uncouth and clumsy.

We split again. Ben and Eric go off to learn about male customs, like talking business and politics over cigars and brandy. They are both given materials to study to keep up with current events of the time and topics of conversation that will probably come up.

Sarah and I follow Dr. McCoy over to a table where a tall woman who looks to be in her seventies is standing. Her posture is rigid and cold, and her eyes look to be examining both of us closely. He introduces her as Renee Vaughn, an etiquette specialist. She looks like she's never slouched a day in her life. Sarah and I look at each other with dread, the first time we've felt bonded over a mutual distaste for something. Renee is here to teach us how to be proper ladies, Dr. McCoy explains. Even the thought of this makes me audibly groan, and Renee immediately gives me a look as if I've been caught whispering in class. I'm going to have to keep my opinions to myself for once.

Sarah and I learn basic mannerisms and etiquette, like how to walk straight and graceful while wearing a corset. Renee has us follow her as she strides grandly around the room, her head held high and her posture perfect. While she cannot see, I follow behind her, comically mimicking her example. Sarah lets out a snort, and it feels like progress.

Ben watches from his table, newspaper in hand, laughing as I wobble around with a book on my head. I flip him off behind my dainty lace glove. He bows in return.

On top of this education, Sarah has to learn the ins and outs of being a maid in 1912. I don't expect her to serve me privately. But I understand she needs to learn to keep up the appearance of it publicly. She'll hear plenty of gossip. The maids always do. She will surely learn many secrets that may be unknown to history.

Over the next few weeks, we learn it all—posture, language, music, dance, politics, gossip, and manners. We study photos of the real passengers we'll soon be mingling with.

The excitement and glamour is intoxicating, but so is the dread.

As our practice schedule nears its end, it becomes even more grueling. Ben now calls these dress rehearsals, since our clothes are ready. I'm brought into a separate area of the room, walled off with a tarp-like fabric for privacy to see my wardrobe. It is a never-ending cascade of day dresses, evening dresses, and nightdresses. The wardrobe also includes linens, gloves, corsets, undergarments, hats, shoes, and jewelry. I run my hand through the rack of fine silks, twisting them between my fingers. The craftsmanship is incredible. Sarah and I spend hours learning how to do authentic hair and makeup.

The last day of practice ends with a private meeting between just the six of us. Dr. Conrad and Dr. McCoy want to go over the last details of how this mad experiment is going to work. Dr. Conrad explains that he and Dr. McCoy will set the target date and engage the time travel, at which point we will vanish before them.

We'll each carry a personal item that acts as our key home: Sarah has a brooch, I have a locket, Ben and Eric have pocket watches. Press the hidden button, and we're pulled back to the lab—no matter where we are. We are told that even though days will pass for us, upon our return, it will feel like no time has passed at all in the present.

Dr. McCoy brings out four large trunks, part of our many first-class suitcases. Engraved on the trunks are our initials. Dr. McCoy explains they are for any artifacts that we stow while onboard. We will each receive items with hidden cameras inside that we can tap to take photos. Simple, inconspicuous everyday items like walking sticks or eyeglasses. We are all given a small box with a biometric lock on it; mine looks like a small music box. He explains we may also pack any personal items to go with us, a comfort of home perhaps.

"Listen carefully, though," Dr. Conrad explains. "Don't let these trunks leave your stateroom. When you are ready to come back, make sure that you are with your trunk and grab it. Try to stay on the ship as long as possible, but if you cannot get back to your stateroom, just press the button and go. Your safety is more important than any artifact you could bring back. Whatever you are holding onto will come back with you when you press the button, so be careful."

Ben grins, always pushing boundaries. "What if you grab the ship? Will that cause it not to sink?"

He's half joking but genuinely curious. I find the question idiotic, but it breaks the tension around this nonsensical project. None of us fully understands how this all works and what awaits us.

Dr. Conrad glares. "We don't know for certain, but it's imperative that you don't do that. When we tested it out, I held that day's newspaper and a Big Mac, both of which came back with me unscathed. We are assuming it will work for the trunks too, though we haven't tried something of their size. But obviously, no, do not just grab the ship. It could change the entire course of history. It could change future world events. The sheer amount of people who would not exist anymore because of their ancestors' changed life trajectory is unfathomable. You cannot tell anyone who you are or what will happen. Please remember, you are there to witness, not change."

After a few parting reminders of last-minute studying, we are dismissed until our departure tomorrow morning. Ben is staying at my place tonight, so we can pack whatever belongings we choose to take with us. I honestly think neither of us wants to spend the night alone, especially not knowing what is ahead.

What if this doesn't work, and this is my last night in the world? I'd like to spend it here, at home, with my best friend. But what if it works? There's no way this experience won't change me.

Chapter Seven

BLAME BRETT BY THE BEACHES

Ben and I arrive back at my house in silence. Dr. Conrad had a car service collect each of us, and we've been told the same black sedans will pick us up tomorrow morning.

Ben and I hardly spoke on the drive, both of us likely trying to sort out the thoughts that are jumbled in our heads.

Ben sinks onto the stool at the kitchen island while I start pulling out pots and pans to cook us dinner like everything is normal. But my hands move on autopilot, and before long I'm just staring blankly at a box of pasta, lost somewhere between panic and disbelief.

Ben snaps his fingers to get my attention. "Hey, Ali. Where's your head at right now?"

I blink and set the pasta down, leaning over the counter toward him. "I hardly know. I mean… can you believe this? This time tomorrow we'll be onboard the Titanic in 1912. Or it won't work and we'll be dust. It's all happening so fast." I shake my head, the weight of it finally settling. "I mean, Christ. What the hell were we thinking?"

I'm having a hard time wrapping my brain around something so ridiculous. The notion of time travel is still utterly insane, and it feels like the last month of practice has flown by in an instant. And despite a month of training, nothing could prepare me for the moment *before* the moment.

Ben leans back. "Hmm. I think I know what we need."

I narrow my eyes. "Seriously? Now?" I can't believe he thinks this is the right time for this.

Ben stands and pulls off his sweater in one dramatic motion. "It works every time. I think this situation calls for it. Pick a song, Al. We've gotta dance it out." He steps backward into the living room, playfully beckoning me to follow. "Come on, Al. You know I'm right. Dance with me."

This is our thing. Our go-to cure for stressful situations, anxiety, or heartbreak. This has been our go-to for stressful situations or decisions. And I will admit that somehow, the invigoration of dancing like fools around the room gives us some sort of mental clarity. Or we're just too tired to care anymore. Either way, it works.

I sigh, but follow, grabbing my phone. I connect to the Bluetooth speaker on the coffee table and scroll through the playlists until I land on our usual standard: *A+B's Life is Chaos Dance Playlist*.

"Hmmm." I tilt my head back and forth as I scroll through the options.

I tap on "Blame Brett" by The Beaches and swipe the volume up, letting the opening riff fill the room.

I let my body loosen up and start swaying and nodding my head. By the time the song hits the first chorus, Ben and I are jumping up and down with our hands in the air, while poorly singing the lyrics with our full chests. We may look ridiculous, but Ben is right. This always works.

When the song ends, we collapse on opposite couches, panting and laughing. I'm dizzy, out of breath, and for the first time all day, at peace. No nerves or trepidation, just a feeling of calm.

Ben was right.

I needed to dance it out. I needed to let go.

We're committed to the project and whatever happens, we just have to let the chips fall as they may. I'm not used to relinquishing control, but maybe it'll do me some good to just jump in fearlessly for once. Maybe there's freedom in that. I've been so afraid of taking a risk. I've spent my life playing it safe. Now is the time to be bold, to be brave.

I get up from the couch and stride confidently back into the kitchen, picking up dinner preparation where I left off; however, this time with much more awareness and concentration.

Ben sits at my kitchen counter impatiently staring down the carbonara I just made for us while I open a bottle of Pinot Noir. Carbonara is Ben's favorite dish. I watched a lot of cooking shows growing up and taught myself to cook so I could make Dad and I dinner every night. It's carried over to adulthood, but now I just enjoy doing it, and I think I've gotten pretty good at it. Aside from the companionship, I think the biggest reason Ben likes to stay here is the food. I thought a home-cooked meal for the two of us before this crazy ride would be just what we needed. Something normal in this long line of uncertainty.

"Up for some last-minute studying?" I ask as I sit across from him.

Ben groans. "Oh, God. Not more of your color-coded flashcards."

He mocks my system of organized flashcards. They may be color-coded and overly detailed, but they've worked. I've used them to study with Ben on topics ranging from current events in 1912 to popularly used words or slang in conversation.

"Not this time, Ben," I say with a sly grin. "I came up with a little something different."

Ben raises a suspicious eyebrow.

I walk over to the closet in the living room where I keep board games, candles, and extra blankets. Sitting on the middle shelf is one of my childhood board games, Guess Who. I spent entirely too much time replacing the names and photographs that came with the game with notable passengers and crew members on the Titanic.

I hold the box up proudly for Ben to see.

He looks at me with a puzzled expression. "I thought you said we were studying?"

"We are." I smile as I pull out the trays from the box, revealing the newly assembled Titanic version of the game.

Ben laughs as he looks at the characters facing him. "Gotta hand it to you, Al. This is good."

I draw the card of my character and hand the box to Ben to draw his.

"Remember, yes or no questions only." I nod towards the board. "You wanna go?"

"Ladies first, Alice."

I roll my eyes and laugh. There he goes, already getting into the 1912 character. "Nice one. Alright. Is your person a man?"

"Yes. Is yours?"

"Nope." We start flipping the panels down in tandem.

"Umm...is he a crew member?" I ask.

Ben glances down at the board. "No. Is yours a passenger?"

"Yep," I reply as I flip over notable crew members like Captain Smith, Charles Lightoller, and William Murdoch. "Is yours known for business?"

"Yup," Ben replies as I flip over more characters, leaving just the richest tycoons that were aboard the ship. Ben giggles. "Does yours look like she's got a dead bird on her hat?"

I laugh. "Kind of."

"Margaret Brown!" he shouts.

"Good job," I say, impressed. "Who did you have?"

Ben shakes his head. "Not telling. Keep guessing."

I stare at my remaining options, looking for distinguishing characteristics that would limit the field further. "Okay...is he under the age of 50?"

"Yes."

I flip over more people, leaving John Jacob Astor, Benjamin Guggenheim, and Edward Harrison.

"Hmm." I stare between the three remaining characters. "Does he survive?"

"Yep."

"It's Harrison."

"You got it." Ben turns his board to show me. "He's kinda cute in an old-timey way."

"Please. Look how smug he looks." He looks to be in his mid to late thirties. His untrustworthy smile curves alongside his handlebar mustache.

"Man, you're just rejecting guys in every century, aren't you?" Ben laughs and I can't help but join in.

"Shut up and eat before your food gets cold."

Ben devours his carbonara, stopping for wine every so often and a gesture showing his enjoyment of the meal.

He puts down his fork, turns towards me, and raises his glass to mine. "Cheers, Al. To taking a risk together."

"Together," I answer as I clink my glass with his.

We spend the rest of our meal reminiscing over our memories together, both trying to avoid the unknown of what is to come. We reminisce on our trip to the Cape last summer when Ben almost fell overboard on a whale watch. We talk about going back next summer—as if tomorrow isn't looming. As if we'll return the same people we left as. As if we'll return at all.

Ben clears the plates and starts washing up. I retreat to my room and fill a small envelope with photos of myself growing up, friends at the Cape, and Ben and I at Christmas. Little pieces of home I can hold onto when everything else becomes unrecognizable.

I get changed for bed and I begin to feel more and more restless. I walk out into the living room where Ben is sitting in his pajamas on the sofa watching the Bruins game.

"Hey," I say quietly. "Can you come stay with me tonight? I really don't want to be alone tonight. I'll put the game on in the bedroom."

He doesn't say anything. Just clicks off the television and stands, smiling as he slings an arm around my shoulder.

"Only time I'll ever sleep with a girl!" he teases as I elbow him in the side.

He slips into my bed and we just talk for a while, with the hockey game on for white noise and normalcy. We lay on our sides toward each other, both grasping at companionship. Platonic as it may be, it's nice to have warmth in my bed and not be alone. I close my eyes and dream of the sea, wondering what it holds for me.

Chapter Eight

LANDSLIDE BY FLEETWOOD MAC

My alarm blares at 6 a.m., slicing through the silence. I roll over to find Ben already awake, lying on his side with his head propped on one arm.

"Morning," he says with a playful wink.

I stretch out in bed, extending my fingers and toes out like a cat. I slept surprisingly well, though I probably couldn't say the same if I had been alone with my thoughts all night. Ben and I take turns in the shower and wordlessly get ready. Neither of us really knows what to say, and I think the nerves are finally hitting him, too. There's not much left to say. We've been discussing the mission as eventually happening, but now here it is right in front of us. Real. Imminent.

I stand in my closet, looking at the racks surrounding me, pondering my choices. What does one wear before time travel? What is the appropriate outfit for the possible end of the world?

It's just another day, Ali.

I settle on high-waisted, straight-cut jeans cropped at the ankle, a square-neck white top, and white low-cut sneakers. Normal, like I'm just heading out for coffee or the farmer's market.

"Al, it's time to go. The car James sent is here," Ben calls from the window. I peek outside and see a sleek black town car idling at the curb.

I nod and grab a black suede moto jacket, putting it on and fluffing my hair back into place. Ben brings our belongings to the foyer while I make us coffee to-go in the kitchen. I brace my hand on the door frame as I reach for two travel mugs. My fingers grasp the growth marks Dad made when I was a child. *Dad. I wonder what you would think of all this. Would you be proud or think I'm crazy?*

I find Ben in the foyer, lights turned off, bags in hand. I pass him his coffee. One last sip of normal before everything changes.

With my small bag of personal items for the trunk in hand, I step out the front door. My gaze moves back toward my house and my chest tightens. Will I ever see this place again?

I freeze, lost in my thoughts, as I lock the front door. Ben's voice calls gently, but I don't move until I feel his hand on my back. He picks up our bags and opens the car door for me. He's really practicing 1900s chivalry.

The drive to Dr. Conrad's lab in Concord takes forty minutes. We sit in silence, cautious not to speak in front of the driver. I'm not sure if he's just a contractor or in on the entire operation. But I assume anyone even breathing near this project is on the payroll. Dr. Conrad and Dr. McCoy would never leave something like that to chance.

Outside, the drive is beautiful. The trees are painted in warm hues of amber, crimson, and gold. We turn off the main road and begin a winding trail deep into the woods. Dr. Conrad's lab sits at the end of the trail, nestled between rows of trees on each side.

As I step out of the car, I breathe in the scent of evergreen and pine. The woods are still and calm. They have no idea we're about to do the impossible in their shelter.

The lab is an unassuming brick building. Anyone who ventures this far into the woods might assume it's a luxury cabin of some kind. It's not even that large, so I imagine a good portion of it is perhaps underground.

Inside, Dr. Conrad meets us and leads us down a hallway to a steel-reinforced arched door. He presses his palm to the biometric touchpad, and the door hisses open. Dr. McCoy is waiting inside, flanked by a small team of staff.

The lab is circular, like a command center. A platform sits at the center of a lower level, surrounded by catwalks and a railing. Offshoot rooms line the walls. Next to the platform is a towering console covered with levers, buttons, and blinking lights.

I gulp nervously as I look around the lab. Shit just got real.

Dr. Conrad leads us into a smaller prep room. Sarah and Eric are already there and half-dressed in their Edwardian clothes.

"Welcome to hair and makeup," Dr. Conrad jokes as if this is the Hollywood set of a period drama.

Sheila and Jane work efficiently. Sarah's hair is almost done; Jane is packing her wardrobe. I'm guided to a vanity where Jane starts brushing my hair. She works methodically, pulling it into a braided knot, leaving a few curls to frame my face.

I plop down in a styling chair in front of a brightly lit mirror. Jane walks over and begins brushing my hair. She works methodically, pulling my hair into a braided knot, leaving a few curls to frame my face. She secures her creation with pins and shifts her focus to my face. She pulls out a container holding little pots of rouge for my lips, eyes, and face.

"You hardly need anything," she says, dusting rouge on my cheeks. Natural is the style." She has no idea that's just my default setting. She gently swoops the brush across my face. When our eyes meet in the mirror, she smiles warmly and looks at me like she's scared for me.

After makeup, I head over to the rack where Jane has laid out a dress and all the undergarments and accessories for me. I stand behind a curtain, remove my clothes, and slip into a chemise. Jane returns to help lace my corset. She tries to pull it gently at first, but she seems hesitant to restrict me.

"Jane, it's okay. We have to be accurate. Tighten me up," I reassure her, gritting my teeth. She looks at me apologetically and tightens the laces, squeezing my waist in. I let out a small gasp. "Perfect."

Jane helps me step into my boarding dress, a dark burgundy suit dress with a matching tailored coat. I place the matching hat on my head, checking the mirror to make sure it's on properly before attempting to secure it with a hatpin. I shove the pin through the hat twice, each time never getting the hat to stay put. I mumble in frustration after each failed attempt.

Stupid hat. Stupid pin. Stupid hair. Why is this so fucking hard?

"Here, let me," Sarah says, stepping in and taking the pin from my hand. She holds my hat in one hand and the pin in another and quickly swipes it through. She makes it look easy.

"Thanks," I say, offering a sheepish smile. The hats are gigantic and they make me feel self conscious, as if they practically double my radius. It feels like I'm balancing a small country on top of my head.

Sarah stands across from me in a black dress with long sleeves and a white apron, a typical maid's uniform. I look over at her rack of clothes and see more of the same. I think of my rack, filled with enough clothes for multiple costume changes a day. Everything from fine silks to jeweled and crystal beaded fabrics. I have boxes upon boxes of hats and jewelry. For a moment, I don't know whether to envy her or feel sorry.

"I hope you know I don't expect you to wait on me," I say, feeling suddenly self-conscious.

She laughs. "Believe me, aside from keeping up necessary appearances publicly, I won't. I don't envy you, Ali. I get to fade into the background. You're the one that's going to be putting on a constant show."

After we finish in hair and makeup, we follow Jane down to the lower level platform where Eric and Ben are waiting. As I walk down the stairs, Ben looks up at me in his brown suit with an ascot tie and a stickpin. He twirls a straw boater hat in his left hand. A walking stick—secretly housing a hidden camera—tucked under his arm. He looks dashing. His eyes brighten as I come toward him and his smile is beaming. This moment feels like the grand reveal after a makeover in every 90s romantic comedy.

"Al, you look amazing," he says as he grabs my hand to twirl me for a better look at the entire ensemble.

"We're about to go to 1912. We should probably drop Al and stick with Alice." I remind him, grinning.

We might as well get used to that now, so we don't accidentally have a lapse in conversation once onboard.

He smiles and dramatically bows to me, one hand behind his back. "Whatever you say, Miss Murphy."

I bow back, matching his theatrical performance. "Wrong again, *brother*. It's Miss Turner now."

I break away to pack my items into my trunk. Each trunk has a small locked box inside it, intended to keep any modern conveniences packed secret.

Dr. McCoy joins Dr. Conrad on the lower level and we begin the final preparations. Everything feels simultaneously hurried and as if it's moving in slow motion. Dr. McCoy holds a small dark wooden box containing our return tickets; the talismans with hidden buttons.

More like a panic button.

Dr. McCoy me and clasps a necklace around my neck, fastening the chain at the nape

"Good luck, Ali," he whispers in my ear.

Dr. Conrad follows behind him and shakes Ben's hand, which turns into a hug. "Good luck to you, Ben."

As Dr. Conrad turns toward me, he pulls me into a hug. "Take care of yourself, Ali. And take care of him, too," he says, glancing over at Ben.

I am not normally someone who hugs. At any gathering, when every-one goes around hugging goodbye, I tense up and become dead-weight. I don't know how to accept love or affection from someone. His hands are shaking as he hugs me, and for the first time, I realize how nervous he is. I feel guilty for just standing here while he wraps his arms around me.

"See you later, James," I whisper in his ear, trying to sound confident to comfort him. When he pulls back, I can see his smile, full of pride. Maybe he didn't expect me to use his first name. Maybe he didn't expect me to come this far.

We assemble as directed onto the platform. Sarah and Eric hold on to the trolleys loaded with our trunks and suitcases. I stand next to Ben, and for the first time, he looks nervous. I look down and notice his hands are shaking. It feels as though we've traded places because for the first time since this all began; I feel calm and controlled. How much crazier can it honestly get?

Dr. McCoy begins the countdown as Dr. Conrad monitors the screen and pushes buttons.

"10, 9, 8, 7...."

Ben leans in. "Are you sure you're ready for this?" he whispers in my ear. Not like I can back out now. We're in this. For better or worse.

"6, 5, 4...."

"You jump, I jump, Jack," I whisper with a playful smile as I slip my hand into his. I squeeze his hand reassuringly, hoping to put him at ease. He looks back at me. Once our eyes lock, his breathing slows down and the nerves disappear from his face.

"3, 2, 1...."

Dr. Conrad pulls the final lever and I'm surrounded by nothing but a bright white light.

Everything and nothing, all at once.

Chapter Nine

BACKWARDS TRAVELLER BY WINGS

April 10th, 1912

The light fades.

Ben squeezes my hand, his voice tight with disbelief. "We did it. We really did it. Open your eyes, Ali."

I hesitate. Even Ben's words aren't enough to make me believe it worked. I need to see it for myself, but a part of me is frightened. And for some reason unknown to me, I'm more scared that it *did* work.

Slowly, I open my eyes.

We're in an alleyway behind a red brick building. The air feels different, heavy with salt and smoke. In the distance, I can hear a muffled flurry of voices and commotion. We all stare at each other in disbelief.

Holy shit. I'm here.

Eric breaks the silence. "I can't believe it."

He has a tinge of surprise in his voice. None of us can believe we're here, that we're even alive.

That triumph is short-lived once a familiar panic washes over everyone like a tidal wave. We've crossed a threshold. There's no going back now, and perhaps that is even scarier than the time travel itself.

"Deep breaths, everyone," I say, slipping into my default role of caring for others before myself. Ben can see it in my face. There's no hiding it from him. We understand the silence in each other.

Ben straightens his posture and clears his throat, slipping seamlessly into character. He offers me his arm just like we've rehearsed. "Shall we, Alice?"

I slip my arm into his and rest my gloved hand on his sleeve.

We walk around the side of the building and toward the front. I kick my dress out slightly as I walk, careful not to trip on the fabric. It would be a shame for me to trip and fall this soon into our adventure.

Above an awning, I can see the words *Platform Tavern*. I know this location from my research. In the years since the Titanic's voyage, the port area has become more of a tourist attraction. But I know that right now, if I dare to turn my gaze forward, across the street, I'll see her. I'll see the Titanic. Then this will all be truly real.

I take a deep breath and turn my head. There she is, moored in the distance on White Star Dock, and even from this distance, she dominates the skyline. In present day, we are used to cruise ships being massive floating cities. But in 1912, Titanic is the pinnacle of luxury and engineering. It feels surreal to even think of her in the present tense.

For now, she is not a tragedy; she is a wonder.

She is the second of three Olympic class ships, the oldest sister being the Olympic, and the younger sister being the not yet launched Britannic, built by Harland and Wolff for White Star Line. Titanic is mountainous, over 882 feet long, 92 feet wide, and 175 feet high from keel to funnel. There are ten total decks, though only eight are available for passenger use. Four funnels extend high above, only three of which are functional. The fourth, for ventilation only, was added to make the ship look even more powerful. She boasts the first swimming pool onboard a ship, among other luxuries like a gymnasium, high-end restaurants, Victorian-style Turkish baths, and squash courts. Even the third-class amenities are superior to that of other ships.

If not for her tragedy, she likely would have enjoyed a lengthy career at sea and a relatively unremarkable place in maritime history. She is astounding to behold. I've only ever viewed her in grainy and distorted archival photos. But here she is, grand, clear, and in technicolor.

I turn my gaze upward and see the lifeboats on the top deck. Something in the sight of them puts a knot in my stomach. The sight of them serves as a stark reminder of the job we're here to do. There are twenty total lifeboats, more than required of a ship her size, yet not enough for all passengers. They will not be filled to capacity, though it is unlikely they would have had time to deploy all of them before the sinking.

A porter approaches us as we walk toward the port side of the ship. Eric and Sarah follow behind us with the trolleys. All of us seem to tense up. This is our first proper test. Ben stands tall and powerful. He reaches into his pocket and pulls out some period-accurate money and hands it to the porter.

"Both to parlor suite B-51-53-55, please. Thank you, sir," he says with practiced elegance.

The porter takes the money gratefully and wheels the trolleys toward the gangway. The four of us exchange barely perceptible nods. First hurdle cleared.

We head for the gangway. Ben leans in, eyebrows raised, grinning. "Showtime," he whispers.

This is it. I clutch Ben's arm a little tighter, and he looks back at me reassuringly. He strides forward and helps me step onto the gangway with our tickets in his hand. The walk up the gangway feels momentous, almost cinematic, though I think that is the adrenaline coursing through me. Eric and Sarah follow as we approach the doorway. Ben presents our tickets to the officer.

"Welcome aboard," he says proudly as he tips his cap toward Ben.

And just like that, we're on the Titanic.

We enter into the First Class Reception, an area located at the foot of the Grand Staircase, and adjacent to the Dining Saloon. It is spacious, encompassing the entire width of the ship. White oak paneling adorns the room, which is furnished with wicker and green fabric. Large leaded glass windows line the room on both sides, allowing gorgeous natural light to illuminate the room. If this opulent space is any indication of the level of grandeur and detail of the rest of the ship, then I must prepare myself to be blown away at every turn.

The officer glances again at our ticket, his eyes scanning for a cabin location, and motions forward to a steward. The young man steps forward and is told to escort us to our cabins. We follow him to the bank of elevators. I watch with curiosity as the lift steward operates the wheel and crank handle to take us up to B-Deck. The elevator opens and we join a gathering of other passengers milling about in excitement. We follow the steward down the halls, desperate to blend in.

Act natural, Ali. Act like you belong here.

I adjust my posture and walk gracefully, trying to remember everything from the etiquette lessons.

As we reach our cabin, another steward is standing outside in the hallway. He appears to be posted outside our door, waiting for us. He stands tall, around Ben's height, in black pants, a white dress shirt and tie, and a blue wool jacket with gold White Star Line embossed buttons. His dark brown hair is slicked back, and he stands formally and at attention.

The guide hands over our tickets. "This is your room steward, Charles Hughes. He will take care of you on your journey."

Charles smiles warmly at us and extends his hand out to Ben. "Mr. Turner, it's a pleasure to have you aboard," he says with a thick English accent as he greets Ben. "I'll be your room steward, so anything at all you need I can take care of, sir."

Ben thanks him as we enter our adjoining suites, beginning with the sitting room. The room is beautiful, paneled in white but furnished in dark woods and green upholstery on the desk, chairs, and sofas. It has a marble fireplace fitted with an electric heater, and an entrance into the attached private promenade.

I walk into my attached bedroom and look around in astonishment. I can hear them making muffled small talk, but I become lost in marveling at the well-appointed cabin. Decorated in the Italian Renaissance style, it boasts high-sheen satinwood paneling and brass sconces. The room has two beds, one closest to the door leading to the corridor, and one on the back wall against the promenade. I take off my hat and place it on the bed nearest the door. Next to the bed is the vanity. A marble washbasin is on the far wall near the second bed. Connected to my cabin is the room containing wardrobes and private bath and toilet facilities. This room connects on both sides between my cabin and Ben's, but is the only room not to connect to the outside corridor.

Ben's cabin on the other side is in the French style with wood paneling, red carpeting, and red upholstery. Even though there are two beds in each of our rooms, and plenty enough space to accommodate the four of us, Sarah and Eric have tickets for inside berths nearby. Dr. Conrad thought they needed to mingle with other servants of the first-class because, as we all know, the help gossips just as much. The goal was that we all glean as much information as possible, running in two separate social circles. I can't say I agree with him. I think it's risky to be separated and vulnerable. It also just seems like a waste of extravagance when we have so much room in the suite; however, the ship is significantly undersold for its maiden voyage.

Charles follows behind us, placing our respective trunks and luggage in our rooms as Sarah helps me unpack. For a moment I lose myself and proper etiquette and move a piece of heavy luggage on my own. I grab the handle and begin yanking it toward me in quite an unladylike fashion.

"Oh no, Miss Turner, allow me."

Charles sweeps in, gallant and startled by my attempt. Our hands meet on the handle. I look up.

And time stops.

I half expect him to suspect something is amiss already. Of course I'd be the one to blow our ruse first. I didn't even make it twenty minutes before letting modern Ali out.

As we both have our hands around the handle of the luggage, our eyes meet closely and I can study his face. He's clean-shaven and beautiful. He smiles at me politely, with a smile that extends to the eyes.

And those eyes.

Warm and kind, they are both soulful and soul-piercing. Twin pools of dark chocolate that I would happily drown in.

"Thank you, sir," I stammer, awkwardly flustered. Ben, of course, notices.

He seems like he's quite enjoying it. He thinks I'm struggling to keep up with the etiquette, when really I just find this man's eyes hypnotizing and I can't quite figure out why. Ben steps away, so no one sees him laugh, leaving Charles and me alone in the corner. I realize I haven't let go of the luggage yet, and for the life of me, I can't figure out how to let go of it without making this moment more embarrassing.

"Charles is fine, Miss," he says politely. His thick English accent is smooth and luscious, like velvet. I could listen to it all day. He almost seems just as nervous as I am. I don't know why. He's not the one traveling from the future pretending to be a first-class passenger. I remind myself this is Titanic's maiden journey. Perhaps he's new in his role. I give myself a list of reasons he might be nervous. It couldn't possibly be because of me.

"Alice, then," I say, a bit too fast. "Please."

All I want to hear him say right now is my name.

Say my name.

He smiles, a little shyly. "Alright Alice, I'm Charlie."

His name lands softly between us. I like the way he says mine.

"Charlie," I repeat back to him with a nod and a smile before quickly turning away to unpack a different suitcase. I feel the warmth in my cheeks as they turn red.

Why did I turn away from him?

Should I have bowed?

What am I doing?

What should I do with my hands?

God, why am I so fucking awkward?

There has to be somewhere in this beautiful room that I can crawl into and burrow forever.

Charlie excuses himself, explaining he has to attend another cabin. He nods towards Ben before his eyes meet mine again and he smiles before exiting the room. It feels as though he was smiling only at me, but I worry I'm reading into it in entirely the wrong way.

Finally alone, Ben slumps down into a chair lazily. "Well, *this* is nice." He's admiring the room, its grand stature, and luxurious appointments. I rip my gloves off so that I can touch everything. I want to create a sensory memory of every inch of this cabin. Every texture. Every detail.

Eric closes and locks the doors while Sarah and I walk around taking photos of the cabins. We have actual cameras in our lock boxes for when we are in private, and hidden cameras for when we are out in public on the ship.

We finish unpacking our things and settling in before Eric suggests that Ben and I walk up to the promenade deck to watch the ship sail away at noon. We can't hide in here forever, so we all nod in agreement and Sarah helps me pull my gloves back on. Eric places the eyeglasses with the hidden camera in them on the bridge of his nose.

"Before we go," I say, spinning toward them. "Everyone's clear on the story, right?" The typical "mother" of the group, I have to check one more time.

Ben sighs, amused. "I'm Benjamin Turner, you're Alice Turner, my half-sister. This is my valet, Eric, and your maid, Sarah. My mother died after I was born, my father remarried and they had you. Our family has made a fortune in hotels and real estate development. We're sailing home together to New York, then on to Boston. Does that pass your test?"

I nod, satisfied. "Alright, alright. I'm sorry." I know I'm being overly careful. "I'm just nervous that we're going to stick out somehow."

"I think as long as we act like we have money, we'll blend right in with this lot," Ben says reassuringly, as he nods his head toward the hallway filled with passengers. "Provided you don't trip and fall over yourself, or try to lift your luggage again."

I chuckle. "Oh, you noticed that, huh?"

Ben smirks at me. "What I noticed was you checking out the room steward."

"I was not!" My voice practically raises an octave the more defensive I get. I'm a terrible liar and it shows. Charlie certainly is handsome. More than handsome, actually. He's fucking gorgeous. There's no harm in acknowledging that, right?

"Whatever you say, sister. Let's go, shall we?" Ben's grin is maddening as he extends his arm out for me to take.

We take one last deep breath before stepping out of our cabin and into the public hallway.

Charlie is out there helping another family settle in across the hall. His gaze catches mine and he smiles. I quickly look away but can feel my cheeks flush with warmth. I don't know why I'm blushing or why he seems to affect me like this.

Situated in the forward part of the ship is the Grand Staircase. Spanning over sixty feet from the landing to the glass skyline sitting above, it is the main connection point between decks for first-class passengers. I run my hand down the seventeenth-century solid oak banister. The staircase features carved paneling throughout, and at the base of the stairs, there is a cherub light and a carved wooden clock. It is a wonder to behold. I have only ever seen grainy black-and-white photos of this space or deteriorated underwater images, hardly able to recognize the beauty that she once was. Time has broken down her appearance, so to witness her in her luxurious glory is truly an honor. It's difficult to comprehend that this beautiful piece of artistry lies in ruin on the ocean floor in a watery tomb.

Via the Grand Staircase, we find ourselves on A-Deck Promenade, an enclosed walking area spanning the length of the ship reserved for first-class passengers. Ben and I walk slowly, arm in arm, as the ship pulls away from the dock. Crowds below are enthusiastically waving us on, not realizing how lucky their fortune is to be on land and not this doomed vessel. Ben and I are whispering to each other as we play a game of who's who. We spent weeks studying photos and biographies of the famous guests and are now covertly pointing them out to each other.

Ben leans into my ear and tips his head toward a mustachioed man with a bowler hat and a walking stick. "Ismay, right?" I calmly nod affirmatively, and he smiles and leans in again. "See? I paid attention."

Ismay tips his head politely toward us as he passes by, which seems to excite Ben. If one of the richest and most powerful men on the ship didn't suspect something was amiss about us, then we surely passed some kind of test.

The ship moves on the brief journey to our first port in Cherbourg, and every so often, I can see Ben tapping the hidden camera he has on his walking stick. The sun has shifted as it enters golden hour, and the ship that seemed vast and marvelous in the bright light now feels even more luxurious and romantic in the dreamy orange glows. I stare out over the water and feel the salt air on my face while Ben pulls out his pocket watch. I'm lost in a daydream until I can hear Ben in the middle of a conversation with someone who isn't Sarah or Eric.

"... No, our family owns a hotel chain on the east coast, but we live in Boston. My sister and I are making our way home now...."

Ben gently puts his hand on my elbow to turn my attention. He's speaking to another man, around his age and height, with light brown hair and blue eyes. He's dressed in a tan suit and matching hat. I recognize him immediately from my research and from the homemade Guess Who game Ben and I played in my living room during a last-minute study session. The man is Edward Harrison, famed steel tycoon.

"May I introduce my sister, Alice Turner." Ben sounds proud to say that. He's always felt like a brother to me. It just feels right to have him introduce me like this. It honestly doesn't even feel like a lie. Though we have only known each other for just over a year, we felt bonded immediately, like platonic soulmates. We just understand each other, maybe even better than we understand ourselves. "Alice, this is Edward Harrison."

Edward takes my hand in his, leans forward, and raises it to his mouth. He kisses it, maintaining eye contact with me the entire time. Without good reason, it leaves me uneasy. He lets go of my hand and smiles at me. It's disingenuous and cocky. He looks every bit as smug in person as his photograph did. His eyes lock with mine and they are a great deal colder and emptier than the comfort I saw in the warmth of Charlie's. He seems to look at everything, and everyone, as if they are objects he possesses. I want to roll my eyes so far back into my head, but social protocol won't allow it, so I stand there like a frozen porcelain doll and smile innocently. The dream girl of this era, it seems.

I stand there smiling politely as he continues speaking with Ben about his business. I already know who he is. He is based in New York and has been groomed by his uncle to take over the family business empire. He talks finance and business to Ben as if I'm not there, yet he clearly wants me to hear it and be impressed by it. Ben does a better job than I do at pretending to care, but luckily my opinion wouldn't matter to him, anyway. He explains to Ben that he and his elderly uncle are traveling back to New York after business took them to London.

He directs his attention back toward me. "Have you been to New York, Miss Alice?"

Of course I have, but I don't think he wants to hear about the time Ben and I went to Pride weekend in New York City on a whim and then waited outside for hours hoping to get Hamilton tickets. So I play the doe-eyed girl once again. "No, sir. I have not had the pleasure." The sickly sweet tone I have to use with him tastes disgusting as it rolls off my tongue.

"Perhaps soon then? I would love to show you around *my* city."

Of course he would.

He speaks as though I'm already wrapped around his finger. He makes it sound like he owns all of New York. God, he's so smug and presumptuous this 20th-century fuckboy. I can't even pinpoint why I don't like him. I chalk it up to a gut feeling. I am not normally a person who rushes to quick judgments or makes assumptions about someone without knowing all the facts. But I have a feeling about him and I just can't ignore it. I'm certain that underneath all that money and propriety, underneath that facade of goodness and civility, is just the hollow shell of a self-important man.

Suddenly the bugler interrupts with the dress call, a reminder that dinner is approaching. It's time for everyone to return to their cabins and change into their most elegant fashions. Saved by the bugle, I think to myself gratefully.

Edward turns back toward Ben, his eyes brightened as if he has just had an idea. I have a terrible feeling this has something to do with me, as his eyes move from Ben towards me.

"Mr. Turner, you and your sister *must* do us the honor of dining with our party this evening, won't you?"

Ben doesn't know what else to say, and I'm not sure he even sees what I see in Edward. "It would be our pleasure, Mr. Harrison."

Shit.

Chapter Ten

April 10th, 1912

"Which one?"

Sarah nods toward the wardrobe, where a line of crystal-beaded gowns shimmer under the light like a row of precious stones. Still in my corset and underthings, I cross the room and run my fingers along the luxurious fabrics. I close my eyes and move my hand back and forth on the rack. My indecision on what to wear extends even into the 20th century. Sarah notices my dilemma and quickly pulls one out, handing it to me with a smile.

"Don't worry. I do the same thing, and it's easier when someone just decides for me."

I laugh. "You might be right."

She helps me into a deep purple gown with an elegant high-waisted columnar silhouette. The undergown is a dark purple silk fitted through the waist. The wrapped overdress is the same color, but is a crystal beaded silk chiffon that sweeps into a train in the back. It has a deep squared neckline, and the bodice has short crystal beaded sleeves. A silk band at my waistline in contrasting lilac cascades down into my train. I lower my head as Sarah tucks matching jeweled pins into my hair.

"There," she says. "Perfect."

I meet her gaze in the mirror and smile. "I wish you could come with us. It doesn't feel right, like we're leaving you behind. Like you're lesser than us."

Sarah waves it off. "Oh, god. Don't feel bad, please. There is not a single tiny part of me that wants to dine with all those people, to have everyone staring at me. I'm glad to dine with Eric in the saloon. I think if we can get the other maids and valets talking, we'll learn just as much as you and Ben will."

She's right, but I think it may take a night or two of rubbing elbows before anyone, first class or the servants, will divulge anything remarkable.

"That's true. The help hears everything, don't they?"

"They sure do," Sarah says with a smile. "Well, you're all set. Do you need anything else before I go?"

"No, thank you. I'm going to relax in the sitting room with my book while His Royal Highness finishes his grooming ritual." I playfully nod my head toward Ben's room.

Sarah giggles as she walks toward the door. "Enjoy yourself tonight, Ali."

I grab my book from the bedside table and head into the sitting room, stretching out on the sofa and opening up to where I left off. I make it two lines in before glancing up at the fireplace. It's fake, of course—electric—but the flickering light still feels real in that comforting way fire always does. There's nothing better than reading in front of a fireplace.

I place the book down and approach the mantle. My fingers fumble for a switch. I feel around uselessly. Nothing. I've built actual fires, real ones, and now I'm defeated by a fake fireplace. A woman with a goddamn master's degree, foiled by 20th-century tech. Fantastic.

I glance helplessly toward Ben's room. There's no way I'm asking him for help. I'll never hear the end of it. I can literally hear him now giggling and asking, "*oh, you need me to turn you on, Ali?*"

That's not an option.

I pause for a moment and think of how to remedy this situation.

Oh, yes. Charlie.

Surely he would know how to turn it on. I walk over to the door and I pop my head into the hallway. He is standing further down the hall, checking his watch.

"Excuse me, Charlie?" I suddenly feel nervous just saying his name.

He looks up, eyes brightened. "Miss Alice, is there something you need?" He strides toward me and faces me in the doorway.

"Yes. I, uh...I need help with the fireplace."

He blinks. "The fireplace?"

I nod, embarrassed.

He smirks, only a little, before catching himself. "Uh... of course." He sounds flustered. I step aside so he can enter the sitting room. He glances at the fireplace. "Is it not working?"

"I don't know," I say, shrugging my shoulders. He looks at me puzzled, with one eyebrow arched. "I can't figure out how to turn it on."

He lets out a small laugh and quickly runs his hand along the side of the fireplace, easily flicking on the switch I didn't realize was there. The fireplace illuminates as soft flames bloom to life.

Charlie leans casually against the mantle, one leg crossed over the other, with an elbow resting just so. "Voilà."

God, he's gorgeous. The fireplace isn't the only thing that just got turned on. *Ali, what the fuck?* I feel a flutter in my chest as my heart beats faster.

He picks up my book and hands it to me. "Always better to read in front of a fireplace, right?"

"Right," I manage.

We both freeze for a moment, holding onto opposite ends of the book. His body looms over mine. Standing this close together, I can hear his heartbeat echoing alongside my own. His brown eyes, dark like wood, but comforting and warm, gaze into mine. I stare at his hand gripped tightly on the edge of the book. *I want him to grip me like that.* He inhales sharply and lets go of the book, his hand flexes as he releases it. Something about that makes my breath hitch. Why is something so subtle, so hot? *What is going on with me?*

"Have a good evening, Alice," he says gently, like the dew on morning grass.

He stops in the doorway and looks back at me once more. His mouth splits into a grin. Forget the fireplace. His smile alone is like a beam of sunlight illuminating the room.

When he's gone, I let out a breath I didn't even realize I was holding. It wasn't even intentional. It wasn't as though I forgot to breathe; it was as if I forgot *how* to.

I have no time left to read my book. As if I could even focus on the words now. I walk across the room to put the finishing touches on my outfit before we have to leave.

I stand in the mirror examining myself as I pull on the matching long evening gloves. I have to admit that I'm impressed by the work of Dr. Conrad and Dr. McCoy's design team. For a moment, I allow myself to feel beautiful. I swish in the mirror with a slight air of playful confidence.

In my reflection, Ben appears behind me, fully dressed and dashing as ever in a black tailcoat with satin lapels and a pointed front waist. He has a white formal shirt, waistcoat, and trousers that match his tailcoat. His bowtie is in hand. He has never figured those out. His hair is combed back into place after sighting slightly from the breeze on deck.

"Wow, Al," he says as I turn around to face him. "You look incredible."

I grin. "Thanks. You—"

"Oh, I know!" He interrupts and moves in a small twirl to show me the entire ensemble.

Always the showman.

Ben is the best-dressed person in any room he walks into, not even for his fashion, but for the self-assurance that oozes from him. I wish I could bottle even an ounce of his confidence.

He looks down at his hand with the undone bowtie and back up at me with a face of childlike helplessness, waiting for me to offer to save him. "You know I'm hopeless with these."

I take it and knot it with ease.

"Hey," I say quietly. "What do you think about Harrison?"

I'm looking for any kind of acknowledgment that the bad vibes I get from him aren't just in my head. History remembers him fondly, but something about him doesn't seem right to me.

Ben raises a brow. "Cute, but not my type."

"Ben."

He sighs. He can tell that I don't want to have dinner with him, converse with him, or even command his attention at all. "Honestly, Al, he's pretty arrogant. He seems like a colossal asshole. But we're supposed to be conversing with the who's who on the ship, and he's unfortunately a member of the elite. If there are secrets to uncover, he might know a few."

"You're right." I smile, reassured for now, and slip my beaded bag around my left wrist. I'm thankful that at least my poor opinion of Edward isn't unfounded, and that Ben shares similar concerns. "Ready then?"

"Always." Ben takes my right arm and leads me out the door.

The Grand Staircase gleams like something out of a fantasy as Titanic's rich and famous all make their way to dinner. Ben and I follow the crowd and he politely bows his head toward the other gentlemen as we walk. Inside the First Class Dining Room, white walls and crystal chandeliers stretch endlessly above patterned linoleum floors. It's grand, but cold. Ornate, but somehow impersonal. Crowded, and yet I feel completely alone.

As we enter the room and make our way toward Edward's table, many guests have grouped themselves into cliques, no doubt discussing any salacious gossip that may have come aboard. High society just feels a lot like high school, and I can feel the eyes of other passengers on Ben and I as we make our way through the dining room. I try to keep my gaze forward and mimic his confidence. Everyone separates into their social circles, judging those around them while hoping no one sees the skeletons in their own closet. Some things never really change, I suppose.

"There you are!" Edward stands as we approach his table. He gestures to two empty seats beside him and dread blooms in my stomach.

My eyes fix on the empty seat directly next to him. *Please don't let that one be mine. Please don't let that one be mine. Please.*

"I'd like you to meet everyone," Edward says, voice theatrical. He gestures toward the large crowded table and suddenly I feel like I'm on a stage intended to perform the song I no longer know the words to. "Allow me to introduce my new acquaintances, Mr. Benjamin Turner and his sister, Miss Alice Turner." He enunciates the word "sister" in a way that makes me internally shudder as if he is not just trying to make it clear that I am single and available, but more so, laying claim that I am his. It's like I am undiscovered territory and he has just planted his flag of ownership in me. I, however disgusted, smile politely and properly greet each guest that I am introduced to.

"Miss Alice, I saved this seat for you, so we can get to know each other," Edward says with a sickly sweet smile as he pulls out the chair directly next to him and waits for me to sit down in it. He goes through the motions of chivalry and gentlemanly behavior, but it's empty and insincere. I glance at Ben, who is helpless to save me and sit down, taking great care to mind the appearance of my gown as I attempt to act like a proper lady.

There are seven other guests seated with us, and they all seem to be in the same elite social circle as Edward. Arthur Harrison, Edward's uncle, sits across the table from him. They're both in the center of the table, no doubt to hear everything and be able to control the conversation. On Edward's left is his cousin, Francis Holt, his wife Helen, and their daughter Daphne. At the far end of the table is Joseph King, a friend of Edward's from university. He travels with his wife Cecilia and her sister Martha. I can see the resemblance between the sisters as they both examine me up and down and whisper to each other. I don't know if they suspect anything or just don't like me. I assume they are uncertain of Ben and me, likely having never heard of our family or our business before. Perhaps they also see Edward's attention directed toward me and are intrigued by whatever attachment they think is forming.

I stare at the table before me, examining the intricate design on the porcelain plates. There is enough cutlery laid out for a family of six, and yet it is all just for me. I panic for a moment, hoping to recall the order of cutlery from the etiquette lessons we took to prepare for this. I glance at the menu for the evening. It lists ten courses. Everything from oysters, to roast duckling, to French ice cream. It all sounds wonderful, but I'd sell my soul for a cheeseburger right now. Not some gourmet burger with farm-sourced cheeses and bacon jam, but the most unhealthy burger you can imagine from your favorite local hole-in-the-wall. The kind of place that is covered in fifty years' worth of grease and oil so thick that you don't know how health and safety inspections have allowed it to stay open. The kind of burger where just from the sight of it, you can feel your arteries blocking up. The image in my head of attempting to eat a greasy burger in my silk gloves in front of this horrified audience is almost enough for me to crack and laugh out loud.

As we work through the courses, the table is robust with conversation. Some of the conversation is quite entertaining and even relatable. I find the banter between Francis and his wife, Helen, quite refreshing and amusing. It is a stark contrast to how rigid and separate Joseph and Cecilia King seem. I can only assume that this is perhaps a difference between a marriage based on affection rather than convenience or gain. I find it interesting that Francis and the Harrisons are related, as Francis is much warmer and friendlier than Edward or Arthur.

Ben is doing his best work filling in the gaps of our life story. He is quite adept at telling somewhat truthful stories about us but sprinkling in enough falsehoods to cover up the modern details. His skill as a raconteur commands attention in any century.

Edward interjects often with stories that are intended to impress me. I suppose on paper, everything he says and the way he acts is entirely normal and proper of the time. This is what he has been taught to do, I remind myself. For a moment, I think perhaps I judged a successful man too harshly, and maybe my prejudice got the better of me. Maybe I wanted to dislike him, and so I found any detail that would make it easy to do so. But then I watch him wordlessly motion to the wait staff when he wants more wine and I realize my first impression was accurate. I thank the server each time they fill my glass or clear a plate. Edward seems impressed by my manners, but doesn't feel the need to replicate them himself. Something in his manner of speaking is just insufferable, and the more he talks and the larger he makes himself seem, the smaller I feel. I've always felt like you can tell a lot about someone by how they treat people in the service industry. Edward clearly sees people as those above and those below.

I don't know why, but the evening gloves are perhaps the worst part. I feel trapped in them. They are more restrictive than even the corset. It feels as though my skin cannot breathe, like every inch of me is caged. I'm grateful that dinner is drawing to a close soon. Edward continues to talk, though I think he just enjoys listening to himself. He seems pleased at how well I listen and smile innocently. Little does he realize I'm really thinking of different ways to remove his head from his body. My fork pierced through his neck. The champagne bottle smashed over his head. Anything for a moment of peace without his incessant fabrications of personal and professional heroics. I find it quite convenient that he is the hero of every story he tells.

As the server clears the last dishes from the table, Edward stands and smooths out his tailcoat. I know what this means. I'm about to be free. *Thank fucking God.*

"Your company has been lovely ladies, but I believe it is time for cigars and brandy. Gentlemen, shall we?"

Ben has been preparing for this, but immediately looks over at me with concern. The confidence he has had on parade tonight drains from his face. I know he's nervous about splitting up for the first time. Will we be able to keep up this charade if we do not have each other to lean on? I admit I am not sure if he worries more about keeping his own appearances up when we're apart, or my ability to do so without his help.

"Do you mind, Alice?" Ben asks like he needs my permission.

We both know how crucial these sessions of cigars and brandy are. He can learn unknown trade secrets of major business empires, secrets that perhaps went down with the ship. In order to keep up this appearance, he really shouldn't be asking my permission. He should take charge, and I should be the quiet follower.

I nod at him sweetly. "Not at all, Benjamin. I am quite tired. It has been a long day and I'm sure you could use company more riveting than mine. I shall walk back to the suite. It won't take long."

It feels weird calling him Benjamin. I only ever use his full name when I'm annoyed, though I know it is proper for the time we find ourselves in. I appreciate his care in making sure I'm okay. I know that underneath the etiquette displayed in his question, he genuinely wants to know if I will be alright. He knows my face and what I try to hide. He could see how uncomfortable I was at dinner. It's difficult for me to bite my tongue and act only as a spectator rather than an active participant.

Ben leans in closer. "You sure you're okay?" he whispers.

Maybe we should have a code word or something, so that we know when a situation is undesirable. He gently kisses me on the cheek before stepping back to examine my face.

I silently nod, fake a smile, and watch as he leaves with the other gentlemen. The ladies stay at the table to continue discussing mundane topics. Apparently, the French lace tablecloths Cecilia King ordered for her daughter's cotillion were not the ones she received. *Oh, the horror!* The dresses are being shipped in from Italy and the designer is taking too long. *How will you survive?* I consider throwing a curveball at them and getting a rousing conversation about women's suffrage going, but decide to just retire for the evening.

I excuse myself from the table and make my way out of the dining room. For a moment, I consider going straight back to the suite, but I know Sarah is likely there waiting to discuss the evening.

I'd like a moment alone, just to feel like Ali for a second. I step out of the first exit I can find onto an outdoor deck. There's a chill in the night air. I enjoy feeling the rush of cold air on my skin. The men are preoccupied with cigars and brandy and the women have all but retired for the night. I am alone. *Finally.*

I lean over the rail and slightly slump my posture. I can breathe and be alone with my thoughts. It's nice to even have thoughts, even if they have to be kept to myself. The ocean stretches endlessly before me.

I hear a door swing open and feel a presence behind me.

Out of the darkness is a voice. *His* voice.

"It's bloody cold out here," Charlie says to himself. He breathes into his hands to warm himself, before realizing he isn't alone out on the deck. "My apologies, Miss Alice."

He seems surprised to find me outside...alone...in the cold.

"It's Alice, please," I say, gesturing to the spot next to me.

He takes a few steps toward me and positions himself against the railing, facing the opposite direction like he's keeping watch.

"How was dinner, Alice?" he asks, tipping his head to the side.

"Cold."

He turns his head and fully glances over at me, brow curved. "The food?"

"The company." I smile wryly at him, my sarcasm having accidentally slipped out. I also realize I've been leaning over the railing this entire time, my posture not at all the image of ladylike delicacy that it should be, though it does not even seem to concern him.

He huffs a small laugh, arching his back over the railing to stretch. "You seem different from the rest of them, Alice."

It's dark, and he can't see me beaming at his observation. I don't know why, but it makes me happy that he thinks I'm different. I should be nervous about his observation. Do I make it that obvious that I'm not from this time? And why do I even care about what he thinks?

I shouldn't care. But I do.

Charlie looks down at me, exhales loudly as if he's made some sort of decision, and steps back from the rail. "Walk with me?" He tilts his head toward the empty walkway on the deck.

"I shouldn't." I can barely muster the words. I don't understand many of the social customs, but I know this is scandalous. I should leave right now before anyone sees us.

He leans toward me, close enough that our noses almost brush against each other. I breathe him in. The smell of sweet vanilla is intoxicating. He looks directly into my eyes and it's hard to remember my own name.

"But do you want to?"

"Yes," I whisper.

He takes a step back and smiles, waiting for me to cave in and follow. It works. He smiles like that, and God, I think I'd follow him anywhere.

We walk for what seems like hours, talking about everything. I tell him carefully edited stories about my childhood, from growing up in Boston to my relationship with Ben. He listens like every word matters.

I'm suddenly very aware that I've probably been rambling, and I worry that I'll slip up and reveal something I shouldn't. Conversation seems to come easily with Charlie, and I can see myself saying something that should be secret. But I also just want to know more about him. He somehow feels mysterious and yet also like someone I've known for years.

"Look at me, spouting off nonstop," I say, suddenly feeling self-conscious. "I feel as though I've done all the talking."

"No. It's fine. I like it."

"Why?"

His voice grows soft. "I just like the sound of your voice."

My voice? He likes the sound of my voice? Why in the world would he find listening to me ramble on enjoyable?

I turn my head toward him in confusion. "Mine?"

Charlie turns toward me fully. His gaze intensifies. It stops me in my tracks. "Yes, yours."

He says that so matter-of-factly, it's as if he's surprised I've never heard that from someone before. To be honest, I don't think I talk enough to anyone else, apart from Ben, for them to like the sound of my voice.

We stand there frozen, only for a moment.

Yes, yours. I let his words linger in my mind, as if I'm slowly savoring their taste. I quickly brush a wisp of hair from my face and attempt to deflect attention from the rosy warmth flushing my cheeks.

"Please tell me about you."

Tell me something awful so I can stop looking at you as if I'll melt. Tell me you hate babies, or sunsets, or Saturday mornings. Anything that will snap me out of this trance I find myself in.

He shrugs. "There's not much to tell, honestly. Your life sounds far more interesting."

"No, really. I want to know," I press.

He smiles to himself and continues walking. "Well, I was born and raised in London."

"What part of London?"

He cocks his head, impressed that I asked for a more specific location. "South London. Croydon."

Admittedly, my skill in geography is severely lacking and hinges solely on my knowledge of sports franchises in the area. I cannot tell you a single thing about the locations of rivers in Europe, but I can tell you which cities have soccer teams and what leagues they're in. You'd think a historian would have an expert-level knowledge of geography, but not me.

"What do you do for fun?"

He seems surprised I asked such a question. It's as if he hasn't thought about life beyond working on ships in quite some time. "What do you mean?"

"When you were home in London, what was fun for you?"

"Hmm." He tilts his head. "If I wasn't working or at home, I was usually at the pitch with my mates."

"So... you like soccer?" I'm trying not to show my excitement. I know a lady of this time wouldn't have an expansive knowledge of sports, but it's one of my passions.

"Like it?" He tilts his head back and laughs. "I love it."

"And your team?"

"A local club, Crystal Palace." He grins as he excitedly turns around and begins walking backward while he gives me a history of the team and his favorite player, Harry Hanger. It's odd to hear an English person using the term soccer, but I have to remind myself the term football wasn't universally used until the 1980s. I wish I could tell him how big the sport has gotten, how wide the audience has grown, and how his small boyhood club now plays in the Premier League.

I notice how well he must know the layout of the ship because he glides backwards easily while maintaining conversation with me. It reminds me of how effortlessly an ice skater can skate backward. His entire face brightens as he talks about his team. The joy he finds in it is infectious.

He turns around to walk alongside me again. "I'm sorry if I prattled on too long. No one has ever asked me that before."

"Why not?"

He shrugs. "I don't know, but I'm glad *you* asked me. It made me happy to share it with you."

This man is a goddamn golden retriever. He's charming, but it's entirely genuine.

I have to keep the conversation going to avoid swooning. "Tell me about your family."

"My father was a carpenter. He owned a furniture store. And my mum, she handled the books for him."

"Do you have any siblings?"

"No, it was just me." Me too. I wish I could tell him that. He sounds wistfully sad. I wish I could tell him I understand what it's like to grow up lonely. "They lost a few before me, and that was hard on Mum. She always said I was her miracle."

"Did you always want to work on ships?"

"No." Charlie's jaw clenches at the question. "My father taught me everything he knew about carpentry, and I was going to take over the shop until…" His voice trails off as if we've landed on a particular part of his history he does not speak of often.

"Until what?"

He sighs, an exhale full of sadness and a sense of remorse. "Mum got sick. She died when I was eighteen. Nothing was the same after that. I just had to get away, so I joined White Star Line, and I've been on ships ever since. Papa died a few years after."

"I'm sorry, Charlie." I wish I could tell him I understand him, that I too am an only child. I wish he could know that I also realize what it's like to lose a parent. Judging from the change in tone from when he spoke about his mother to his father, I wish I could also share with him that I understand the concept of having a difficult relationship with a parent. We have more in common than he realizes, and it pains me that I cannot share that with him or comfort him.

"It's alright, Alice," he says, but I can feel the weight of it still pressing on him. I want to tell him I understand. That I know loss. But I can't.

"Do you enjoy working on ships?" I ask, trying to redirect the conversation toward perhaps a lighter topic.

"It has its moments, but it's a place for me to rest my head every night. I was on the Olympic for a while. When spots opened up for Titanic, my friend Alfie was going to take one. But his mother got sick, and he went home to care for his family, so I offered to come in his place. I like the ships well enough, but it's an odd feeling sometimes."

"What do you mean?"

"Spending your life traveling, always moving, but never feeling like you actually go anywhere. I'm nearly twenty-eight and I feel like there's so much I haven't seen. It's not bad though, living on a ship. Sometimes I get lucky and meet interesting people." He smiles and winks at me.

Charlie looks down at his watch and shakes his head. "Time flies. It's eleven. The parlors are closing soon and people will be out here. You should get back before anyone sees you."

I don't want to leave. I don't want this to end. I don't even care who might see us walking together. I look down and see his empty hand and want to weave my fingers with his. He escorts me over to a walkway to B-Deck, remaining outside as I stand in the doorway.

"Tomorrow?" I ask.

I want to meet here again. I am hopeful that he does too. I don't know what this is, but I know I want more of it.

He looks at the ground and smiles. It looks like he's blushing. He's nervous.

I'm making him nervous.

He looks back up at me and smiles. When he smiles, it's like he does it with his whole heart.

"Tomorrow, Alice."

He says my name like a promise and it feels as though my heart is free-falling from my chest.

I walk back to my cabin grinning like a fool, already counting down the hours.

Chapter Eleven

CHICKEN BY YOUR NEIGHBORS

April 11th, 1912

We are approaching Queenstown, Ireland, to take on additional passengers and supplies. The morning air carries the faintest tang of sea salt through the open saloon windows, and the low hum of conversation blends with the clinking of teacups and the occasional scrape of silver on china.

Ben sits across from me, recounting his night as he pours himself a cup of tea.

"Well," I ask, slicing into my poached egg. "Did you learn anything in your first cigars and brandy session?"

Ben grins from around the rim of his teacup. "Well, I learned that Mr. Harrison fancies *you* quite a bit."

I shoot him a look, and he seems completely unbothered. Amused, even. He's enjoying this. Of course he is.

"No, he doesn't," I reply flatly. Absolutely not. Do not pass go. Do not collect $200.

Ben chuckles. "What do you mean?"

"He likes the *idea* of me," I say, setting down my fork. "Not *me*. I think he's interested in any single woman of sufficient fortune and acceptable breeding that he deems worth the chase. I'm just unfortunately positioned in his line of sight."

Ben raises a brow. "That's your expert analysis?"

"I think he's bored," I continue, folding my napkin with perhaps more intensity than necessary. "And men like him don't see women as people so much as puzzle pieces to fit into the life they've already envisioned for themselves. Just a trophy to add to a cabinet."

I suppose I don't fully know Edward enough to say he is a truly reprehensible man. Perhaps he is simply a product of his time and upbringing—shaped by expectation rather than intent. He was raised with wealth, groomed to inherit power, and with that came standards as to how he should live his life. Aren't we all just products of the expectations laid upon us? I can't truly fault him for that. He has been expected to take over the family empire, marry well, and continue the cycle. It's likely never even occurred to him to question it. I suppose maybe his true fault is that he just doesn't realize he's barking up completely the wrong tree.

Ben snorts. "Fair enough. Though it's amusing watching him lay the attention on you so thick."

I stop myself from rolling my eyes. "Thanks."

Ben shifts in his chair. "What did you do last night? Sarah said you got in pretty late."

"Nothing," I answer quickly, too quickly. "I just went for a walk."

Ben's brow furrows. "By yourself?"

I shake my head, avoiding his gaze. The less said, the better. My eyes drift around the room, looking for any reason to remove myself from this line of questioning and the inevitable lecture that will follow.

I reach for my teacup and stir it, even though I've already added sugar and milk. It gives my hands something to do—something other than fidget beneath his scrutiny.

Ben and I sit in a silent standoff, each of us waiting for the other person to break first.

Then Charlie enters the saloon, carrying a note he hands off to a well-dressed gentleman two tables over. As he turns to leave, his gaze snags on mine, and for a moment, the room drops away.

His brown eyes are calm but observant, and I forget how to breathe properly. My heart is beating so loudly I feel as though the entire room can hear. My hand moves in a frantic, subconscious swirl, my spoon spinning faster and faster in my tea. I'm not even aware of it until my cup slides off the saucer with a clatter—and in my attempt to catch it, I somehow launch the spoon across the table.

Charlie smirks, then disappears out the door.

Ben watches the entire embarrassing scene unfold with growing amusement. When I finally turn to meet his gaze, he looks positively gleeful.

Here it comes. The Spanish Inquisition.

He leans forward, voice low and teasing. "Al, what the hell was that?"

"Nothing," I say, brushing at my skirt. "Absolutely nothing." I grab the porcelain teapot and lift it with the air of someone trying very hard to change the subject. "Do you want more tea?"

Ben leans back in his chair, laughing under his breath, delighted at my embarrassment. "Well, I don't know. Are you planning on throwing the whole pot at him next time?"

My cheeks go hot. I want to crawl under the table and disappear forever, but once I look at Ben, the absurdity of it all hits me and I let out a reluctant giggle.

"My, my, my," he says, hands folded like a smug bastard. "Do my eyes deceive me, or are you blushing?"

"It's, uh… very warm in here," I lie shamelessly. "We should go."

Ben chuckles as we stand, but I'm too distracted to care. I have no idea what's happening to me. I don't recognize this version of myself—the one who blushes, fumbles teacups, and fantasizes over a pair of brown eyes.

And yet, I don't mind her either. And if she gets me near Charlie again, she can keep hold of the wheel.

We head up to the promenade deck, eager to walk breakfast off in the fresh air. The breeze is brisk and cool, carrying the scent of the Irish coast. We pass a particularly contentious game of shuffleboard in progress. Ben slows to observe, likely trying to brush up on the rules before being roped into a game himself. Ben is competitive. He plays to win, always.

And for purely selfish reasons, I hope he does. Ben is unbearable when he loses. The only thing worse than losing Ben is a sick Ben. He becomes a melodramatic wreck, and will act like a Victorian child on their deathbed even when he has just a minor cold.

I walk on ahead, following a similar path to my walk with Charlie.

I'm so lost in the memory that I step on the pale blue ruffled skirt of my dress and trip forward.

A gloved hand reaches out to grab my arm, sparing me from my usual clumsiness.

I look up at the mystery figure who has just rescued me from mortification and see a pair of eyes that are familiar to me.

Because they're my eyes.

Or rather, the eyes of Violet Kelly, my great-great-grandmother.

Chapter Twelve

FALLS BY ODESZA FT. SASHA ALEX SLOAN

April 11th, 1912

Violet Kelly.

I knew it was her the moment our eyes met. Her resemblance to me or mine to her is uncanny and instantly recognizable. It is astonishing to feel as though you're looking into a mirror from another time. It's not just the freckles, or the high cheekbones, or the bridge of the nose.

It's the eyes.

My eyes.

Her eyes.

Our eyes.

"Thank... thank you," I manage, breathless.

I knew she was here, somewhere on the ship. I had only hoped I would be lucky enough to meet her. I told myself I wouldn't seek her out in order to keep the secrecy of our project aboard. But I convinced myself that if I found her organically, it was okay. I'd let fate play it's hand. But even that logic was thin.

I feel a sharp pang of guilt for not informing Dr. Conrad, and even Ben, that I have a relative on Titanic and that I knew about it before signing on to the mission. I convinced myself that it wouldn't change anything and that I was still committed to our job. I believed, perhaps recklessly, that the likelihood of meeting her among the thousands of people aboard the ship was near impossible.

But now, here she is. Standing before me, very much alive. I hate myself for not knowing what to say to her. Thankfully, my awkward nature does not appear to be hereditary because she takes over the conversation with ease.

"Are you alright, dear? You nearly took a tumble there," she says with a soft laugh.

"I'm well, thank you. No harm done to me or the dress."

"Wonderful." She gently presses my hand in hers. Even through her glove, I can feel the warmth of her touch. Kindness radiates from her eyes. "I'm Violet Kelly. A pleasure to meet you, Miss...?"

"Alice Mur—Turner." I correct myself quickly, stumbling over my alias.

"It is lovely to meet you!" She looks toward the shuffleboard game. When my gaze follows hers, I see Ben approaching, having noticed my near trip and fall.

I smile and gesture toward him. "And my brother, Benjamin Turner."

Ben takes her hand to greet her. As his eyes meet hers, he too realizes where he has seen them before. I can't tell if he suspects anything or if he is just shocked at the resemblance. He looks back at me, puzzled, but before he can say anything, she motions toward a gentleman approaching us.

"This is my husband, John Kelly," Violet says brightly. "Darling, this is Alice Turner and her brother Benjamin."

John greets Ben with a firm handshake and a pleasant smile—just as warm and kind as Violet's. They engage in polite conversation, which frees me up to speak more privately with Violet.

I turn fully toward her, trying to commit every detail of her to memory. If my recollection is correct, she's thirty years old right now, two years older than me. She's beautiful. She stands taller than me, dressed in a pale green day dress that brings out the green in her eyes. Her dark brown hair is twisted into a graceful knot. Her skin is fair and freckles dance across the bridge of her nose. Her green eyes look at me in confusion, likely wondering why this awkward young woman is just staring at her. Or, perhaps, she too sees the striking resemblance between us.

Say something, Alice. Anything. You're being weird.

"Are you enjoying your journey?" I ask, painfully aware of how dull the question is.

Is that the best thing I could think of to say?

"Indeed," she says, smile widening. "I have never seen a ship this grand before. I confess I do not particularly enjoy sailing, but I did not want John to travel alone. Is it just you and your brother here, or are you married?"

"Oh no, no, no." I laugh loudly and wave off the notion before realizing I'm being a little too casual and all too awkward.

Thankfully, she laughs. "That would have been my response if I had not found John. He is my match in every way. When you find that, you will just know. It just takes time."

Time. She doesn't realize I'm quite familiar with the concept of time right now, especially given the method of travel that's brought me here.

I have to make myself ask her questions about her life as we walk, many of which I already know the answer to. I've studied our family records and ancestry, but something about hearing it directly from the source makes everything feel more real, more legitimate. It brings them to life.

"Do you have children?" I ask.

Her face brightens the moment the question leaves my lips. "Oh, yes! We have twins, Diana and Evelyn. They are back in Boston with my mother. She cared for them while we traveled. We cannot wait to return home to them. I miss them so much."

"Twins, how lovely. That must be an adventure!" Evelyn was my father's grandmother. She eventually married Thomas Murphy, and their son George was my grandfather.

She smiles appreciatively at me. "Thank you. They certainly keep us busy. John proposed we take an extended trip to have some time together, just the two of us. I thought I would enjoy the peace of our travels, but now I long for the loudness of our home. It's not without its difficulties, of course. They are twins, but they could not be more different."

She unclasps the gold locket that hangs around her neck. Etched into the outside is a rose pattern with the letters V and J interlocked. I recognize it immediately from a box of family heirlooms I have in storage. Inside is a small black-and-white photo of two small girls in front of a grand staircase.

She points to a little girl sitting on a stool. "Here, that one on the left, that's Diana. She's my wild one. She's loud, theatrical, and vivacious. When she enters a room, she barrels into it. If she has a thought, you're going to hear about it. And she has *many* thoughts!" Violet is laughing as she points to the other little girl, standing behind her sister. "On the right, that's my Evelyn. She's quieter, a thinker. You can see the wheels turning when you look at her face. I have to coax her feelings out sometimes. She guards herself a little too well, I think. See how she has her hand on her sister's shoulder? She tries to take care of everyone and protect them like that."

Evelyn sounds so much like me, it leaves me speechless. I recognize the setting of the photograph right away. From the placement of the windows to the staircase in the background, it's quite clear the photograph was taken at home. Their home. *My home.* The same staircase I slid down as a child, the same windows I peer through to watch a thunderstorm. They've always been with me. Perhaps I've never truly been alone.

My voice breaks slightly. "They're lovely," is all I can muster with a grateful smile. "Thank you for sharing them with me."

What a gift it is to meet my family, even more so to see myself in them, in their physical appearance and their character. It comforts me to know that perhaps some of the way I am isn't because of any trauma, but that it runs in the family.

The bugle calls for dinner, interrupting my gaze upon the photo of my great-grandmother and her twin sister. I quickly hand the locket back to Violet and try to compose myself. I don't want to scare her off with my emotions.

"Perhaps we will see each other again tomorrow?" I ask, hopeful but cautious.

"I would like that very much," she says warmly. Violet smiles as John and Ben approach to escort us back to our cabins before dinner.

I walk in silence back to the cabin with Ben, replaying every word of my conversation with Violet. Every second felt like something out of a dream I hadn't dared to hope for.

We reach our cabin, and I quickly kick off my shoes with a dramatic groan of relief. I need a moment's rest without them. They've been hurting all day. I like to wiggle my toes when I'm fidgeting, and these shoes do not allow even the tiniest space for movement.

Ben stands in the doorway between his room and mine, removing his jacket and tie while recounting his day to me.

"John was really nice. He's a funny guy. Not at all arrogant, like some of these people. How was his wife? Violet, right?"

I nod, heart hammering.

"She's just lovely," I reply dreamily. I sound like I'm in awe of her, which truthfully, I am.

Ben narrows his eyes. "It's wild. She has the same eyes as you. I had to do a double-take when you introduced us. With a resemblance like that, you'd think you were family." He says it so innocently, as if genuinely surprised by how similar two strangers can look.

There's no getting around this now, I suppose, and I'm a terrible liar.

I sigh, fiddling with the hem of my dress. "She's my great-great-grand-mother, Ben."

Ben's eyes widen in shock. "You never told me you had..."

"I've never told anyone," I say quickly. "I didn't even tell Dr. Conrad. I was afraid if they knew, I'd be removed from the mission. I never expected to know her, let alone find her. I convinced myself the odds were impossible."

Ben runs a hand through his hair, still stunned. "Ali..."

"Don't worry, you can save the lecture. I know I can't tell her anything. It would put my existence into question if I did and anything in her life were to change."

I try to reassure him as best I can. I'm not about to risk anything.

Ben nods slowly and I am grateful he doesn't scold me further.

"What happens to them?" he asks softly. "Do you know?"

I nod. "She will make it off the ship. But John...he won't survive."

The room falls silent.

Ben's shocked expression turns to sadness. "Oh, Ali. I'm so sorry."

I nod, blinking away tears. "I'm sorry too. I shouldn't have kept it from you or Dr. Conrad. It was wrong and I know that. I think once I had my mind set on coming, I didn't want anything to prevent it from happening. I was finally doing something brave, and I just didn't want it taken away. I assumed he would do some kind of background check or look through records and see I had a relation here and immediately disqualify me from the project. When that never happened, it just became easier to not mention."

Ben places a hand on my shoulder. "I'm just sad for you. You've found her, a piece of your family. It's another person for you to lose, and that worries me, Ali. You've already endured more pain and loss than I think is fair to one person."

"I appreciate that, Ben. I really do. But I promise you, I'm okay." I meet his eyes, steady. "I've always known what happens to her and John. I wish it could be different. And I know for the sake of my existence that I can't alter their lives. So for now, I'll just enjoy the time I have with them and I just have to be content with that."

Chapter Thirteen

ELECTRIC TOUCH BY TAYLOR SWIFT FT. FALL OUT BOY

April 11th, 1912

I dress for dinner in a midnight blue crystal beaded gown that has loose sleeves and a multi-layered skirt that cascades down to the floor. I fasten on my black silk shoes just as a knock sounds from Ben's door.

I pause, already dreading the voice I know will follow.

"Mr. Turner," Edward says from the hallway. "I was wondering if I might escort Miss Alice to dinner this evening."

God, help me. I know we're stuck dining with him again, but I don't want to walk with him, too. I hate the idea of being seen on his arm, paraded around like I'm a prized heifer that he owns, makes my stomach turn.

"Oh, I'm sure she would be delighted," Ben replies, to my horror.

I glance over and Sarah is looking at me apologetically. She despises Edward as much as I do. She has the luxury of gossip from the other maids and staff, and they do not hold back on his arrogance.

Ben enters my room, preparing to deliver the blow in person. I don't even give him the chance. When I greet him with an icy stare, he knows he's in trouble.

"Al," he says with a wince, "what was I supposed to say?"

I roll my eyes. "Tell him I'm seasick. Tell him I went overboard. Hell, you can tell him I was a figment of his imagination for all I care. Anything except, 'oh, I'm sure she would be *delighted*.'"

Ben stares at me like he knows he crossed enemy lines but didn't see an alternate route. "Ali…"

Eric appears behind Ben like a diplomatic referee. "Ali, he didn't have a choice. We have to play whatever hand is dealt to us, and right now, Harrison's the card we've got."

And I'm the sacrificial lamb. Cool. Glad we're all on the same page.

I appreciate how well Eric and Ben get along, but I hate being out-numbered. Especially when I know Ben is right.

I groan, dramatic and entirely justified. "Fine. Let's get this over with."

I pull on my black silk gloves. Tonight I am thankful for them. At least he won't be able to touch me. It's as though I'm wearing armor, shielding me from his touch.

I pace in a few circles, trying to hype myself up with the energy for an evening of empty smiles and fake politeness. Sarah gives me a reassuring smile and I walk over to the open door in Ben's room.

"Mr. Harrison, how nice to see you," I say, saccharine and sharp. I think I'm getting the hang of the doe-eye damsel play-acting.

"Miss Turner, you look exquisite," Edward says, words dripping in manufactured charm. It's an innocent-sounding compliment, but it's laced with lust. Not for me, or my status. I'm merely a trophy, a conquest that he needs to win over. The challenge is all that excites him. With him, it's never "you *are* exquisite" as if he's complimenting or admiring me for me. It's simply "you *look* exquisite" as if I am merely ornamental, adorned with the highest fashions, styles, and jewels. He speaks as if the appearance of goodliness matters more than actually being good.

He holds out his arm, and I flash a fake smile as I take it. The moment he looks away, my eyes go dead.

As we step into the hallway, I can see Charlie watching from down the hall. In the crowd of people he can see me, but only as I move closer can he see I am on Edward's arm. He looks upset, and when I try to make eye contact with him as we pass by, he looks away from me.

I feel guilty, and I worry Charlie will think something is going on with Edward. Why am I even worried about that? I don't understand the thoughts I'm having. .

I spend dinner listening to Edward's extravagant tales of his time at university. He is, conveniently, the hero of every outlandish story he tells. I have to hold back my extensive education and pretend to be fascinated and in awe of such a worldly man.

His uncle Arthur is almost as arrogant as he is, but at least he has decades of success to warrant it. Arthur built the business empire, but all that work came at the sacrifice of never having a family, leaving his nephew as his heir. It still surprises me that Francis is related to Edward or Arthur, given how different his character is compared to theirs. He and his wife Helen, and their daughter Daphne, are surprisingly kind, and I feel a twinge of guilt for judging them initially.

I block out the table conversation and focus on the orchestra in the background, smiling politely every few moments to give the impression that I have been listening. As dinner draws to a close, I sit and wait for Edward to take his leave with the other gentlemen. I try not to show my excitement, but their outing signals that I am free for the evening. Right on cue, he stands up, thanks the ladies for their company, and asks the other men to follow him for cigars and brandy. I find it amusing because they make snide comments about the ladies gossiping over tea every afternoon, but in reality, that's exactly what the men are doing every night over brandy.

Ben rises from the table but stays beside me. "Do you need an escort?"

"No. I'll stay here," I whisper.

I watch as he leaves, waiting till he is out of sight to make my escape. I quickly take my leave from the table. I tell the ladies I had too much sun today and am quite tired. It works like a charm, and I'm on my way out to the spot where Charlie found me last night.

But he isn't there.

I tug at my dress nervously while pacing back and forth on the deck.

Maybe he isn't coming. Perhaps last night was an anomaly. A right place, right time kind of situation. Maybe I read all the signals wrong. Did I wrongfully perceive his friendliness to be chemistry? Maybe he doesn't feel whatever it is I'm feeling. Is this all in my head? Perhaps his appearance of disappointment when he saw me with Edward has something to do with this.

I pull my gloves off, and it feels like my entire body can exhale.

I get inside my head and convince myself he's not coming and turn to leave. The door creaks open and he walks out tentatively, as though surprised to see me.

"I didn't think you'd come," I whisper.

"I didn't think you would either." His voice is flat, and as quiet as mine, as if he also is unsure if last night was a one-off situation.

"Why not?"

"I thought you'd be preoccupied with Mr. Harrison." There's a bitter edge to his voice that sounds almost like jealousy.

"Absolutely not." I scoff at the mere thought of being involved with that man. And it hurts me even more that Charlie would think that would be the man I'd choose. "I would never."

He looks at me, studying. "So you're not attached to him?"

I shake my head. "I'm not attached to *him*."

Why did I say that? And why did I say it like *that*?

I've known this man for twenty-four hours and I'm worried he thinks I like someone else? Is this how much my personal life is lacking? I'm flirting and I don't even realize I'm doing it?

Charlie smiles wordlessly and gestures toward our walk. His smile is different. It isn't polite or innocent. He seems almost devilishly pleased that I said I wasn't involved with Edward.

As we stroll along the deck, conversation flows more freely than I expect. My guard slips. I let out glimpses of the modern version of myself that should raise red flags, but Charlie doesn't seem fazed. He *likes* it. All the sharp edges I feel pressured to file down for others don't seem to bother him at all.

"You're quite the reader," he says. "You had a different book today than you did yesterday."

My eyebrows raise with intrigue. "You notice a lot, don't you?"

"I notice *you*."

The words stop me in my tracks.

"Me? Why?"

"You're not like everyone else. There's just something about you. It's different."

"Oh." The disappointment in my voice is clear, as if this is yet another expectation I fall short of.

"No!" Charlie quickly interjects. "Not like that. It's a good different. It's like every day I wake up and the world looks the same, and then I meet you, and I look at it now, and it's like everything is in color. There's just something about you."

I don't know what to say. My mouth opens, then closes again.

"You're the only person who's ever seen me like that, I think," I admit.

"Really?"

"Most people think I seem too closed off, or damaged, or messy."

"I don't think you seem like that at all."

We reach the back of the ship. No one is out here. The ocean stretches endlessly beneath a canopy of stars. I walk casually, less of the prim and proper ladylike way I've had to grow accustomed to lately. There is a small square platform in the walkway that is raised, large enough for someone to stand on to get a better view of the water.

"You don't?"

"The woman I see is intelligent, independent, opinionated." Charlie notices me looking at the platform and then around as if I'm calculating how to best get up there. I hop up unaided, for a moment forgetting that I should have done that a bit more gracefully. "Alice, be careful," he says with a tone of concern, yet his face appears amused. "Maybe she's a little stubborn, too."

The water is calm. The waves ebb and flow rhythmically, as if lulling us or even pushing us closer together. I tilt my head back and stare at the night sky, breathing in the cold air and letting the breeze blow the hair around my face. My arms stretched out at my sides. I just feel free.

I marvel at the sight of nothing around us but gentle waves. It's hard to tell where the sparkling navy sky ends and the dark ocean begins.

"It's so beautiful," I whisper.

"It is," Charlie replies softly, but when I steal a glance in his direction, he's not looking at the sea. He's looking at me.

And his eyes.

Those goddamn eyes.

They flicker in the moonlight, still full of so much warmth even in the dark.

As I step down from the viewing platform, Charlie offers both hands to assist me. I take them and for the first time find my gloveless hands in his. They're warm despite the cold air. His touch sends an electrical current through my body like I've never felt before. Something inside me has awakened. It's as if we have something inside each of us that has been waiting to be connected. It's crazy, but it feels as if these are the hands I'm meant to hold for the rest of my life.

That's ridiculous, Ali.

We stand frozen for a moment, my hands in his, lost in time. I don't know if thirty seconds have passed or thirty years. Neither of us wants to move, or perhaps neither of us can. I feel magnetically pulled to him, and all I want is to get even closer. We stand beneath a twinkling sky, and somehow the only stars I see are the ones in his eyes. It takes everything in me not to bring my lips to his. I am utterly mesmerized by him. Our eyes remain locked together until we're both jolted back to reality by a familiar voice.

"Alice!"

Ben's voice comes toward us. I drop Charlie's hands and we separate like shrapnel. I feel like I've been caught after curfew in the backseat of a boy's car.

"Alice, what are you doing out here?" Ben asks, confusion and concern etched across his face. I'm still not used to him saying my full name instead of Ali.

I struggle to find the words until Charlie steps in to rescue me. "Miss Turner had requested a tour of the ship, sir."

Ben raises an eyebrow. "In the cold? Out in the dark?"

Charlie looks tongue tied and I realize it's my turn to step in and aid. "Well, the tour *was* inside, Benjamin. But then Charlie mentioned how clearly you can see the stars and constellations in the sky when out at sea. We stepped outside so I could see them."

Ben looks both of us up and down carefully, but appears to believe the story. "It's late though Alice, we'd best retire for the evening."

He turns toward the path back to our cabin and holds out his arm for me to take.

As we walk away, I glance over my shoulder.

"Goodnight," I whisper to Charlie.

Ben leads me away, slowly at first, nodding politely in the hallways to other passengers. As we move closer toward our cabin, I notice he picks up a brisk speed. We reach our rooms quickly and Ben leads me inside. Barely a second after closing the door, Ben turns on me, the politeness gone from his voice.

"Since when do you care about astrology?" Evidently, he saw straight through the constellation story we attempted to weave.

"It's astronomy, Ben."

He rolls his eyes. "Oh, come off it. Don't be cute. I don't believe for a second that you were out there looking at the stars or whatever bullshit you said."

"I don't know what you mean."

"Yes, you do! I saw you, Al! I saw the way you looked at him. The way you touched him." His voice grows quieter. "I've never seen you look at someone like that."

I have no defense. He's right.

Charlie makes me feel something that I can't explain. I am careful, calculated, and consistent. But right now, I'm reckless. I'm heading down a dangerous road without a map. And the scariest thing about it is that it doesn't scare me at all. Something feels right. It feels as though I've just been searching for Charlie. And as much as I realize it's dangerous, or even perhaps stupid, I can't stop myself from wanting to be near him.

"You're right," I say finally. "But, it's not what you think, Ben."

I decide to cave in a little and admit to some flirtation, but not to the extent of what I feel. If Ben knows everything, he'll feel the need to be overprotective. I don't want to stop seeing Charlie, so for now, it's better to keep him in the dark. I also can't give Ben the answers he wants, because I don't even fully understand what I'm feeling. All I know for certain is that I feel drawn to Charlie.

Ben exhales, frustration giving way to concern. "Al, I'm not mad. I promise. A little attraction is normal. Maybe not what you're used to, but it's normal. You're allowed to have some fun. Flirt all you want, I don't care. Just be careful, okay? You know why we're here. Remember what's going to happen."

My eyes go cold, as if the light has been snuffed out from them.

Remember what's going to happen.

I've been avoiding that significant detail. Whether I've been actively avoiding it or too distracted to think about it, I'm not sure. But now that Ben has planted the seed in my brain, it's consuming me.

I know the ship sinks. I know there is a significant loss of life. Why did it never occur to me to wonder what becomes of Charlie? Am I really that lost in a haze, or did I just not *want* to know? Even if he makes it off the ship, we still live in two different centuries. Where did I think this was going? I can't believe I let myself get caught up in this. It's as though I know the ending of the book but won't read the last chapter, just in case something could magically change.

When Ben retreats to his room, I scramble to my trunk. Besides the small locked box, I have a stack of papers, blueprints of the ship, photos, and the item I'm looking for — the list of crew and passengers. I frantically rifle through the papers, my eyes rapidly scrolling for his name. Finally, I see what I've been avoiding. Right before me are the words that feel like a stab to my heart.

Hughes, Charles Frederick- Deceased

I collapse down to the floor, crumpled paper in hand, and weep.

Chapter Fourteen

HOW LONG BY SUFFS

April 12th, 1912

I lay awake in the stillness of morning after a sleepless night, the fabric of my pillow damp with guilt-stained tears. I am *not* the girl who cries over a boy, especially one she doesn't even have. This sudden show of emotions feels foreign to me. I want nothing more than to just stay in bed and wallow in self-pity, but I know I need to go through the motions and do the work we came here to do.

Perhaps if I occupy my time with our work, I can avoid whatever it is I'm feeling. I look in the mirror and see my eyes are red and swollen. I go to my trunk and pull out the vial of concealer I have hidden. It should cover enough that I look halfway normal.

I put on a pale blue silk dress with a lace cover that has long sleeves and begin pulling back my hair. I'm hoping to spend most of my day in the Reading and Writing Room and escape into someone else's world instead of my own.

Truthfully, I also want to hide from Charlie. I somehow find this ridiculous ruse easier to maintain if I don't have to look into his eyes and continue lying. Maybe I can get through the next few days if I just cut off whatever this is right now before it has the chance to root itself inside me.

Ben knocks at the adjoining door and enters my room. He is fresh-faced, clearly having had a much better night's sleep than I have. He looks ready to greet me energetically until his gaze sets upon the reflection of my face in the mirror.

"Geez, Al. You look like shit."

I glare at him through the mirror. "Why, thank you," I mutter. I can't even muster up a retort.

Ben hesitates, his expression shifting from teasing to concern. He can tell I'm not myself, but I can see in his face he's debating whether to press the issue. Is it safe to engage or am I a bomb just waiting to detonate? He is used to me being his calm and consistent friend and not the curveball of chaos I seem to have become over the last few days.

He tilts his head. "Al, I can tell when something's wrong."

"Ben, please. I don't—"

"But I also know you enough to know when you're not in the headspace to talk." Ben cuts me off before I become defensive, raising his hands in a soft surrender. "Take the morning to yourself. I'll come and find you later. We've been invited to dinner again with Mr. Harrison's party."

He adds that last detail nonchalantly, like he was hoping I wouldn't notice it.

I curl my nose at the thought of another forced outing with Edward. Two evenings were bad enough, but now more? Ben catches me without even looking at me. He just knows me that well.

"Don't even make that face, Al. It's not getting you out of it." He stops himself, walks back over to me, and plants a gentle kiss on my cheek. His eyes scan the emptiness in mine with concern. I can see how deeply my pain unsettles him. "I'll come get you later."

One thing I've always loved about Ben is that he never pushes me to talk when I don't want to, or better yet, can't find the words to convey my feelings. He always gives me time and space to process and think. He knows I need to analyze an issue from every angle and just really chew on it for a while. However, judging by the look of concern on his face, even he hasn't seen me in this much of a rut before.

What I wouldn't give for a session with Dr. Kassen right now to untangle the myriad of feelings I'm having, though I'm not sure that even she is equipped to deal with this situation. Time-traveling to the Titanic, falling for a boy I can't have, and mourning something that never was? It sounds like the plot of a bad novel.

I grab my book and walk to the Reading and Writing Room, slipping onto a settee near the window. The page is open in front of me, but the words blur. My eyes are fixed, but my mind is elsewhere.

"How is the book?"

Violet's familiar voice snaps me back to reality.

Startled, I fumble the pages in my hands, losing my spot. "Oh, um...It's good."

Violet laughs. "Really? You've been on the same page for ten minutes."

She's caught me there. I guess I didn't realize how much I'd spaced out.

"Oh, it's quite a good book, but I think I've done enough reading for today. I'm finding it hard to focus," I admit.

I try to regain composure. I don't want to incur questioning from Ben *and* Violet about why I seem so melancholy and withdrawn.

She smiles kindly. "Perhaps you need some air. Would you care to walk on deck with me?"

I rise, grateful she doesn't press me further. I don't know how to convey the mixture of feelings brewing inside me in a 20th-century socially acceptable way right now. I can barely make heads or tails of them myself.

As we exit the Reading and Writing Room, I spot Charlie in the hallway. He's speaking with another steward, but notices me out of the corner of his eye like he senses my presence. He turns his head and glances at me, inhaling sharply as if suddenly nervous.

My cheeks grow red. My legs feel weak.

Don't engage, Ali.

I try to move to Violet's left, hoping to use her body to block him from being able to see me. It doesn't work, Violet assumes she's in my way and steps aside, so I end up looking ridiculous trying to hide behind a figure that is no longer there.

Fucking smooth.

When I glance up, Charlie is looking directly at me, and my heart practically leaps out of my chest. It's so fucking hard to avoid him when he looks like that.

Violet and I make it to the promenade, a breeze curling around us as we walk towards the rear of the ship where it's emptier. I lean on the railing, watching the waves form in Titanic's wake, the pale blue ribbon it leaves behind. It's comforting.

We pass a gaggle of first-class ladies chattering in hushed tones and I feel their judgemental stares rake over Violet. But then they line up like ducks in a row and politely nod as they walk by. It's like that group of mean girls in high school that smile to your face and talk behind your back. I still find it comical how similar human nature is, even though the world is wildly different.

Violet chuckles. "I always find that amusing."

"You find what amusing?"

"The routine of propriety. Smiling and nodding to someone's face, but continuing in scandalous gossip once out of earshot. I know what they say, you know. I've heard the whispers."

I glance at her. She's smirking, but I see the tension behind it.

I don't know what she is talking about. Does she assume I know, or is she trying to say something? I don't know if I should pretend to know what she means. Luckily, before I can decide to play along, she continues.

"We have the fortune to exist in high society," she says, "but we are not truly part of it."

"What do you mean?"

I assumed anyone first class, anyone with enormous wealth, all ran in the same social circle. I suppose I mistakenly believed that as long as you had the means, you were in the club. I know there is a difference between old money and new money, generational wealth versus self-made. Perhaps she is referring to that.

"It's complicated." Violet gazes out over the ocean. "We're included in the sense that we attend the same events and the same parties. We support the same charities and our children attend the same schools. But there's a disconnect."

"Why?"

"I think we scare them, John and I. We challenge the very framework of the society they live in. They're afraid of new ideals, and new ways of doing anything. John and I have been very vocal supporting women's rights in society. But it's not just about securing the right to vote for women, that's only the beginning. What I want is for their lives to be entirely their own."

My heart quickens. "I understand. And I wholeheartedly agree with you."

It's important to me she understands she can tell me anything that's on her mind. I have a feeling whatever is weighing on her right now is something I'd want to know as part of her family and as part of the work we were sent here to do. I wish I could tell her where the world is now. How far we've come. How far we have left to go.

She seems to take my agreement as a sign of support to continue further, as if she has encountered a trustworthy and sympathetic audience. She sighs for a moment and quickly wipes her brow. The exhaustion of putting on the constant demure expression of femininity, at least publicly, is finally breaking her.

Violet takes a deep breath in and out. "It's just so difficult to have your life reduced down to a single moment, a transaction. An arrangement involving a woman, made entirely by gentlemen, as if we are something to trade and own. We breed young girls to be the perfect, mild, obedient wife. We make them believe their entire purpose is to marry and marry well, for the future of their family may depend on those connections. They have to produce as many children as their husband wants, because they're his children, after all, not hers. They're expected to manage the home, but not allowed to own it. And then we raise our boys to expect it. Your partner should be challenging you, to be better, to be more than you are, not serve you. I want my children to have love if they want it. But I want them to have a partner that basks in their light, not one that snuffs it out or feels threatened by it. And the cycle just repeats itself, over and over, like a carousel. It is utterly exhausting."

"They're lucky to have a mother like you," I say sincerely. It's strange—to be so close in age to her, but also feel like she's the mother I never had. The mother I wish I'd had. We've only just met and yet it feels as though I've always known her. When I hear her talk so passionately about feminism and equality, it feels as though she's speaking the truths that are alive within my heart as well.

Her voice breaks slightly. "I want more than that. I want more than that for my girls. I want them to be bold and ambitious. I want them to look at the world with kindness and see not what it can give them but what they can give back to it. I want them to make their own choices and blaze their own path."

Violet leans in closer. "Women are capable of so much more than they, or anyone else, realize. We're not looking to turn society on its head or take over. We just want a seat at the table."

I freeze, my breath catching in my throat.

"Wait..." My voice trails off as I think about what she's said and why it sounds so familiar to me. That phrase. *We just want a seat at the table.* It's the same quote that's printed on the cover of the Boston Suffragette Weekly that hangs in my office. The author, Alice Carney, wrote the most controversial and progressive pieces in the journal. Historians have searched endlessly through records to find a trace of her, but none have been able to locate her. The consensus in my profession is that it must have been an anonymous pen name.

I realize now that Violet may be the key to unlocking the secret of who Alice Carney is. Is this the moment I've been waiting for? That I've been working toward for years? There are likely many women on board who share the same sentiment as her; however, Violet, so freely and casually using the phrase, has to mean something. Surely it doesn't show mere agreement with the movement, but participation within it too? Perhaps she even knows Alice Carney herself, if she is indeed a real person, as some believe. Or perhaps, closer to what I and many others believe, she may know who created Carney. I don't know why, maybe it's just sheer intuition, but I feel as though Violet is the key to unlocking her identity.

"I've read that before," I whisper. "I have the journal it's printed in. Are you telling me you know Alice Carney?"

Violet smiles, chuckles to herself, and leans closer to me. "I *am* Alice Carney."

I blink. My mouth opens, but no sound comes out.

Holy shit.

"Oh, my... how?"

I'm in sheer disbelief. I don't know what I expected her to say, but this admission was not it. I suppose the information was all in front of me the entire time, yet I could never see the finished picture. I knew Violet was involved in the suffrage movement, but maybe the link between her and Carney was too obvious a possibility that I just couldn't see it. I searched only for the most difficult, hard-to-find theories.

"It's safer that way," Violet says with a smile. "I knew my opinions were, shall we say, ruffling some feathers in society? I decided to start publishing under a pen name. John has read everything I've written and has even helped fund and distribute the journal, but I knew I needed to keep him and the girls safe. I'm trying to change the world for them, but I have to protect them too. It's my job as their mother. As the movement grows in strength, I can only imagine it will grow more violent as well. So I created the character of Alice Carney. The goal was that if I funneled my thoughts and opinions into the character of Alice, then perhaps women would resonate with her more than someone they already knew. Secrets travel quickly in our society, and they can bring someone down just as quickly as they build them, which is why I felt it necessary to spread my opinions through a character. A beacon for the movement, an ideal we could all hold ourselves to or see ourselves in."

"I understand," I say, nodding slowly. It all makes sense now. The mystery. The voice. The pen name that captured the spirit of a movement.

Her explanation aligns with the theories of most historians, that Carney was used as a unifying character for the movement, an image to stand behind, similar to Rosie the Riveter.

"Why the name?" I ask, wanting to know everything I possibly can.

"It's quite simple, actually. Alice means noble and Carney means victory. And that's what I see for our mission. It will be a noble victory. And we will not stop until it is so."

My heart hammers. "Why have you told me this? I mean, I hardly know you." It's not lost on me that I am a stranger to her, and she has divulged something so personal to me.

Her gaze holds mine. "I... I just feel connected to you. There's something about you. It's like I already know you. It's hard to explain, but I just knew I could trust you."

Her words strike me right through the heart. I wish I could tell her the truth about who I am and why I'm here. I know I can't, for so many reasons. It would be impossible for her to believe, even if I could tell her. But her saying that she also feels connected to me without a reasonable explanation is enough for me.

It feels as though pieces of a puzzle, that I've had all along just floating, are finally locking into place. Anytime I asked Dad why he named me Alice, he always told me it was after Alice Carney. He never indicated that he had any idea about who Alice truly was, although we never got the chance to discuss it as adults. Did he know of the connection between Alice Carney and Violet Kelly? Is it some family secret he held onto until I was ready to know? I'll never be able to ask him or know for certain. He always just said I'd understand one day. But understand what? I want to believe that he knew the full story and thought he was giving me a name that truly meant something. I can only assume he was keeping the family secret until I could comprehend and appreciate the weight of the name he'd given me. A name that inspires one to be noble and brave, even in the face of the impossible. I am beginning to realize that perhaps it isn't a burden to be named for someone, it's a gift. It's a small light to reach out and grasp, to find warmth in when the world feels at its smallest and darkest. I could only hope to be as brave or noble as Violet.

"Do you ever think about revealing who she is? Who *you* are?"

She smiles wistfully, as though she's had this thought many times. "All the time, actually. I've started writing it a million different times, in a million different ways. I can never find the right words to tell the story of it all."

"All?"

"The movement. The progress. Where we started, why we did it, everything. But to publish it, we have to achieve something greater first. A real equality. Something tangible, legal, and permanent. Something that can't be taken away from us. Until then, Alice Carney has to remain a mystery. She still has a job to do. Her work is not complete. She still needs to inspire and unite women to believe their voices are louder as one."

"Well, I, for one, can't wait to read this one day when it happens." I lean in closer to her. "And it will happen, Violet." I try to sound confident to encourage her, though I know it truly will happen. I know the progress that will be made towards equality, in her lifetime and within mine. Violet speaks with such passion and conviction that I'd be proud to be in the trenches with her, arms-linked and fighting for equality.

"I hope you are right. I've only ever written one chapter, and it's not even really a chapter. It's more so a collection of thoughts that need to be stitched together coherently. It's hidden away, though. I suppose I'll pull it out again one day when we're ready."

"It's hidden? Where?"

She winks, grinning at me. "Under a floorboard in my closet. For safekeeping."

Holy shit.

The loose floorboard in my closet. The one I keep meaning to fix and never do?

Are you telling me this monumental piece of history and potentially the key to understanding who I am, has been literally under my feet for years? You've gotta be kidding me.

"Though I suppose the important thing isn't to tell the world that I am Alice Carney," Violet says, her voice turning serious. "Maybe it's to show women she could be any of us. All of us."

She motions toward some of the other first-class passengers mingling around us. "Most of society is so preoccupied with building their empires, ensuring their names are carved into stone or printed to paper. They believe that's their legacy." She shakes her head. "My children. And my children's children. They are my legacy. Their courage. Their freedom. I want more for them, for all of them. Even if I never get to see it, I want it. Even if nothing ever changes, I still have to try. I have to keep knocking on the door of change."

"Don't just knock on the door, Violet." I say with a smile. "*Bang it down.*"

Little does she know that not only will things change, but she will live to see it. In less than a decade, Violet and her daughters will win their right to vote. Not only that, but she will grow old and be able to watch them carry on with her work.

Her loud and fearless Diana will become an actress and will use both her platform and her wealth to care for impoverished women and children. Evelyn, her quiet and thoughtful child, will find her voice in calls for equality. As Violet said, the right to vote is only the beginning. Evelyn will be among the first women that enter the workforce as World War II rages on. After the war, she will advocate not only for continued employment opportunities for women but fair wages as well.

And generations from now, a girl named Alice will follow in their footsteps.

I share her eyes, her name, and her dreams.

She hopes to leave a legacy.

She doesn't realize it's standing right in front of her.

Chapter Fifteen

THIS IS ME TRYING BY TAYLOR SWIFT

April 12th, 1912

I sit at the table in the sitting room, feet propped on the other chair like a rebellious teenager, while Ben finishes getting ready for dinner. His reflection moves in the mirror as he grooms his hair into obedient submission with a silver comb and a dab of pomade.

"I have to tell you something," I say.

Ben doesn't look up. "What's up?" he asks, half-focused on taming a particularly unruly lock of blonde hair.

"Violet is... she's uh..." I stammer, mouth going dry. The words are there—I have them—but they won't come out. Saying them out loud feels unreal.

"She's what, Al?" Ben glances at me briefly in the reflection.

I take a breath and just say it. "She's Alice Carney."

Ben freezes, comb in hand. Slowly, he turns to face me, his expression shifting from mild curiosity to full-blown shock.

"Stop," he whispers. "You're kidding."

"I'm serious," I say. "She told me today. We were walking on deck, just talking and life and women and everything. She said something that made the wheels start turning for me. I got suspicious that maybe she knew who Carney was. I don't know why it never occurred to me that Violet and Alice Carney were the same person."

"How did this happen?"

"You know that cover that's framed in my office?" Ben nods, having seen it daily. "She quoted it. Word for word. I mean, she's said a lot of feminist things that made me think she was part of the movement. It could have been coincidental. I mean, she's from Boston too, so of course she would have access to reading the magazine herself to know the quote. But something deep in me kept saying there was something more. It's silly because all the evidence was right there, and I never even thought about the possibility that she was Carney. I just overlooked it, like I had a blind spot. I think I was so preoccupied with getting to know her, I just didn't see what was right in front of me. So I just straight up asked her if she knew who Alice Carney was."

"And she told you the truth?"

"She told me *everything*."

"Can we trust her?" My eyes narrow on Ben, ready to pounce in defense of Violet. He raises his hands to stop me. "I just mean, could she be covering for someone else?"

"I suppose anything is a possibility, but I believe her. She trusted me with this information and I believe what she's told me. Plus, as records show, Alice Carney disappeared and didn't publish for six weeks in the spring of 1912. Those six weeks line right up with the sinking. She was grieving. Or Violet was."

Ben nods slowly. "Wow. This is incredible. You've been working on this for so long. Do you realize what this means, Ali?"

"It's like finding a living piece of history," I say, nodding my head. "It's as monumental as Robert Ballard finding the Titanic wreck in 1985. I get that. I dreamed of uncovering her identity for so long, and now that I have, it means something entirely different to me. I finally realize why I am named for Alice Carney. It was for Violet. It was for Violet all along."

Ben sinks onto the edge of the chair across from me, stunned. "What are you going to do now?"

I shrug. "I don't know. She told me she wants to reveal everything at some point, but obviously, we know she never did. I'm hoping Violet leads me to the answer somehow."

Ben pulls out his pocket watch and checks the time. "Are we ready to go?" He checks himself over one more time in the mirror, fixing the last stray hair.

There's a sharp knock at the door and I know immediately who it must be at this hour. Edward.

"Ugh!" I groan as I tilt my head back and slump down in the chair like I've been mortally wounded. I feel like a child throwing a tantrum. I want to make my body into dead weight. The only way you're getting me out of here is if you drag me. I want to become the child throwing the explosive tantrum in the busy grocery store, and Ben, the embarrassed and mortified mother.

"Ali, I'm going to answer the door. Can you sit up and try to act like a lady?" Ben asks calmly, as if he's negotiating with a petulant child.

I cross my arms like a toddler. "I *am* a lady. A lady that doesn't want to go to dinner with that prick."

"I said a lady, not a baby," Ben says over his shoulder as he makes his way to the door.

"No promises."

I stand up and swish my gown into place. The underlayer is a red wine-colored silk with chiffon sleeves. It has a scalloped gold lace overlay and a matching wine-colored velvet sash around my waist. It feels the least ladylike, the least demure of any options the stylists sent me with. Its bold, powerful colors feel almost like battle armor tonight.

Ben opens the door and my scowl turns to an empty, placid stare at the flip of a switch. I will go through the motions, but I will not be happy about it. I find it more and more difficult to even pretend to be pleased in Edward's presence.

Edward stands in the hallway with his usual pomp, offering his arm like he's doing me a favor. Ben discreetly rolls his eyes behind him as he hands me off. We walk together toward the dining room, Ben trailing close behind.

We are dining again this evening with the Holt family and Edward's uncle. Luckily, the King family is not here tonight, so I am safe from the judgmental stares of Cecilia and Martha. Small mercies, I guess.

After my conversation earlier with Violet, I observe Daphne's mannerisms, looking for clues that would show she feels trapped within the confines of her life. Her mother seems intent on finding her a match during this voyage. The topic of marriage keeps coming up at the table, with questions about mine and Ben's parents and stories of Francis and Helen's wedding day.

Edward leans across me to speak to Ben. "Say, Turner, when will *you* settle down and choose a wife?"

Ben's nervous gulp causes him to briefly choke on his potatoes. I bite back a laugh.

For once, he's squirming, and I find it thoroughly amusing.

Daphne straightens in her seat, her back going rigid as if someone pulled a string. She adjusts her posture and shifts her gaze toward Ben. It's subtle, but I see it: the silent audition for male approval. Poor girl, she doesn't even know him and yet she feels the need to present herself to him.

"Yes, brother," I chime in playfully, patting Ben's back like I'm helping dislodge the potato from his throat. "When *will* you choose a wife?"

Ben stiffens his posture to regain control over the character he has been carefully crafting while on board. He laughs, smoothing his expression. "I suppose I haven't found the right woman yet."

He winks. Just for me. A private joke in a room full of performance.

"Oh, surely we can remedy that with such fine stock to choose from just here in this room," Edward says, pointing his fork outward toward the other tables of guests.

I freeze.

Did he really just say that?

Stock?

Are you fucking kidding me?

My fist curls beneath the table.

Violet was right. The life of a woman, her entire purpose, truly is reduced to the singular transaction of a marriage agreement. I can't quite decide whether his use of the word stock infuriates me more, or whether it is his implication that men need simply to choose a wife. As if she has no say in the matter. As if we just wait, always at attention, for their favor. She may accept a proposal after courtship has been initiated, but she cannot pursue a suitor herself. She must wait to be chosen off the shelf like the perfect doll.

I glance around the room. No one else reacts. No one blinks. Because this is normal.

This is expected.

It's like a professional sports draft. An athlete hones their skills their entire life. A hockey player, for example, will spend years perfecting their skating, their goal scoring, and their stick handling, all in preparation to present themselves as a package for choosing.

A woman does the same. From childhood, her education is based on the expectations and skills needed for marriage and managing a home. She hones her skills of sewing, playing instruments, learning languages, and other activities to fill her day as she pretends her life is exactly as she wished it would be. She learns it all not because she wants to, but because she has to. Because marriage is the only success route. Because her value is determined by how well she can perform.

And then she waits.

Waits to be noticed.

Waits to be chosen.

Waits to be owned.

A man decides her worth and it's utter fucking lunacy.

I am so exhausted from keeping up this performance of being an impeccably bred young woman. I'm tired of smiling when someone else wants me to, and not when I'm genuinely happy. The pressure to be the perfect blend of beauty, charm, and submission is crushing.

At this moment, I am incredibly grateful to be me.

Maybe I'm alone. But I'm free.

I may be faking smiles and choking down rage, but no one owns me.

I don't wait to be chosen.

I choose myself.

And tonight, that's enough.

Chapter Sixteen

April 12th, 1912

Luckily, dinner is over quickly and the gentlemen withdraw themselves right on schedule, allowing me to make a quick escape.

I come straight back to my cabin from dinner and slump into a chair, exhausted from the brave face I've been wearing all day. I hastily pull my gloves off and throw them on the table. I'm determined to stay in the room this evening. It's a half-hearted attempt to minimize the damage I feel I've already done.

Sarah enters with her journal in hand, but the second she sees me slouched in the chair, she sets it down and joins me.

"Ali," she says softly. "Are you alright?"

I exhale. "No. I'm not," I admit. "I feel like I've completely messed everything up."

"So fix it." She sounds so matter-of-fact—almost frustratingly so. She doesn't understand how tangled this all is. Or maybe she does.

"It's not that easy."

I don't know how transparent I am. Does she think this is just about playing the first-class part and pushing myself through performances? Or does she realize how complicated things have gotten now that I've let my feelings get involved?

Sarah's voice turns gentle, her hand warm against my back. "Ali, come on, none of this is easy. We didn't sign on to this for easy."

"I know," I mutter.

I have no experience with it, but it feels like I have a big sister comforting me.

"Look," Sarah says, voice softening. "I know we haven't known each other for very long, and maybe this isn't my place. But I can see you. And I can see that something has changed within you. I won't speculate who or what it is. That is yours to keep until you're ready. But, you should know, it's not something that happens all the time. And if you sit here and let it pass you by, Ali, you'll regret it for the rest of your life."

She doesn't elaborate, but she doesn't need to. I can feel the ghosts she carries, as if she has loved and lost, or perhaps been too afraid to love at all. I want to ask—but I don't. She's given me enough, and I think in some way, we understand each other now without words.

I sit in silence, sorting through the wreckage of thoughts in my head. I've never been this girl before, one who is reckless and acts on emotion instead of logic. Everything in my brain says run. It's what I always do when things get hard. I could get hurt. And even worse, he could.

But then there's something in my heart, magnetically pulling me to him, as if beyond my control. Lonely, intrusive thoughts fill my head. But with him, it's clear. Everything makes sense.

Perhaps what I need at this moment is one of Ben's patented dance-it-out sessions, but I haven't divulged to him the entire scope of what's going on in my head. He knows about Violet, but he doesn't know about Charlie—not really. I think if I brought him up to speed, we'd be arguing, not dancing. And I don't need to be under his watchful eye the rest of the time we're here.

"I think I need some air," I say, rising with a heavy breath. The fresh air, I'm convinced, will clear my head. But truthfully, I think I'm hoping to find Charlie outside, though I know I shouldn't. I glance back over at Sarah. "Thank you, Sarah."

I slip my gloves back on and walk towards the door, taking a deep breath to compose myself before heading back out.

The night air on the promenade bites my skin, but it's a welcome sting. I take great care to avoid the aft of the ship. The views of the deck from the smoking room and lounge would surely provide Edward with an invitation to join me. I am not in the mood to entertain him, or speak to anyone, for that matter.

I find a secluded area of the deck, out of sight from any windows, to just lean out over the rail and try to make sense of all my thoughts.

But clarity doesn't come.

Instead, I feel his presence behind me before I hear anything. There's no noise, no swing of a door, or even footsteps. Just a quiet sense of comfort and warmth glowing behind me.

"Alice?"

A light touch to my arm startles me, sending another electric current through my body.

"Charlie," I whisper. I don't even feel worthy of speaking his name. I need to get out of this situation. I came out here for mental clarity, but the sight of him clouds my mind even further. It's like a drug you know you shouldn't take, but it gives you such relief and pleasure you find yourself unable to leave it. The longer I stand in his presence, the more I will crumble.

"I called your name three times," he says gently. "What's going through that head of yours?"

"I have to go," I say coldly, like it's the only defense I have left. I hate that I'm using such an empty, lifeless tone to rebuff him. I'm convinced it is what's best for him, though I can't help but feel guilty.

"Are you unwell? Please let me walk you back to your cabin," he says.

He takes my hand in his to lead me and it's too much. It's too kind. Too warm. Charlie is the epitome of sunshine. He is the bluest skies. And I am a dark storm cloud, bringing only rain and thunder, set on destruction. I can't bear to dim his light.

"No, please." I yank my hand back. My voice rises as I hyperventilate. "I just... I can't do this."

"Do what, Alice?" he asks.

"I can't lie to you anymore."

I pull back and push through the door leading back toward the staircase, not fleeing toward peace, but desperately trying to escape the weight of the truth. I'm convinced that removing the privacy of our conversation will end it; however, I can see Charlie following me through the corridor.

"Alice," he says behind me, his voice urgent but low. "Just tell me what's going on."

"I can't." I walk faster. I don't want to destroy him. Maybe if I keep moving, he won't follow.

But I want him to follow.

He catches my arm. "Why? Alice, please. Just tell me."

I sigh and turn to face him. I take one look at his eyes and I break.

"Charlie, I have to *show* you. Otherwise, you will never believe me."

He frowns. "What?"

"Do you trust me?"

"Alice—"

"Do you trust me?" I repeat, firmer.

"Yes," he says, without hesitation.

"Then follow me."

I motion for him to follow my lead back to my cabin. By the time we get there, I'm barely breathing. I check the hallway. Luckily, there are no passengers nearby to notice any impropriety. I pull Charlie into my room.

Sarah has left for the evening, though I'm not sure if that is fortunate or not. It allows me the privacy to speak with Charlie. But it also means there is no one of sound logical mind to pull me back from the ledge right now.

Charlie hovers by the door, uncertain. I don't blame him. He has no idea what's coming.

I pace the room, back and forth, trying to think of the right words to say. Where do I even start? How could I ever expect him to understand or believe me?

Charlie is the first to break the silence between us. "Alice, what is going on?"

"I'm not like everyone else."

He laughs, trying to lighten the moment. "I know that. You're unlike anyone I've ever met."

"No," I say quietly. "I mean it."

"Alice, what are you—"

"I'll tell you everything. But I need you to listen first, okay?"

He nods tentatively. "Okay."

"I'm not from *this time.*" I exhale deeply. "My name is Alice Kelly Murphy, and I was born on April 29th, 1997. I'm from the future, Charlie."

"Alice…" Charlie tilts his head, growing impatient as if he thinks I'm using a delaying tactic, stalling him from the truth with some outlandish story about being from the future.

"Haven't you ever wondered why I'm so different from anyone else? You have said it yourself. I seem so modern, not like any other woman you've ever met. Why do you think that is?"

He shakes his head in exasperation. "Alice, what are you saying?"

"Charlie, I mean it. I'm from the future," I say, voice shaking. The details of Dr. Conrad and Dr. McCoy's discovery pour out of me. "I work at Chisholm University in Boston. I'm a historian there, and so is Ben. His godfather is a scientist, and he and his research partner discovered time travel. Eric and Sarah are scientists. Ben and I, as historians, were asked to come along on this project to time travel to the Titanic."

I realize this has to be an impossible story for Charlie to comprehend. Saying it out loud makes it quite apparent how ridiculous it sounds. How could I ever expect him to believe what I've just said?

I watch the disbelief wash over his face. He raises a hand, almost like a plea. "Alice, stop."

"I can show you, Charlie," I whisper.

I open my trunk and pull out the small locked box. I press my fingerprint to it and it opens. The advanced technology widens Charlie's eyes enough to be intrigued. I can see the curiosity fighting his instinct to dismiss my outlandish story. I pull out a small stack of evidence—the photos I had packed.

I hold them in my hand for a moment, debating whether to continue. I want him to understand and believe me. But I also know I'm about to shatter his world. I just don't want to lie to him anymore. There's no going back now. I'm past the point of no return. I hand a few of the photos to Charlie to look through.

Charlie stares at the first glossy photo. I'm posing with Ben in front of a Christmas tree at last year's university Christmas gala. Ben is in a modern, dark green three-piece suit and black tie with his arm around my waist. We were allowed plus ones but opted to attend together. I'm wearing a crimson red sequined fitted midi dress with a scoop neck and spaghetti straps. It's a far cry from the layers of silks I'm currently wearing. Charlie's eyes flicker with interest; however, I can't tell if it's the clear technicolor photo or the sight of so much bare skin.

He looks back at me, struggling to understand, and flips to the next photo. I'm moving into my college dorm, standing in blue jeans and a cropped Pink Floyd tee shirt next to my packed Jeep. I remember that day vividly because it was one of the few times Dad ever showed emotion. He acted all nonchalant the entire day, like me going off to college and leaving him for the first time was no big deal. Yale was only two hours from home anyway, and I'd travel back to Boston frequently. But we hadn't spent more than a few nights apart my entire life, aside from soccer camp a few summers during high school. He helped me unpack, bought me beer and groceries, and then we went to dinner. When he said goodbye, he acted like he'd see me the next day, but I watched out the window from my dorm as he cried on the way to his car. He couldn't show me his emotions, but he felt them.

The third photo is of Dad and I in 2011 at game six of the Stanley Cup Finals. We had just watched our beloved Bruins force a tie-breaking game seven, after scoring four quick goals in less than five minutes in the first period, the fastest ever tallied by one team in the finals. Dad's friends had seats behind us and took the photo. Late in the third period, as we waited for the final whistle to blow, Dad wrapped his arm around my shoulders and I put mine around his back. You can't see either of our faces, but somehow the pure joy is so clear.

"Alice, how…" He loses his words as he flips to the next photo. In the most revealing photo in the stack, I'm standing on a large rock formation in front of the shoreline in Cape Cod wearing sunglasses, a Bruins cap, and a black bikini. Ben took the photo when we were in the Cape over the summer, capturing me during the golden hour with a bright smile and a hand on one hip.

He looks flustered, and he drops the photos as he tries to compose himself and form a sentence.

"I'm sorry," he says nervously as he picks them up off the floor. I remain focused on the task at hand and wait for him to wrap his brain around what he's been told.

Finally, he sits, elbows on knees, eyes still on the evidence of a life he can't fathom. "Tell me everything."

"Well…my name really is Alice. Most people call me Ali. Ben isn't my brother. He's my best friend and we work together as historians at Chisholm University in Boston. I really have lost my parents. My mother left us when I was a child. My father raised me, but he passed away four years ago." It all just starts flooding out. It's like one of those buckets at a water park that builds and builds until it tips over, flooding everywhere. Everything pours out of me.

I watch his face as he takes in everything I'm telling him, looking for some indication of where his head is at.

"You lied to me, Alice."

"I didn't have a choice, Charlie," I whisper. "I swore never to tell anyone. We all signed a contract. I never thought I'd meet you, that I'd..." My voice trails off, unable to complete the sentence. I'm not even sure what I was about to say. My emotions are running at a completely different pace than my brain. "I promise you, I'm the same person as before. But there is something else I should tell you."

Charlie places the photos gently on the table and stands. "How could there possibly be more?"

"Charlie...."

"Go on then." His tone is flat, and I can hardly blame him for it.

"That woman you saw me with earlier. Do you remember?" He nods, unsure of where I'm going with this. "She is my great-great-grandmother."

He reels. "Did you know that before you arrived? That she was here?"

I look down at the floor. I can't bring myself to keep his gaze. His eyes, which normally shine when he smiles, are now full of hurt. It's a pain that I have inflicted on him, and I don't know how I'll ever live with it.

"Look at me, Alice. Did you know?"

I meet his eyes and answer, barely above a whisper. "Yes."

His voice and body language shift as if he's crossed over from confusion to anger. "So you've been lying to everyone? Is anything you told me true?"

"Charlie, yes!" I say, voice cracking. "Everything I've told you is true except for where I'm really from. I'm still me! I'm still Alice, I promise you. I never wanted to cause you, or anyone, any pain."

Charlie paces the room, thinking quietly, stopping momentarily in disbelief. He seems to be summing up a total of everything. He appears to almost be somewhat accepting of everything he's learned until something in his face fades, as though he's come to a realization. He finally breaks with the question I've been dreading.

"Why Titanic?"

I don't know how to answer, and he deserves to know the truth. Whatever I say will hurt him.

"It's…" I stop myself. I can't jeopardize the work we're doing, or even history itself. I can't be selfish. My selfishness is what's gotten me into this mess. "I can't tell you. I have to let history unfold or else the entire future is in question."

I cannot plant the seed in his head for what is to happen. He is a selfless man. He will surely single-handedly try to ensure the collision does not happen, without realizing the catastrophic ramifications that act of heroism will have. My breath is rapid, almost as if I'm hyperventilating.

He takes a step toward me, eyes pleading "Alice, please. Have I given you reason not to trust me?"

"Charlie," I whisper. I am faltering in my resolution. I am begging him not to press this further, but he remains determined.

"I believe you owe me this, Alice. I deserve to know."

His voice is broken. So am I.

"Titanic will sink."

He stares at me in disbelief, his face turns ghostly pale. "How?"

"Iceberg. Most of the passengers will not survive."

He takes a step back. "And me?"

"Charlie." I shake my head frantically. "Please don't make me say it."

"What happens to me, Alice?" he demands.

I stare at the ground. I can't even look at him. He doesn't deserve this. My silence answers before my words do. "You'll die."

"You tell me I'm going to die and you can't even look at me?" he chokes. "You can play judge and jury, but not executioner? These are people's lives, Alice! *My life!* We are not some experiment for you in the future to conduct to explain away your failures."

Charlie stares at me, a blazing combination of tears, hurt, and anger welling up in his eyes. I try to meet his gaze, but he looks away from me, shakes his head, and walks out of my cabin.

I want to go after him, but truthfully, I don't even deserve his attention or his forgiveness. There's nothing I can say to make this easier, or even stop anything from happening. I've done enough damage. For a moment, I consider grabbing my locket and holding the button, just running away right now. But that feels almost like a hit and run, a coward's retreat.

I pick up a crystal glass sitting on the table and hurl it at the wall. It shatters.

So do I.

I collapse on my bed under the weight of what I've done, hands pressed to my mouth to muffle the sobs. There's no undoing what I've just done. I deserve his anger, and I hate myself for hurting him. I can't believe the position I've put him in.

How can I expect him to hold that information to himself?

What if he doesn't?

What if he warns someone?

Chapter Seventeen

THE REASON BY HOOBASTANK

April 13th, 1912

I'm resigned to the fact that Charlie must despise me now, and any feelings I perceived he might have for me, romantic or otherwise, arc long gone. How could I even blame him? Not only have I lied to him, but he now also shoulders the burden of knowing what will happen.

Selfish doesn't even begin to cover it. I let my feelings cloud my judgment and get the better of me. I've sacrificed Charlie's peace for the sake of my happiness and the joy I found in spending time with him.

And it isn't just Charlie that I've endangered.

Ben, Sarah, and Eric.

I've put all of them at risk. The mission, our safety, and history itself.

And for what?

I climb out of bed and slip into a pale pink silk tea dress with long lace sleeves and a dark pink accented velvet sash at the waist. The colors make me look far brighter and happier than I am.

I wanted to hide today—to vanish into solitude with my shame. But Ben insisted I have breakfast with him and I promised Violet I'd walk with her while Ben and John play shuffleboard. As much as I'd like to crawl into a hole of self-pity, I want to savor every moment I can with Violet. Especially when so little remains.

Breakfast in the saloon passes in a blur. I hardly notice plates of food put in front of me. I don't have an appetite, but I sip tea to keep up the appearance of normalcy. My entire focus is on finding ways to distract Ben so that he doesn't see the fault lines cracking beneath my surface.

If he sees how much I'm struggling, he'll ask why. I'll pivot the conversation, try to distract him with a sarcastic joke, but eventually, I'll crumble to his questioning. I can't tell him what I've done.

"So Edward made a weird comment last night," Ben says, mercifully cutting though my intrusive thoughts.

I freeze as I spread jam on the scone I don't plan to eat. "Weird how?" I ask, my throat tightening. *Please don't let this be about me.*

Ben leans forward, brow furrowed. "Francis was going on about some mutual acquaintance. I think the guy is in steel or lumber or something? Anyway, it sounds like he's about to go under. I think the guy stands to lose a fair bit of money with the closure. I was only half listening. Normally when they talk about finance and business, it's so god-awful dull. I rarely have much to offer to the conversation because Edward loves to hear himself talk so much he constantly pivots everything back to himself. But he made a passing comment about how things like that are avoidable with a little strategy and ingenuity."

"Strategy and ingenuity, huh?" I repeat cautiously.

Ben nods. "I don't know. I could be reading into it, but it felt like he was implying something. Like it was a flex. Maybe it's just the way he said it. I mean, you know how his tone can be so..."

"Sly? Manipulative? Egotistical?" I rattle off every fault I can think of about the man whose only true love is himself.

Ben smirks. "Yes! That's exactly it. It felt like he was saying something without saying it, you know?"

I nod. I understand him completely.

On the surface, Edward seems the pinnacle of wealth and propriety. It's underneath that you realize he's a charlatan, merely selling the appearance of a respectable man.

History remembers Edward Harrison as a financial titan, with unquestionable success and an impeccable reputation. I don't buy it. After spending time with him the last few days, it's impossible to believe he didn't step on people or cheat the system along the way. No one gets that big without some skeletons.

"I have a theory," I say, pulse racing. "But I'll need your help testing it."

Ben perks up. "I'm listening."

"When you're with him tonight, tell him one of your hotels is failing. Tell him occupancy is down, the building needs costly repairs, and it's bleeding you dry. Really sell it though, Ben. Can you do that?"

Ben squints at me. "Sell it how?"

"Don't act like you care about the people. Be as cold as possible. All business. Your only concern is profit. Make that abundantly clear—that you're willing to do whatever it takes to turn it around, even if it's unethical. Be ruthless, Ben."

"So, you want me to act like a total jackass?"

"Exactly." I nod. "Lay the douchebaggery on thick. He won't be able to resist the bait."

Ben chuckles. "Douchebaggery? Is that even a word?"

"It is now."

"I shall put in my best performance, I assure you." Ben laughs again, and it loosens the tension in my chest slightly. "What's your play here?"

I shrug. "He's gotta be doing something shady. I know he didn't say anything incriminating, but I'd bet money that he's committing some kind of fraud. There's no way he took the clean path to success, and there's no way he won't brag about it if you make him feel like he's among similar company. Just hand him the rope, Ben. He'll hang himself with it."

"Alright, let's do it." Ben grins, lifting his tea cup like a toast. "Here's to brandy, cigars, and baiting a fraud."

"Cheers to that," I say, taking a sip of my tea. I still feel completely broken over the mess I've made with Charlie, but this distraction gave me a flicker of relief.

After breakfast, Ben walks me up to the boat deck where Violet waits, her face lighting up when she spots me. Ben departs with John, no doubt on a mission to destroy other passengers at shuffleboard. Violet and I link arms like schoolgirls and begin to stroll.

We talk about books as though there is no gap between our respecting time periods.

"I'm surprised Austen is your favorite, Violet," I say truthfully. Admittedly, Jane Austen is my favorite author as well, which makes me feel even more connected to her. I just never expected it from Violet.

Her eyes sparkle. "Name me a character more spirited and headstrong than Elizabeth Bennet, or more gracious and selfless than Elinor Dashwood, or more clever and thoughtful than Anne Eliot. Maybe they are romances, but at their very core, they are stories about strong women. Women who endure and overcome."

I smile, continuously in awe of her. She speaks with such conviction, it's as though she was born to make you believe in something. I think she could sell me a used car that doesn't even work with how easily she speaks from her heart.

I want to know everything about her, her life, her interests, all of it. I know I should focus on Alice Carney, but I just want to know more about *Violet.* I want to memorize her laugh, the way her eyes sparkle when she smiles, the way she talks with her hands when she's really passionate about something.

"Do you like music?" I ask, suddenly embarrassed over subjecting her to a game of twenty questions. I can't help it. I just want to soak in every moment with her, because soon enough, I will be without her again.

"I love music," she says, brushing a strand of hair from her cheek. "I actually play piano, though most of what I play now is lullabies and amusements for the girls."

"I play too.." I suddenly realize that the piano that sits in my formal living room is Violet's as well. Our hands have grazed the same keys, possibly playing the melodies of the same songs.

She smiles. "What's your favorite song, Alice?"

Shit.

Do I even know a song from this time? I'm sure I know many, but I'm not entirely certain of the exact dates they originally came out. I don't want to name one and find out it came out five years later. I have to take a complete stab in the dark here and hope for the best.

Think. Think. Think.

I remember a song from when I was a kid watching *Anne of Green Gables.* Anne Shirley and Gilbert Blythe danced to it at their wedding.

They were the quintessential enemies to friends to lovers trope, and I grew up adoring their slow-burn romance.

"Uh, 'Let Me Call You Sweetheart.'"

Violet's smile deepens. "Oh, yes. That's a lovely song." She tilts her head in thought. "I think mine is 'It's Hard to Kiss Your Sweetheart When the Last Kiss Means Goodbye.'"

"I don't think I know that one."

Without hesitation, she sings.

> *It is hard to kiss your sweetheart*
> *When the last kiss means goodbye*
> *You are grieving all the while*
> *No matter how you try*
> *Although your lips are smiling*
> *From your heart there comes a sigh*
> *It is hard to kiss your sweetheart*
> *When the last kiss means goodbye*

Her voice is soft, but it pierces straight through me. The lyrics are hauntingly beautiful, and I can't help but feel guilty as she sings. I can't help but think of her and John.

She doesn't know what is coming for her and how quickly it approaches. She doesn't know that she will lose her sweetheart, that their last kiss will mean goodbye. History has already written her heartbreak. I blink hard, begging the tears stinging my eyes to retreat.

And then, selfishly, I think of Charlie

Though I have not kissed him, and that's certainly not for a lack of desire to, our goodbye is also drawing near. He may never speak to me again, and I understand his reasons for that, but I can't help but grieve what I've never had. I will lose him, and Violet, sooner than I am ready for.

Sometimes life is unexplainable. Sometimes it hands you the right people at the wrong time.

I know in my heart that I met both Violet and Charlie for a reason. And maybe they are temporary, but the lessons they both have taught me are permanent.

They have both left handprints on my heart.

And no amount of time or distance can ever take away.

We are interrupted before I can awkwardly ask any more questions. Sarah appears, stepping into character seamlessly.

"Miss Alice, it's time to get you ready for dinner. Mr. Turner has already returned to the cabin."

Behind her, John approaches, ready to escort Violet.

Violet looks at the sun settling into golden hour. "Oh goodness, we've completely lost track of time."

I was so wrapped up in conversation with her, I never heard the dinner call.

"I'll see you at dinner, Alice," she says warmly, pressing my hand.

I watch her disappear into the golden light, wondering how many more moments like this I'll get.

And whether I'll have the strength to let go when the time comes.

Chapter Eighteen

MIRRORBALL BY TAYLOR SWIFT

April 13th, 1912

Sarah and I make our way back to the cabin to prepare for the evening. As we pass one of the first-class lounge areas, I catch a glimpse of Charlie out of the corner of my eye. He's carrying a box of clean glassware toward the supply closet next to the lounge. His posture is tense, shoulders drawn high, like he's methodically going through the motions.

He sees me, but quickly looks away, as if the sight of me burns.

I want to speak with him, to hear his voice. Every part of me knows I shouldn't, that I've done enough damage already. But my heart refuses to listen.

"Sarah, go on ahead. I want to grab a book from the reading room for later. I'll join you momentarily, okay?"

It's a weak excuse, and I think she knows it. Her brows twitch, but luckily, she nods and continues down the corridor. I wait until she's out of sight before pivoting toward the supply room Charlie entered moments earlier.

I pause outside the door, bracing myself for the conversation ahead, and then quietly slip inside. I close the door softly behind me and quietly latch the lock. The small closet is dimly lit and smells like polish.

Charlie doesn't turn around at first. He continues stacking glasses into neat rows. He takes a deep breath in and his whole body tenses as he catches the scent of my perfume.

"You shouldn't be here," he says low and cold, still not facing me. "If people saw..."

"No one saw," I promise him. "I don't care if they did. I just.... I needed to see you."

He turns slowly, reluctantly. His face is unreadable, his voice icy. "Did you need something, *Miss Murphy*?

The formality punches me in the gut.

"I deserved that," I whisper.

He doesn't answer me, but he doesn't have to. The tension in his jaw says enough. He's trying so hard to come across as unemotional, but I can see it in his eyes. The pain. The pain *I* caused.

Every word is detached and hollow, like he's holding back what he really wants to say. I deserve every sting or barb his words could hurl at me, and I'm prepared to take them as a deserved lashing. Instead, he just stares, as if he cannot bear to inflict pain on me, even though I have drawn the first blow.

"I have to get back to work," he says, stepping forward, trying to pass me. Acting on instinct, I reach out and grab his hand. He freezes.

"Charlie, please."

His eyes meet mine and I see the conflict in him, as if he's torn between want and betrayal.

"Just let me get this out, and then I'll leave you alone. I'll stay away. I promise."

He doesn't answer me, but he doesn't pull away either.

"Charlie, I'm... I'm so sorry," I say, my voice catching on the weight of the words. "It was never my intention to hurt you or to burden you. You don't deserve this. None of this is fair to you. I don't deserve your forgiveness, I know that, nor could I ever ask for it. I don't expect anything from you. And I know these are all just words to you now, and maybe you find it impossible to believe anything I could have to say after such dishonesty. And I deserve that. I know I do."

I blink, trying to keep my tears at bay. "But Charlie, if there was anything, even just *one* thing, you could choose to believe, please let it be this: what we've shared the last few days and the feelings I have for you, that has *never* been a lie. Not for one second. I just need you to know that."

I can feel the tears welling up in my eyes and I can't bear to cry in front of him, to make him somehow feel even worse than I already have. I don't want him to feel obligated to say anything just because I got emotional. He has every right to feel betrayed or angry, and I don't want to take that away from him.

Before he can respond, I slip past him and leave the closet. I'm not even sure if he was going to say anything. I just had to get away before I completely broke down.

I reach our suite through my private room, avoiding the sitting area in case Ben is already there. I just need a moment to myself to collect my thoughts. I lean against the door behind me, the tears finally spilling freely. My solitude is interrupted when Sarah steps out from the bath facilities and notices me.

"Ali?" Before I can even speak or pull myself together, she walks toward me with her arms outstretched. "Oh, Ali. Come here." She pulls me into a hug and I let go—of everything. For once, I let someone hold me.

We don't speak for what feels like forever. She just lets me cry, like I'm an infant that just needs to self soothe. Eventually, she brushes my hair from my damp cheeks, taking stock of the mess my emotions have made.

"We need to get you ready for dinner, Ali," she says gently. "Do you think you're up to that?"

I nod, barely. I don't want to spend another evening in Edward's company, but I also don't want to send Ben into the lion's den alone. I can easily sit there and go through the motions.

Sarah helps me switch into an evening gown for dinner. She selects a steel blue silk gown with a silver crystal beaded overlay with draped sleeves. It's beautiful, but the color feels melancholy and seems to match the ache I feel inside. The steel blue with icy gray undertones makes me feel like a rain cloud.

She helps me pull back my hair, securing it with a silver crystal comb that matches the overlay of my gown. I slip on the long white satin evening gloves that make me feel imprisoned and slouch down into a chair to wait for Ben. Somehow every evening I'm waiting for him to be ready, even though I have far more preparation than he does.

Eventually, Ben knocks and enters, sharp in his tuxedo. He offers me his arm and we head toward another night of Edward's heroic greatest hits.

As we make our way to the table, I catch Violet's gaze from across the room. Her warm smile reaches me like sunlight through fog. I manage a small one in return.

As our table carries on in varied conversation, I disassociate and stare at a chandelier hanging from the ceiling. Large and exquisite, the crystal droplets shine brightly and reflect angles of light around the room.

What would happen if that chandelier were to fall, I wonder? Would anyone even notice it thunder to the floor and shatter into thousands of glistening pieces? Pieces that still shine, but now as angular shards, can pierce at any touch. Beautiful, but dangerous.

I feel like that chandelier.

Suspended. Nothing more than a grand, lustrous ornament. Everyone has their eyes on me. Not to marvel at me or watch me shine. They're waiting for me to fail. They're waiting for the car to crash so they can watch it burn.

What I'm realizing now is that this feeling isn't just about the shimmering facade I've been maintaining this week. This is a performance I've mastered my entire life. I've always tried to be everything to everyone, like I don't need anyone else's help. I've operated on this "fake it till you make it" mentality for so long that it's hard to distinguish between truth and reality anymore. I strive for perfection in everything I do, not because I want to succeed. I want the validation and the assurance of not upsetting someone or letting them down, because then they'll leave me.

But I am exhausted.

Pretending that I am strong has left me no strength to actually *be* strong. I feel like I'm carrying the weight of the world, or at least the weight of everyone else's expectations, in my arms. My muscles ache. My mind aches. I want to drop it. I'm tired of pretending to be perfect. It's all a performance. A circus. Don't accidentally swallow the sword. Don't fall from the tightrope. Don't make a single mistake, because they'll notice that. They won't notice you shine, but they'll sure as hell notice when you're cracked.

I'm tired of showing everyone the versions of me they want to see. The dutiful daughter. The successful historian. The strong and independent woman. Beneath all that is someone desperate for rest. I want to let it fall to the floor and shatter, along with everyone's expectations.

I am fully capable of breaking at any moment.

Would anyone even notice if I did?

Chapter Nineteen

I FOUND BY AMBER RUN

April 13th, 1912

After dinner, I make my way back to the cabin while Ben retreats for another evening of cigars and brandy. He doesn't question me. He doesn't need to. My silence at dinner spoke for itself. There will be no detours tonight. No walks on deck in the moonlight. Just me, hiding in the one place I can drop the mask I've worn all evening.

When I enter the room, the lights are dim and Sarah is already gone for the night. I'm not sure if I'm grateful for the solitude or afraid to be alone once my intrusive thoughts come creeping in. I lock the adjoining doors on either side of my room, craving privacy. I just want to be alone.

With a sigh, I remove my gloves finger by finger and toss them onto the vanity. I begin to unfasten my shoes but freeze at the sound of a soft knock at my door. One knock. Sarah usually knocks twice and then comes in. Perhaps she thought I was asleep and didn't want to disturb me. Or she saw me come in and just wants to check in on me.

I walk cautiously to the door, pulling myself together in case it *is* Sarah. But as I open it, I find him.

Charlie.

He's leaning slightly in the doorway, one arm propped against the wall, his brown eyes unreadable.

My breath catches in my throat.

"Why... why are you here?" I can barely get the words out, too stunned to even mask the hope and fear tangled in my voice. I can only imagine he's finally processed the truth and is back to deliver the harsh words I truly deserve. The words I cowardly ran away from earlier today.

"I had to see you," he says.

I shake my head in disbelief. "Why?"

I expect anger, a scathing speech about lies, but instead he looks calm.

Charlie glances down the hallway, checks both directions, then without a word, steps inside. With a firm kick, he shuts the door behind him. Before I can respond, or even process what's happening, he closes the space between us, cups my face in both hands, and kisses me.

His lips find mine with urgency, but not aggression. The kiss feels like a question and an answer all at once.

It's... everything.

My body presses against his, and I feel the wild pounding of his heart in sync with mine.

"Alice," he murmurs against my lips, his voice trembling. His growing arousal is unmistakable as his body presses tighter to me. I feel like my knees will buckle beneath me at any moment.

The sound of his voice is intoxicating, even more so when he says my name. Growing up, I never cared for my name. It always felt foreign, like it belonged to someone else. I insisted on being called Ali. Now I would jump through hoops, walk through fire, anything, just to hear his voice say my name.

Our eyes lock and I tremble—not with fear, but with longing. Nothing has ever had this effect on me before, like I'm standing on the edge of something dangerous and divine. I want more of it. I want more of him. I want *all* of him.

He pulls me back toward him and his mouth has mine captured in a deep, mesmerizing kiss. I let out a small moan of pleasure. I've never had such a primal reaction to just a kiss before, but I feel as though he is masterfully stoking a fire burning deep within me. He smiles against my lips, clearly pleased.

He pulls his head back momentarily, hovering his mouth close to my ear. "Do you want me to stop?" he whispers.

We float in the moment briefly, as he waits for my consent to go any further. His breath is warm and seductive. If I paid any attention to logic, we should stop right here. But where has logic ever gotten me before?

My body screams no, but I whisper it. "No."

Every feeling, every desire that's been burning within me for days is finally boiling over, no longer able to be contained. I want him inside of me, to feel the weight of him above me. I want to feel every pulse as he buries himself in me.

A desperation pools in my belly, growing stronger and stronger. I slip my hand around his waist, pulling him into me as our lips crash again with heat and need. My fingers find the buttons of his jacket and begin undoing them one by one. He watches me, eyes burning, seemingly nervous and invigorated. I slide the jacket down from his shoulders as he hastily pulls on his tie.

The clothes fall to the floor as we leave a trail lining our steps toward the bed. I grab the hem of my gown, but he gently takes it from me and lifts it over my head. The beading snaps slightly as it comes over my hair. I tug the comb free and let my hair fall in soft waves.

Charlie gently strokes a few wisps of my hair back behind my ear before caressing my cheek with the backs of his fingers. It's so gentle I could come undone right now. I slip the suspenders from his shoulders, letting them fall to his waist. He reaches down and pulls it off in one smooth motion, exposing his broad, sculpted chest.

My breath catches in my throat.

Fuck, he's perfect.

And somehow—tonight—he's mine.

Charlie gently turns me around and begins loosening the laces of my corset. His fingers tremble slightly as he pulls the strings. I feel my whole body exhale as I tilt my head backward, surprised that the slightest removal of fabric could send a shiver down my body. He presses his lips to the back of my neck and I shudder, gripping the raised end of the bed for support.

He turns me back to face him, eyes locked on mine as the corset drops to the floor. He slips a hand around my back and takes a portion of my chemise into his fist. His other hand gently runs along my collarbone, the simple graze of his touch sending an electric charge through my body and down between my legs. He pulls the chemise over my head and I feel a quick rush of cooler air. I instinctively cover myself with my arms.

"Stop," he says softly, taking my hands in his and pulling them down, exposing my body. "You're *so* beautiful."

He stops for a moment, eyes widened at the sight of my nude figure. I have never felt so exposed, yet so completely safe, in my life. His hand runs down my body to the curve of my hips, causing my muscles to quiver. With his left hand around my waist, holding me close to him, he brings his right hand up to cup my breast. My nipple hardens under his palm. His eyes devour me first, then his lips. With my tongue exploring his mouth, we move together toward the bed.

I lay down, and he settles himself above me, nudging my legs apart. His eyes move back toward mine as he pauses. "Are you sure?"

"Please," I beg. I desire him with a desperation that has grown relentless, as though I will combust if I don't have him.

He gulps nervously and slides into me with aching slowness. He lets out a soft groan as our bodies finally meet. I gasp, wrapping my legs around him, pulling him even deeper.

Charlie's eyes ignite and he thrusts inside me, slowly at first. My hips rise to meet his, and our bodies find their rhythm like the waves outside.

"Alice," he murmurs, as if my name is a prayer.

With each thrust of his body, his breath becomes faster and faster. Every gasp, every moan seems to ignite his passion even further. With my hands clenched around his back, I feel as though I might burst wide open. I cling to him like he's the only real thing in the world.

My head tilts back as I reach my climax. I cry out his name, over and over, not because I'm lost, but because I think I've finally been found.

He groans deeply as he follows, his body shuddering above me. He exhales and his whole body collapses, warm and heavy against my chest. His head nuzzles into the curve of my neck, softly grazing my skin with his lips.

Fuck.

It wasn't my first time, but it was the first time it ever felt like *this*. Like something whole. Something real.

This feels like how it's meant to be, how it's meant to feel, when it's the right person. It's as though our bodies fit perfectly together, just like our souls.

Chapter Twenty

EASE MY MIND BY BEN PLATT

April 13th, 1912

Charlie rolls onto his back, staring at the ceiling as he attempts to catch his breath.

I shift to my side, propping myself up on my elbow to face him. His expression is caught somewhere between awe and uncertainty.

Then he turns to me, and suddenly he's not the confident man who was just inside me, touching me like he's known every inch of me forever. He looks shy. Boyish.

"Was that... was it okay?" he asks, his voice breathless.

I blink, startled and amused by the question. Hadn't it been obvious? I don't have a ton of experience with this. I'm not a nun by any means, but after a short time in college where I thought having someone in my bed would fill the emptiness in my life, I haven't really gotten to this part of a relationship. Intimacy always went hand in hand with being vulnerable, and that's never been easy for me. Until now, apparently.

I smile softly. "Are you kidding? It was perfect."

Relief spreads across his face like sunshine.

I hesitate, then ask the question that's been sitting in the back of my mind since he knocked on my door. "Can I ask you something?"

"Of course."

"Why did you come back?" I try to keep my voice steady. "I didn't think I'd see you again. I thought after everything you'd be angry, or hate me."

He exhales, his hand resting gently on his chest. "I *was* angry. I was confused. But then I started thinking," he says, his voice quieter now. He turns to me, his eyes locking with mine. "If this is where my story ends, I want it to end with you."

Tears prick the corners of my eyes. I don't know what to say. Is this what it feels like to be chosen? To be wanted not out of need or obligation, but desire? I lean down to plant a kiss on his lips, before settling down onto my stomach, half laying on his chest. We lay there for a moment, silently, just holding each other.

Charlie gently strokes my arm with his fingertips. "Tell me about your life, Alice."

I smile. "What part?"

"All of it. Tell me everything."

"Well, I grew up in Boston. I left for university, but I came back when I graduated. My mother left us when I was little, so it was just Dad and I for years. I live in the house I grew up in. It's huge, and beautiful, and luckily it has been in my family for years, otherwise I could never afford it. Dad left it to me when he passed."

"What was he like?"

"Oh gosh, Dad. Well, his name was Samuel, but everyone called him Sam. He was a lawyer, so he taught me to argue." I laugh, though it's tinged with nostalgia. "He took me on all kinds of adventures when I was growing up. We went to Civil War battlefields, museums, every historical landmark you can think of. He's the reason I love history."

Charlie smiles while listening to me gush about Dad, though I suspect it must be difficult for him to hear, considering his complicated relationship with his own father. I recount stories of our adventures that are locked away in my head, like the fine china you only pull out on special occasions.

"He had such a busy work schedule, but he never missed our Saturdays in the park when I was a kid. Never missed a soccer game when I was older. He was always there."

Charlie perks up. "Soccer? You played?"

"Yeah!" I giggle. "I think he was worried that I was lonely and needed some kind of social activity. He tried a few different sports with me and nothing clicked. But he took me to a field one day and handed me the ball and I took to it like a duck to water. So he put me into soccer when I was nine and I played all throughout school. I played midfield. I was always good at protecting myself from attacks and tackling opposition."

"Sounds about right." Charlie laughs. I suppose that I've put up walls in more ways than one.

"I mean, we did everything together. Everything except talk, that is. At least about the important things. I grew up wanting to ask so many questions, always wondering if I had done something wrong. Why didn't she want me? Why wasn't I enough? I didn't ask those questions out loud because I was afraid of the answers. I didn't know that he couldn't be what I needed him to be, because he was in so much pain himself."

Charlie listens in silence, his thumb drawing gentle circles on my hand.

"I decided early on I'd do everything possible to take care of Dad. I'd make myself so invaluable that he wouldn't leave me, too. But then he got sick, and he faded so fast. For the longest time, I thought he died because I wasn't taking care of him anymore. Like I was being punished for wanting to do something for myself. That's silly, I know, but I felt more alone growing up with one parent than I do as an adult with none."

"Alice," Charlie says, squeezing my hand. "I don't know why your mother left. But please understand, you have been and you always will be enough." He tilts his head forward to lock his eyes with mine. "You are worth staying for."

I reach to squeeze his hand. He may never understand how much that means to me to hear from someone, but I let the words wrap around me.

"You know, I tried to find her once," I admit. "My mom."

It feels good to admit that. I've never told anyone, not even Ben. I've just bottled it up inside me, the pressure of it pushing against my chest for years.

Charlie sits up. "You did?

I sit too, facing him now, knees drawn to my chest. "A few years ago, right after Dad died. Once I got through the haze of funeral decisions, flower arrangements, caskets, all that, I had a realization. She was the only parent I had left. I wanted to track her down. Not with any deep desire to meet her or rekindle anything. I think a part of me just wanted to know she landed somewhere safe. And deep down, I think I wanted to remind her that I existed."

"Did you find her?"

I weave the sheet in between my fingers to fidget with as I talk.

"Yeah, I did. And she lived less than an hour away. Would you believe that?" I shake my head, laughing bitterly. "She wanted to leave us so bad, but she didn't even go far. It's like her ghost loomed over me my whole life, so close, yet I can't reach out and grab it. That's why I figured she would obviously hear of his death or see the obituary in the papers. He was a pretty high-profile lawyer, so his death got some media attention. I thought if she even lived with the smallest amount of regret, or had any curiosity about me whatsoever, this could be her moment to face me."

"Did she?"

"No," I say flatly. "But I decided not to let her get away with it. I read an article in the paper showcasing her art, and at the bottom of the review it stated her next art showing would be the following month at a gallery not too far from me. It was the perfect opportunity to face her. I had no idea what I would say to her. I think I just wanted to see her, or have her see me. I thought maybe, just maybe, if she saw me, she'd want to know me. At any rate, I knew she wouldn't be able to avoid me in a room full of critics and buyers. I went to the showing and spotted her in the crowd straight away."

"How?"

"She ran her hand through her hair, shifting her weight from foot to foot. It's a thing I do, too."

I remember the moment I saw her. It's seared into my brain. She was beautiful and looked like she'd hardly aged at all. Her brightly colored maxi dress swayed as she flowed effortlessly around the gallery. I felt grateful that I look so much like Dad, because I couldn't see myself in her at all. Until she ran her hand through her hair and shifted back and forth. I've done it ever since I can remember. Whether I'm in conversation or teaching a class at Chisholm, I'll subconsciously shift my weight back and forth and run my hand through my hair. It's fascinating that someone can skip out on raising you, but you still carry parts of their personality. My heart dropped when I saw the similarities in our mannerisms. I was angry. I didn't want to be anything like her. But now, I realize, if the worst thing I inherit from her is a nervous tick, that's not bad. I'll take it.

"What happened?"

"I circled the room for a while, mostly hyping myself up for a conversation with her. I viewed her paintings, looking for some consolation in them. I think I hoped to see some kind of hidden meaning in them, like feelings of guilt or regret. But I saw nothing. I waited, and waited, and watched her work the room till I saw her coming in my direction. She finally reached me, looked straight into my eyes, and..."

Charlie leans forward. "And?"

"And *nothing*. Absolutely nothing." Subconsciously, I run my hand through my hair. "Maybe it's crazy, but I had this wild idea that she'd see me, and just know that I was her child. I thought maybe some maternal instinct would finally kick in for her, and we'd finally have this moment. I wasn't even sure if I wanted that moment to be of connection or confrontation. I didn't even know if I wanted to tell her I missed her or that I hated her. But there was nothing. She didn't even recognize me. I was just like any other stranger in the room to her. I think part of me was sizing up the competition, in a way. Like, this is what you left me for? Was it worth it? Is this what meant more to you than being my mother? I had a thousand questions for her in my head, and yet, only one really mattered: Why? Why did you leave me? Why wasn't I enough for you? I decided not to say anything to her or make a scene, no matter how much I wanted to."

"How come?"

I wrap the sheet tighter around me. "What purpose would it serve me? It wasn't going to magically fix anything. It wouldn't undo the years of pain. I think I finally realized I can't expect her to give me the answers to heal myself. If I lay that expectation on anyone else, I'll set myself up for disappointment. She may have given birth to me, but she certainly wasn't my mother. I couldn't give her the satisfaction of being the victim. That was the day I began therapy. I was determined to become a better, happier person because of my parents, not in spite of them. I don't want to inherit their mistakes. I decided if I was going to live a full life, I had to stop waiting for someone else to give me permission."

"You're extraordinary, you know that?"

I smile faintly. "You're a little biased."

"Maybe. But that doesn't make it less true." Charlie leans forward on the bed to reach my hand, squeezing it in his. "And just so you know, she missed out on knowing the most incredible woman."

I smile back at Charlie and lean forward to kiss him. He slips his hand around me and pulls me toward him, before flashing a wicked smile and playfully flipping me over onto my back. He moves himself over me, as his lips journey up from my navel, to my chest, to my neck, gently caressing each region.

"And just so you know," he murmurs between kisses, "I'm enjoying knowing *every inch* of this incredible woman."

"My goodness." I giggle. "Does the White Star Line know their stewards are so devoted to their work?"

"Mmm," he whispers, in half chuckle and half moan. "I think you'll find that I am quite attentive to my favorite passenger."

We lay together through the night, bare in every sense of the word. I tell him everything. I want him to know every inch. Everything from my job at Chisholm, my life in Boston, my friends, to the ache I carry.

Charlie's fingertips gently swirl in circular motions on my bare back as we lay up all night, lost in each other, in conversation, in companionship.

Eventually, our conversation drifts to love and relationships.

"Has there ever been anyone for you?" I ask softly, suddenly nervous.

Charlie chuckles to himself. "No. Never really cared, to be honest. Growing up, I was always with my friends and playing games. Once Mum passed, I just kind of kept to myself, and then eventually I wound up on ships. Never really had time for it, or interest, I guess."

"Weren't you lonely?"

"Sometimes, I suppose. But I got used to it. What about you? There ever been someone for you?"

"Nothing serious." I shake my head. "Teenage flings. College mistakes. Ben has tried setting me up a few times, but it never works out. Usually because of me. Actually, *always* because of me."

"Because of you?"

"I either find reasons not to go on the date at all, or I sabotage it while I'm there. I just can't get out of my head."

Charlie raises a brow. "And you and Ben never...?"

"Oh god, no." I laugh. "He's like a brother to me. Besides, I think *you* have a greater chance of catching his interest than I do."

Charlie freezes slightly. "Ah," he says, softly. I watch as his face processes what I said. "Got it."

I realize this is probably hard for Charlie to comprehend. I don't know where he stands on an issue he likely has no previous experience with. It's hard to expect him to be accepting or tolerant of something he perhaps has no exposure to, but I will defend and protect Ben with my last breath if necessary.

I watch him closely. "Charlie, he's my family."

He nods. "I know." Charlie leans in and gently kisses my forehead.

"That's it?"

"What?"

"No judgement? No questions?"

"Why would there be?" He tilts his head. "It exists now, you know. And like you said—he's important to you. So he matters to me.

He doesn't know how comforting this kind of acceptance is to hear from someone, in his century or mine.

There's a kind of peace that settles over me. The kind that tells me I'm safe. With Charlie, I don't need to hide the damaged parts of me. Most of my life, I have guarded my weaknesses, fearing that they would be used against me, or would even scare someone away. But with Charlie, it feels as though every part of me, even the darkest corners, is completely safe with him. I can lay my pain, my dreams, my fears, and my hopes in his hands and they are protected.

If only Dr. Kassen could see me right now. Well, maybe not *right now*. Every week I sit on her sofa with her explaining to me how my mother leaving caused me to have a fear of abandonment, and therefore a fear of attachment.

If she could see this reckless, impulsive woman I've become this week, I don't know if she would call me brave or stupid, or maybe both. I'm not sure if she would be proud or want me committed. Truthfully, I don't even know which of these options I am. All I know is that the woman who fears attachment is currently yearning for more of it.

Chapter Twenty-One

HURT BY JOHNNY CASH

April 14th, 1912

The sun peers into my room through an opening in the curtain. A golden sliver of light shines on my face, waking me from the most restful sleep I've had in ages. Out of the corner of my eye, I spot Charlie's arm draped over me, his chest rising and falling in a slow, peaceful rhythm against my back.

Tonight, the ship will sink. But right now, wrapped in the safety of his embrace, the looming tragedy feels like a distant dream. For just this moment, I let myself believe that all my wildest hopes, dreams, and fears have settled into something real. Something I never thought I'd find. Him.

But I lay here now, feeling his chest peacefully breathe in and out, and I can't help but believe that I was meant to find him. And though this perfect moment is fleeting and cannot possibly last forever, I want to hold on to it until the last possible second.

I shift to face him. The movement stirs him awake, and when his eyes meet mine, he smiles and kisses me. It's a soft kiss, the kind that feels ordinary, as though we'd be doing it every morning for the rest of our lives.

His eyes flick over my shoulder toward the window, and I watch the sleepy tenderness fade away from his face.

He bolts upright. "What time is it?"

I look over at the clock on the end table. "It's half-past eight," I say groggily.

"Shit!"

Charlie scrambles out of bed, frantically searching for his clothes amidst the tangled sheets. I quickly slip on my breakfast dress—a pale lilac silk with a delicate lace overlay. I glance at him, half amused, half entranced. Part of me hopes he never finds his shirt, so we can stay here, suspended in time, forever. Plus, the sight of him in my room, topless with his suspenders hanging from his waist, has me wanting to return to bed.

I spot his shirt peeking out from under the bed. I casually toss it to him, then slip on my shoes as distant voices filter in from the hallway. I can hear Ben and Eric fading away as they head off for the morning.

Movement comes from the next room.

Sarah.

Fuck.

Panic stabs through me when I realize she's coming over. I motion for Charlie to stay quiet and sprint to the adjoining door, intercepting her before she can enter. I swing the door open and hold it behind me, blocking the doorway into my room.

I plaster on the fakest, brightest smile I can muster. "Good morning!"

God, that was stupid. That was the exact opposite of what I should do if I was hoping to fly under the radar. I attempt to smooth my hair into place with my free hand. The mixture of bed head and sex hair might be what blows my cover right now.

Sarah blinks at me, clearly taken aback by my breathless energy. "Jesus, Ali. What are you doing?" She looks annoyed, but also confused. I move and block her as she attempts to look around me. She lets out an exasperated sigh, her eyes narrowing with suspicion. "Ali, what's going on?"

I hesitate.

Do I trust her? Charlie being late for his duties is only half the battle. I have to get him out of the room unseen, especially by Ben or Eric. A steward leaving my room wouldn't be a scandal, technically. But the disheveled state of the room tells a different story. I have to roll the dice and hope to hell I can trust her.

I look through the crack in the door. Charlie is fully dressed, his jacket is on but unbuttoned.

"I have a boy in my room," I whisper, as though a parent has caught me past curfew.

Her expression stills and I immediately regret telling her. No doubt she will tell Ben. I look back at her, expecting to meet a lecture or a face full of disapproval. Instead, she's laughing. And not just a small chuckle, but a full laugh from down in her belly.

"Good morning, Charlie!" she calls out, shoving past me into the room. He freezes like he's been caught red-handed, halfway buttoned, looking like a deer in headlights. Neither of us is sure what her play will be. She glances around the room at the bedsheets and pillows strewn around and smiles. "Well, I'd ask if you had a good night, but it looks like you did."

I turn every shade of red possible. "Sarah—"

A sharp knock rattles the door to my room.

I frantically look at Sarah, my eyes widening and pleading for her help. She raises a finger to her mouth and silently points toward the left side of the room. Charlie moves first and I follow. I stand up against him and he wraps his arms around me protectively. My pulse thunders in my ears as Sarah walks toward the door and opens it, but remains careful to block the doorway.

I can tell by the way Sarah's body stiffens with a cold professionalism that it isn't Eric or Ben. They would have likely entered on their own, anyway. "Good morning, sir. How can I help you?"

The voice that replies makes my skin crawl. Edward.

"I'd like to escort Miss Alice to breakfast."

Shit.

This is it. I don't want to go with him, but if I do, it buys Charlie enough time to get out of the room unseen. I wish I knew what Sarah was going to do. I stand in the corner at her mercy. One swing of the door and everything falls apart. I brace myself for exposure.

"I'm sorry, Mr Harrison, but I'm afraid Miss Alice has already stepped out for the morning."

She covered for me. I can't believe it. I hear Edward walk away. He doesn't even acknowledge Sarah. *Fucking asshole.*

She watches him leave the hallway and shuts the door. Still in his arms, Charlie and I breathe a collective sigh of relief. I can feel Sarah watching us, and when I look over at her, she's smiling.

"Thank you, thank you so much," I say breathlessly. Charlie follows and nods in her direction with silent appreciation. I'm grateful that she covered for us, even more so that she didn't sacrifice me to a morning of Edward's extravagant bragging. It's hard enough in the evening, and there's at least some alcohol at dinner. She looks surprised that I'm thanking her. Or perhaps she's surprised that I assumed she wouldn't help me.

"Ali, I've got your back." Sarah smiles at me. Her words land deeper than she knows. I know we've had moments where it's felt like the ice has thawed between us, but I suppose I never realized we were forming a friendship. I thought we were being friendly, but I wasn't sure if that meant we were friends. I'm not used to having many friends, especially female ones, and I find myself completely at a loss with how to navigate this.

Sarah presses her ear to the door. "I don't hear anyone. Charlie, I think this is your chance to slip out."

He nods, then turns to me. "I'll see you later, love." He slides his hand around my waist and kisses me. "I promise."

Sarah quickly opens the door and Charlie slips out into the hallway, buttoning up his jacket as he leaves. I have only a moment of relief before I hear Ben's voice in the hallway.

"Good morning, Charlie?"

Shit. He sounds confused. He has to be wondering why the steward is leaving our cabins while buttoning his jacket. He opens the door to his room and I can hear him briskly coming toward our adjoining door.

Sarah and I stare at each other with matching deer in headlights expressions. I suddenly don't know what to do. I stand there completely frozen, partially in disbelief at the turn of events that have brought me to this moment. Sarah, clearly more quick thinking than I am, sprints to the adjoining door and blocks the doorway.

"Ben! You're back! I didn't expect you back so soon." Her voice is energetic, albeit lacking sincerity. She tries her hardest to distract him.

"I forgot my pocket watch," he says flatly, pushing past her.

His eyes lock on the unmade bed.

Then on me.

Ben's jaw tightens. "Sarah, can you leave, please? I need to speak with Ali alone."

She takes a step toward me, positioning herself between Ben and I, as if she's going to battle with me. "I think I'd like to stay."

He doesn't even blink. "I think you'd like to go." He looks like he's about to burst.

Sarah looks at me for direction. As much as I would love her to stay for moral support, I want to spare her from any more involvement. I nod at her, indicating it's okay to go. She steps out, giving me a parting glance of solidarity.

I'm ready for whatever he has to say. I'm prepared to take it on the chin. There's nothing he can say at this point that I don't already know. I'm well aware of my recklessness, but I am also not ashamed.

Ben stares at the floor for a moment. When he finally speaks, his voice is quieter than I expected.

"Ali, what the hell are you—"

"I know what I'm doing, Ben," I cut in. There's no use lecturing me. I know the risks and the consequences, and I did it anyway. I'd do it again, and truthfully, my entire body yearns to do it again.

"Come on, Ali!" Ben shakes his head furiously. His fists are clenched and whitened. "This is fucking risky."

I walk from my room into the adjoining sitting room, trying to get away from the scene of the crime.

"Aren't you the one who told me a little risk is good for you? Didn't you tell me to have some fun?" I try to mitigate the tension in the conversation, but even I know Charlie wasn't just a little risk or a little fun. He was and is so much more than that.

"This is not what I meant and you know it! We can't risk anyone possibly knowing the truth. What if he found out? Did you even think of that?" Ben scolds me as he follows me into the sitting room.

I stop right in my tracks and turn to face him, he in the doorway and me across the room in front of the fireplace, just a table and chairs separating us.

"I've told him everything, Ben."

His whole body recoils. "What?!"He's furious, and I don't think I've ever seen him so angry.

I shrug apologetically. "I'm sorry. I couldn't lie to him. It didn't feel right. He deserves better than that."

Ben explodes. "Do you have any idea what you have done? You've put our work into jeopardy! Our safety! For what? A crush?"

"It's not like that. It's not a crush. He's more than that."

He takes a few steps toward the table, grabbing the top of a chair to lean against. His voice shifts into grave concern. "Al, this isn't like you."

I exhale sharply, tears prickling. "Ben, you don't understand. All my life I've felt this pressure. It's like a weight has just been constantly pushing down on my chest. I couldn't breathe. I don't know where it came from, or why. Maybe it's because of my past, or maybe it's the way I've chosen to cope with everything I've been through. I don't know. I feel like I don't know anything anymore." My voice breaks. "But what I do know is that when I'm with Charlie, there's no weight, no insufferable pressure. It's just him, and it feels like I'm finally breathing. He makes me feel like I've come up for fresh air."

"Ali, this is dangerous. This was dangerous from the start, but now you've made it even more complicated."

"What am I supposed to do, Ben? Let him go? Let *this* go?" I cry as I clutch at my chest. I can feel myself losing my breath and swirling into a panic.

Ben steps closer, his expression a mixture of fear and fury. "This, what? What are you talking about? What is *this?*"

"Ben, please—"

"Come on, Ali. You sound like you're—"

"In love?"

He's not even looking at me. He sighs and tilts his head, as if that isn't even a possibility. "Ali...

"Yes," I cry. "I *love* him!" The words surprise me as they escape my lips. But I know it to be true. *I love him.* I think I've always known. I realize how ridiculous this all seems. Can you really fall in love—truly in love—with someone in only four days? Can you belong to someone so wholly it's as if you were destined to find them? I know attraction and infatuation can be instantaneous, but until now, I never imagined that love could be as well. After all that has transpired since Dr. Conrad's suspicious note, I'm not sure I know the difference between the possible and the impossible anymore. Perhaps the impossible is just a dream waiting to become possible.

Ben laughs bitterly. "*Love*? What do you fucking know about love?"

"What?"

"You push everyone away!" Ben yells. "You always have. You wouldn't know love if it was right in your face." That was a fucking low blow.

He knows exactly what buttons to push to get a rise out of me, and unfortunately, I know the same for him.

My jaw clenches. "Well, what about you, huh? You had love right in your hands. Someone who wanted to grow old with you and you bolted. At least I'm not running away from it." I sound petulant and I hate it. I purposely hit Ben where it hurts, and judging from his face, it's worked.

His eyes blaze. "Yeah? Well, maybe you should! I mean Christ, Ali, he's walking around with a death sentence for fuck's sake and you're avoiding it."

I lurch forward. "How dare you…"

"And when this doesn't work out, and it won't because, spoiler alert: the goddamn ship is going to sink, I'm the one that's gonna have to pick up the pieces!"

"Ben, that's not fair." I have never asked him or expected him to take care of me, and his implication that he feels obligated to has me seething.

"None of this is fucking fair!" His voice is thunderous as he slams his fist on the table. His anger startles me and I flinch.

We stand on opposite sides of the room, staring at each other, licking our wounds. I'm wondering which of us will strike next. I don't want to. I hate myself for the things I've said. I knew bringing up Ryan would hurt him, and I did it anyway. I wanted to hurt him. I wanted him to feel the pain I felt. The tension in the room is so thick, and I don't know how to break it. All that exists between us is the debris from this explosion of anger and guilt. I want to apologize, take back every hurtful thing I've said, but I'm terrified. I feel remorse for what I've said, but I don't feel sorry for what I've done. Is there any way to go back to the space we occupied before we deliberately hurt each other? Can we ever look at each other the same again? As angry as I am right now, this right here, this friendship between us, is precious to me. And it is worth protecting.

The tears break free. I turn away, covering my mouth with my hand as a sob escapes. I stand up against the far wall of the sitting room, closest to the promenade. My eyes are closed and I don't hear Ben move across the room until I feel his arms wrap around me.

"Ali," he whispers, voice cracked and raw. "I'm... I'm so..."

"Me too," I choke, squeezing him.

We hold each other, bruised but still intact. I can feel the beat of his heart descend from a rapid pace to one more calm. We're both still clearly hurt by the sting of our exchanged words; however, we recognize the love and respect between us is more powerful than anything else. Neither of us wants to lose the other, and I personally cannot bring myself to continue to hurt him. When he finally pulls away, his eyes are wet, but his voice is steady.

"You know I've got you, always. You'll always have me." He tucks a strand of hair behind my ear. "I've got to get back on deck before they wonder why I'm taking so long. Are you going to be alright on your own?"

"I'll be okay," I whisper, wiping away tears. "I told Violet I'd have tea with her." It always feels weird referring to my great-great grandmother by her first name.

Ben tilts his head. "Are you seeing him again later?"

"Of course I am." I know what little time we have left. I want to savor every moment I can with him.

Ben nods at me with a half smile. He knows it's no use stopping me. I know he just doesn't want to see me get hurt. I pull myself together, wipe my swollen eyes, and force a smile.

"Do you need me to escort you to tea?"

"No, Sarah will walk with me. She needs to help me fix this." I point to my unkempt hair. Ben walks across the room and opens the door, motioning for Sarah to enter. She had stayed in the hallway nearby, likely in case I needed backup.

"Okay, I'll see you in a bit." Ben gently kisses my check before leaving the cabin. As much as I want to apologize and clear the air between us, I think we both need time away from each other to cool down and digest everything.

Sarah brushes out my hair, giving me a crystal comb to hold on to until she's ready to secure her creation.

"Thank you," I say softly, looking up at her in the mirror.

"You're welcome," she mumbles. I sense a bit of sadness in her voice, as if she feels responsible for the confrontation with Ben.

"No, not for the hair. For everything. I've been so wrapped up in my own things that I haven't acknowledged or recognized how much you have helped and supported me these last few days. I just want you to know I see it and I appreciate you."

She smiles. "You're welcome, Ali. I meant what I said. I've got your back."

"Thanks, that's nice to hear. I know I've put all of you in an impossible position. I've kept things hidden from you all, and I'm sorry."

"You're not hiding things as well as you think you are," she says with a wink.

"Fair play," I acknowledge with a giggle. "But what I mean is, I know I've put you all in a risky position. By being with him, telling him the truth about it all. I tried to stop myself. I really did. I tried to cut and run. I just can't. Something always pulls me back toward him."

"What do you mean, Ali?"

"I just...I can't shake this feeling. I don't know, Sarah. I thought our purpose here was our work. To find out what happened and why. But the more time I spend here, the more clear to me it all is. It's like... like I've been going through life, constantly searching for something, something I didn't have. Like I've always lived a half life. Alive, but never fully living, or loving, or hoping, or anything really. I've lost everyone. And I thought getting the best education and focusing on my career would fill that hole inside me. But it hasn't. It's been like a bandage. It covers it up so I can ignore it and pretend I'm fine, but the hole is still there, you know? But now... now I think the missing piece of me was him. It was him all along. I think I was meant to find him." I shake my head and laugh. "I know that must sound crazy to you."

Sarah smiles to herself. "Not as crazy as you think."

"What do you mean?"

"I followed my heart here too, you know."

It takes me a second. "Wait. Eric?"

She nods. "I've been in love with him for the last two years."

My jaw drops. "Seriously?"

It all makes sense now. Ever since we started preparing for this project, I've watched her eyes follow him out of the room or brighten when he entered. Every time I felt guilty for eating in the main dining room, she said she was happy to just eat with Eric. I always assumed it was some kind of us versus them, or scientists versus historians bond that they shared. I didn't realize she had feelings for him. But now that I have all the clues in front of me, it's quite clear to see.

"Yeah, since we both started working with Dr. Conrad," she explains. "And I never told him. I was scared. But then this opportunity came up, and he jumped at it. And with all the uncertainty about whether it would work or what could happen, I couldn't bear the thought of something happening to him. Without a thought, I volunteered to come too. I followed him here, I guess."

I shake my head. "I had no idea."

"No one did. Until now. I wanted to thank you, Ali. For showing me how important it is to let people in and how rewarding it can be to take a leap of blind faith."

"What do you mean?"

"I mean, you're nothing like the girl I met weeks ago. You've been so brave, and I decided it was time to be the same. That's why I wasn't here last night. I found Eric and told him everything."

"And....?" I smile as I press for more.

She blushes. "And it appears we've both been afraid to tell the other anything about how we felt."

"Oh, Sarah. I'm so happy for you," I gush. This kind of sweetness and joy is exactly the silver lining I needed to hear right now.

"And I'm so grateful to you," Sarah says, smiling. "You showed me that fearlessness is sometimes the most beautiful thing a person can choose."

Tears spring to my eyes again, but this time they're warm.

"I have to thank you, Sarah. For showing me that first impressions are not always correct, and that sometimes a cover is not the book. I judged you, and for that, I'm sorry. I didn't know how to be your friend."

"You do now." She squeezes my hand warmly. "Now let's get you to tea."

Chapter Twenty-Two

KEEP MARCHING BY SUFFS

April 14th, 1912

We step out of the cabin and into the corridor. Charlie is nowhere to be seen, but I assume he had to rush to attend to one of his other cabin assignments. I feel so much better after talking to Sarah.

The First-Class Lounge feels like something from a painting: warm oak walls intricately carved, polished brass fixtures shining in the morning light. I scan the room and find Violet sitting at a table in a plush green velvet upholstered chair. Her smile brightens when she sees me walking toward her. She stands to greet me in a yellow silk tea dress that looks like a ray of sunshine when the light hits just so.

"Good morning," she says with the kind of smile that feels like home.

We settle in, sipping tea and talking for over an hour. Conversation with her flows easily, like a river running its natural course. With her, I feel an openness I didn't expect. It feels like talking to a big sister or your best girlfriend, or maybe even the mother I always wished for. I thought I knew her life story from family records, but I'm realizing there is so much more to her. She kept so much hidden in the character of Alice Carney.

Eventually, she suggests we stretch our legs on deck while we wait for Ben and John to finish their game. I gratefully accept. I'm eager to spend any moment I can with her. She doesn't know how limited our time is—but I do.

As we reach the deck, the sun is warm against my skin. We approach the shuffleboard court just as a loud cheer erupts from the men. Ben is grinning, John laughing with him. I don't know how Ben has energy for all this physical activity, from squash this morning to shuffleboard this afternoon. I'd need a nap from just watching him play squash.

The moment snaps when Edward spots me. He plasters that smug, infuriating smile on his face and calls my name like it belongs to him.

"Miss Alice!"

I force a delicate smile and nod in acknowledgement. Once his gaze drifts elsewhere, I roll my eyes and look out at the water.

Violet notices my disgust and laughs. She touches her gloved hand to her lips, shaking her head. "Oh, goodness. And to think I thought the two of you were involved." The way she tilts her head back to laugh looks like my dad, and for a moment I feel him here with me, too.

"Absolutely not, no. I would never." I get so carried away by denying involvement with Edward that I stumble over my words. "He's not the one I—" I stop myself when I realize what I've almost said. But it's too late. She's perceptive, and she's noticed my almost admission.

Her smile sharpens with intrigue. "Oh," she says, her voice teasing and light, "so there *is* someone?"

Suddenly it feels like we're two school girls talking about the cute boy on the playground.

I hesitate. But then I cave. It feels good to share this with someone. Sarah has been my anchor in all this, but Violet offers something different. She knows nothing of my truth, of time travel, or Titanic's fate. She knows nothing of Charlie or the obstacles between us. And because of that, she sees me in a way no one else can.

"It's complicated," I say quietly.

"The best ones are," she replies, her smile softening. She nods toward John. "Fight for what you want, Alice. Whatever complications there may be, surely they must be worth the risk. Love is a rare thing. If you find it, cherish it, and hold it near. Don't be afraid to be loved, Alice. Promise?"

I nod, swallowing past the emotion rising in my throat.

"Promise."

Her words comfort me. And even though she's only a few years older than me in this time period, I can't help but wonder if this is the comfort most girls seek from a mother. I know she's right, but it's not as simple as she might think. I know what lies in store tonight. The hourglass of Titanic's life is swiftly dwindling. My time here is running out, with her and with Charlie. This peace is temporary.

I turn around to face the ocean. I just want to watch the waves while they still pose no threat. While they sparkle, innocent and endless. Soon enough, this water will be a graveyard and the world will remember the devastation. But right now, I want to remember these small moments. Being with Charlie and getting to meet my great-great grandmother. These are the moments I'll carry with me for the rest of my life.

I stand leaning over the rail with her, the salt breeze sweeping over my face. As she looks out over the peaceful waves, I just take her in. I want to study her features, ingrain them permanently in my memory. Her eyes, like mine, are watching the water with tranquility. The breeze is brushing her soft auburn curls onto her face. I watch as she lifts her lace gloved hand and delicately sweeps the hair out of her eyes.

She turns to look back at me, and I pretend I too have been staring out at the water. I can't let her see the guilt on my face. I know the foreboding secret this water holds for her and so many others. I want to throw my arms around her, tell her what's coming and that it will all be alright. But I can't. Dr. Conrad warned us of the potential catastrophic ramifications if we warned anyone what is to happen.

Everything must go on as history has allowed. I keep reminding myself of his words. I've already told Charlie about the disaster. I can't let myself tell anyone else, especially someone whose survival ensures my existence.

I want to tell her to go walk on the deck with John. Walk with him, slowly. Hold his hand. Take in every morsel of time. Study his face in the sunlight. The way the light hits his black hair, making it look almost midnight blue. The way he walks beside her, stealing glances back at her. The way he still looks at her as if it's the first time he's ever seen her, as if she makes his heart stop even after years together. But I can't intervene, and my complicit silence eats away at me.

John will go down with the ship.

Ancestry records show he placed her into lifeboat eight and then made his way toward where other men were convening, hoping for a remaining spot. Eyewitness records show him aiding others into boats, refusing a spot for himself when he realized how many women and children had not yet boarded. He accepted his fate with quiet, determined grace. He watched over the rail as lifeboat eight made its way away from the ship and out into the cold ocean. He looked out over the water, seeing nothing but the waves and his own breath in front of him. He stole one last glance in the direction of his wife, and was never seen again. His body was never recovered.

Thirty-year-old Violet Kelly will become a widow tomorrow, with two children. She doesn't know it yet, but a third child, a son she names John, is safe in her womb. She will raise her children alone. Her broken heart will become her strength. She'll spend her life raising them with love and kindness to provide them with the best opportunities. She'll advocate fiercely on behalf of women's suffrage in a world not ready to hear her voice. Her children will marry, thrive and have families of their own, leading eventually to me.

I wish I could tell her she'll be okay. I wish I could comfort her, and tell her that the tragedy and destruction that will soon come for her will not pull her under. She will be stronger than the current meant to drown her. More so, I wish I could tell her what a beautiful thing she made of it all. The more I know this strong woman, whose own strength is yet unknown to her, the more I realize why I'm named for her. I can only hope to live a life worthy of her legacy and sacrifice.

More than anything, I wish I could thank her. For changing the trajectory of my life, and for the lessons I am still learning.

Instead, I say nothing.

For now, we stand here, watching the ocean, wrapped in the kind of peaceful silence only real friendship can have.

These are the moments I'll carry with me. Not the grandeur of Titanic, nor the looming disaster. I'll remember the sun on our faces, the laughter shared, and the strength of the bond between two women separated by time but linked forever by blood and grace.

Chapter Twenty-Three

AND SO IT GOES BY BILLY JOEL

April 14th, 1912

The sound of the dinner bugle snaps me out of my trance.

Ben and John appear like clockwork, arriving to escort us back to our cabins to get ready for dinner. *The last supper.* I'm dreading an evening stuck at Edward's table when I want to savor every moment that I can with Charlie.

Ben talks about the shuffleboard games the entire way back to the cabin. He's very excited that he's finally gotten the hang of it and is winning consistently. His voice is lighter, looser than it was earlier this morning. I hear him, but my mind is somewhere else. I'm not sure if he's genuinely excited about shuffleboard or if he's trying to fill the space between us with lighthearted conversation. Are we just avoiding how things went earlier?

We reach the suite, entering through the sitting room. Ben kicks off his shoes and collapses dramatically into a chair.

"So I set the trap for Edward last night," he says, grinning like a cat who's cornered a canary. I'm hoping this means that I was right somehow.

My eyebrows lift. "And?"

"And you're a genius, Al. He took the bait instantly. He's running all kinds of schemes. He's hiding money in other accounts, so it's untouchable. I told him about the underperforming hotel and he suggested an accidental fire that would allow me to recoup the insurance money. He even suggested it would be far more believable to be an accident if it happened during the daytime when employees were present. He's an absolute swine."

I can't say I'm surprised that he's scheming and manipulating his way to the bank, but being willing to sacrifice innocent people for his own gain, that's a new low, even for him.

"What an asshole," I say, the bile rising in my throat.

Ben glances at his pocket watch. "Shit, I've gotta get ready for dinner." He gets up and walks through my room toward his cabin. He's gone before I can bring up this morning's confrontation.

I sit for a beat, staring at the closed door between our rooms. I don't want to keep digging his issue back up or opening the same wounds over and over, but I feel like we need to talk about it. It's not enough to just move on and ignore the elephant in the corner of the room. We need to address it. Are we really going to just act like nothing happened? Is this how it's going to be now? We'll just pretend we didn't say the most hurtful things possible to each other?

When I enter my room, Sarah is waiting with a gown laid out for me. The under dress is an emerald green silk. The lace over dress is emerald with ornate crystal beading. The sleeves are sheer, and a black satin sash cinches the waist. It is truly exquisite, and it is one of the first dresses I feel genuinely like myself in. I slip on black satin gloves as Sarah finishes arranging my hair.

I sit and wait for Ben to be ready for dinner. I look at the clock on the table and grow impatient. I just want to get this over with, and I assumed he would be ready by now. He's the benefactor of not having to wear multiple layers of undergarments and have his hair intricately styled. He finally knocks at the adjoining door and enters as he finishes fastening his cuff links.

He smiles when he sees me, but then looks at Sarah. "You ready?" he asks her.

She nods, smirking.

Where's she going? They're up to something.

Ben turns to me, his eyes gleaming. "Oh, you're not going to dinner, Al. At least, not in the dining room."

"What?" I blink. "Then where—?"

He walks over and takes my hands in his, warmth radiating from his palms. "Look, I know time is running out. I can't give you much. I can't give you forever. But I *can* give you tonight. I've arranged for you to have dinner here on our private promenade." Ben pauses for a moment. "Charlie is on his way."

My mouth opens, then closes again. I was not expecting this, especially after everything that happened this morning.

"You set up a date for me?" I ask, stunned.

He smiles, sheepish. "Well, yeah, but Sarah and Eric helped, too. Sarah delivered the message to Charlie. Eric coordinated room service with the stewards.

Tears sting the corners of my eyes. "I don't know what to say." I am almost at a loss for words and I can feel the tears coming into my eyes. "Thank you."

I suddenly feel nervous about this date, which I don't fully understand considering the intimacy of last night. I excitedly pull off the evening gloves. There's no need for such formality in my room. I'm not sure how Ben pulled this off, but I am grateful.

"I can't believe you did this for me," I say, still in shock. "I thought after this morning that you were angry with me."

"I was. I was angry with you. I was *so* fucking angry. I felt like you betrayed me, betrayed all of us, by doing all this. By pursuing this relationship, and telling him everything. It made me even angrier that you didn't tell me. That hurt me the most."

"Ben, I'm..."

"And I thought about it all day. *Literally all day*. Honestly, my squash game was horrible this morning because of you." He laughs, trying to break the tension. "But what I realized is that my anger wasn't that you didn't tell me, it's that you didn't think you could. You thought you had to go through this alone. That's what truly angered me. You finally fell for someone, and you couldn't tell your best friend. I hate that you felt that way. Even more, I hate that I *made* you feel that way."

"You didn't, Ben," I insist. "It was all me. I was trying to protect you. And it was wrong. I know that now. Trust me, I wanted to tell you a thousand times."

"I'm always in your corner, Ali. I don't care what you do, you're my family. That shit's unconditional. That's why I set this whole thing up."

"Why?"

Tears shimmer in his eyes as he takes my hands in his. "Because once I realized I couldn't pull you back from the ledge, I figured the best thing I can do is jump with you and hold your hand on the way down."

I feel my eyes welling up, overcome with emotion, and I pull Ben into my arms. "Thank you," I whisper in his ear as I tightly grip him. He may never fully understand what this all means to me, this gesture, his friendship.

He exhales deeply as we step apart, his smile bittersweet. "Okay," he says. "Tell me about him."

"What do you mean?"

"We missed this before. It's what I should have asked you instead of being angry. But I'm asking now. Tell me everything. What's it like?"

I pause. Then, slowly, the words spill out. "It's...it's kind of like my soul recognizes his. It's like we belonged to each other before we ever even met. I don't know. I've never felt like this before. He just makes me feel brave. I can share the deepest, darkest parts of me, and instead of a fear of being vulnerable, I just feel honest, safe, and bold. Whenever I'm with him, time feels suspended, as if nothing else exists but us. I just look at him and feel like I'm home."

Ben stares at me, then lets out a low laugh. "Wow."

"What?" He must think this all sounds crazy.

"You're not just in love, Ali. You're *really* in love."

"I am," I say, smiling so wide it aches.

"Are you going to tell him?"

"I... I..."

A soft knock at the door interrupts us.

Perhaps that is for the best. I don't know how to answer Ben's question. I don't know if I am going to tell Charlie how I feel. Part of me doesn't see the point. It won't change anything. Titanic will sink by morning and I'll be back in Boston. Telling him I love him won't stop any of that from happening. I think I'm scared that he won't have the same feelings. I know we've shared something special these last few days, but I don't know if he sees it the way I do, and I'm afraid to find out.

Ben studies me, then grabs both my arms gently, pride in his eyes. He nods toward Eric, who opens the door.

Charlie steps into the cabin as Eric and Sarah step out, leaving just Ben and I. Charlie smiles at me. His smile is always magnificent, but this one is magical.

"You're beautiful," he says, taking my hand in his.

Ben steps back, placing a firm hand on Charlie's shoulder. They exchange a silent look of respect.

"Thank you, Ben," Charlie says quietly.

Ben gives a half-smile and disappears out the door, leaving us alone.

Charlie smiles, straightens his posture, and clears his throat before extending his arm out to me.

"Miss Alice, may I escort you to dinner?" His tone is a comical parody of the formality of the first-class passengers.

"Oh, I would be delighted," I respond, matching his theatrics. I happily take his arm and walk out to our private promenade. A selection of food from tonight's menu, including filet, lamb, potatoes, asparagus, and fresh peaches, is arranged on a small table. Crystal goblets and silver cutlery shimmer in the candlelight.

He pulls my chair out for me. It's an act of chivalry I've grown used to this week, though it comes across as more sincere from him than it did from Edward. His eyes grow wide at the sight of the feast before us. "I haven't had a meal like this in years."

I smile, but also feel a reminder of how privileged my time on the ship has been. While lower classes dine on basics like bread and stew, I've eaten ten course meals with wine pairings.

I'm able to be more myself in his presence, especially now that the truth is out in the open between us. I relax my posture slightly and have my elbows on the table. Charlie unbuttons his jacket and sits down across from me. I pull the crystal comb out of my hair and let my brown waves fall loosely to my shoulders.

"I cook a lot at home, actually," I say as I pour us both wine. "Not anything this fancy, but I do pretty well. Ben seems to like it at least. I taught myself to cook when I was eight so I could take care of Dad. He was hopeless in the kitchen."

I laugh to myself, remembering the time Dad scorched the ceiling in the kitchen one Thanksgiving trying to make us a traditional dinner. We ended up with takeout Chinese food that year and watched *The Wizard of Oz*. It was the best holiday I can remember.

Charlie smiles, as if fondly recalling a memory. "I used to watch my mum cook. She made the most amazing roasts. It's the thing I remember most about her, how much she loved to cook. She always gave me the best piece of crackling off the pork, even though it was her favorite part, too."

"What about your father?"

Charlie hesitates, and I can see the pain in his face. "He...he did his best. When Mum was alive, the three of us did everything together. He taught me everything he knew about carpentry, and it was the plan that I'd take over the shop when they got older. When she passed, he and I were never the same. I take after her so much. I think looking at me was too hard for him. Part of him died when she did, and I was just a reminder of what he had lost. He closed down the shop. He couldn't bring himself to make furniture anymore. Everything she loved he just shut out, including me. He did odd jobs to make ends meet and took up drinking heavily to pretend he wasn't so lonely. I struggled with how much he changed. He was so angry. I was angry too. I was furious he sold the shop without even telling me. It felt like my entire life plan got tossed away without a care. Eventually, I grew tired of it, and I joined the White Star Line and started working on ships. I just wanted to get away. Far away. I was at sea when I found out he'd died. I'll always regret that...not being there when he needed me most."

"Charlie, I'm so sorry," I say, stroking his hand gently.

It breaks my heart that he felt like his father didn't love him just because he was so similar to his mother, though I had similar feelings growing up from time to time. Physically I take after Dad. I have a lot of his features, and obviously my eyes are from his side. But he always told me a lot of my mannerisms are textbook Katherine. I have to wonder if that was hard for him, too. To be faced every day with a living reminder of the person who left you. It is a slight comfort to me that although our lives are quite different, Charlie and I have taken a similar path regarding the complicated relationships with our parents.

"It's alright, love." He smiles, but it's a sad smile. "I've made my peace with it. I choose to remember him now as she would have, when it was just the three of us."

"She would be so proud of the man you are, Charlie." He smiles, and I can tell that means the world to him. I squeeze his hand. "And I know your father would be too." Charlie's eyes glisten with the tiniest flecks of tears.

He clears his throat to compose himself. "What do you remember about your mother?"

"Not much, really. I was four when she left." I exhale, tilting my head back and forth. I'm trying to think of something I remember about her that isn't specifically linked to the day she left. "Although I suppose I remember little things, fragments of memories. She was beautiful, stylish, and fiercely independent. It's silly, but I remember her perfume. It smelled like lilies. I used to watch her get ready in the morning and sometimes she'd lightly spritz me with her perfume, and I thought that made me so grown up and sophisticated." I chuckle to myself as I place two fingers on my forehead and trace my eyebrows. "God, I haven't thought about this in years. But sometimes, when I think about her, I swear I can smell her perfume. That's crazy, right?"

"Not at all. I understand it completely. Sometimes, when I'm all alone, I feel like I can close my eyes and smell London. The wet pavement, the smoky air, the smell of a soccer pitch, I don't know. It doesn't make sense."

"I think sometimes, when a memory is really strong or meaningful, we wrap everything into it. The smells included, you know?" He nods in agreement. "What do you miss most about London?"

"Easy: the food." He laughs as he points his fork down toward his plate. "But sometimes I also just miss going home to the same thing every night, you know? I like life on the sea well enough, but I miss having a home. What about you? What do you miss most about home?"

Home.

If he had asked me that a few days ago, my answer would have been so different. I'd miss small luxuries, like the internet or my coffee maker. But after these last few days with Charlie, it's hard to answer what I miss about home when home is what I see when I look at him. I look into his eyes and feel like I'm exactly where I should be. Home is the space between his arms. I try to think of another answer, something without my powerful feelings attached. I suppose I could say I miss my work, or my house, or Bruins hockey games. But after a few days aboard this ship, in this century, the answer is more meaningful.

"My liberty." I pause for a moment before continuing. I know we grew up in different times, with different customs, and that some freedoms I am used to having may be hard for him to understand. "I have freedom over my voice, my body, my entire life. I have an education, a career, and I own my home. I vote and I make my own choices. I don't need anyone's permission to do the things I want to do. I've taken that liberty for granted. This week has surely shown me that. Does it bother you if I talk about this?"

"Not at all. I like you like this." He listens intently, soaking in everything I say.

"What do you mean, *like this*?"

"When you're Alice. Just Alice." He sits back in his chair, almost as if he's marveling at me. I feel so relaxed in his presence. It's like the truest, most honest version of me is safe to exist with him.

"You know, I've spent a lot of time this week with my great-great-grandmother talking about the expectations put upon women and the confines they live in, and it's made me realize something about my mom."

"What's that, love?"

"I've been trying to make her the villain in my story for so long, and maybe she is. But I guess I never stopped to consider that maybe she was a victim, too. I think what I've learned is that both things can exist side by side. She was clear that she didn't want children, that it wasn't the life she saw for herself. They got pregnant with me by accident, and her family's expectation was that she would wed and do things according to what they saw as the proper way. And she tried. I really think she did. I've always thought her leaving was because of the contempt she had for me, like resentment for the life I stole from her. But maybe—I don't know—maybe it was love? Maybe she loved me enough to realize she couldn't give me what I needed or deserved?" My voice shakes, years of suppressed feelings finally bubbling to the surface. "That's what I believe. That's what I *choose* to believe. And honestly, I think I...I..."

"What, Alice?" Charlie's voice is soft and concerned. He instinctively grabs my hand.

"I forgive her." I lean back in my chair, surprised at the words that I've just said.

Fuck.

This must be what Dr. Kassen's epiphany felt like the day she finally got me to explode. The lightbulb went off. It's as if I've been in a darkened tunnel for years, trudging through, never knowing when it will end, and then suddenly there's light. There's a way out. It all makes sense. I can finally let the pain go. I didn't need any kind of revenge or confrontation. I just needed to understand and forgive.

Charlie was right. I *am* enough. I can see it now as clearly as the magnificent man sitting across from me, with pride bursting from his eyes.

"Fuck." I laugh quietly with surprise, wiping a tear from my eye.

I am not healed, or cured, or anything grand and miraculous. But this is something I now know how to live with, not run away from or ignore. My pain is a part of me. It broke me to pieces, but those shards have been put back together, like a stained glass window. The glass is broken, the cracks are clear to see, but they are rearranged into the most beautiful kaleidoscope of colors. And aren't we all broken in some aspect or another? What I've learned this week is that it's okay to be broken. It's okay to feel lost or overwhelmed. Life is hard. I don't need to have all the answers. It's okay to not have a brave face on all the time. Take it off. Let it rest. Let *yourself* rest. Cry. Scream. It's okay to let yourself fall apart, because putting yourself back together is what makes life beautiful. The past will only control me if I let it. I've learned to let go of what I *should* have done and focus on what I *can* do. Just show up and try. It's that simple. Just keep trying.

"Do you think you'll ever try to find her again?"

"Honestly?" I shake my head. "No. I think a part of me will always want to have some kind of relationship with her, or some kind of resolution. I'll always want to know her. And I'll always want her to want to know me. But now, I realize I don't *need* to know her. If you live your life looking for closure, you're not really living it, are you? I used to think I needed some finality with her to close that door and move on with my life. But I don't think it was ever about her. It's always been me. I can't rely on anyone else to make me feel better, or healthier, or more complete. I had to find it for myself." I straighten my posture slightly. "And in forgiving her, I've realized I had to forgive my dad too, which was far more complicated because I didn't even realize I was angry with him. That's something I'm only realizing now after talking with you. I've never told anyone all this before."

"Well, I'm glad you are. You can tell me anything, Alice."

I feel empowered to keep laying my heart on the table. He makes my pain feel safe in his hands and, for once, I actually want to talk about all this.

"I think I felt like I was a monster if I had anger toward him. When everything happened with my mom, he stayed. He picked up the pieces. I put him on this pedestal because he was the parent that didn't leave. But I'm realizing now that even though he didn't physically leave, he wasn't emotionally there either. He was at every school function or soccer game, but he always had a case file in his lap. He probably missed the best part of my piano solos and most of the goals I ever scored just because he wasn't looking up. He was there, but he wasn't *present*, you know? That's the thing about my childhood that hurt the most. Feeling like I didn't belong anywhere, or to anyone. Mom left. I didn't belong to her. Dad stayed, but he never fully let me in. We existed together, our lines parallel but never crossing. The loneliness of being alone I could manage. But having someone with me and still feeling lonely? God, that almost killed me."

Charlie refills the glasses of wine and raises his eyes to meet mine. "It's understandable though, Alice. You stopped everything to take care of him when your mother left. It's natural to be angry at him. You were a child. You resent him for the loss of your innocence. I know he stayed, but you're still allowed to feel like he failed you. You can be angry and grateful, Alice. You need to give yourself the space to be both."

"You're right," I agree. "Sometimes it feels like we went to a restaurant. They ordered the most expensive things on the menu and then walked out. But I'm still sitting at the table trying to find a way to pay for the bill. They both loaded me up with as much trauma as possible, and then left me to figure out how to fix it." I laugh to myself, surprised at how honest and fluid this conversation has been. "You know, normally conversation doesn't get this deep and emotional on a first date. Though I suppose we have a pass on that for special circumstances."

Charlie raises a brow. "What is a date like in your time, then?"

I laugh. "Well, it's a lot different from here. Not that I have gone on a lot of them. But there's no courting or chaperones. I guess the stereotype is dinner and a movie, drinks and dancing, that sort of thing."

"I'm sorry we don't have any music in here," he says, looking disappointed.

"This is perfect," I reassure him with a smile. This night with him is enough. I don't need any of that. I pause for a moment and quickly realize I actually can remedy the situation. "Wait, hold on, I may have something." I get up and walk over to my trunk. He follows me curiously. I open my lockbox and see it: my phone. "I forgot I brought this." I pull it out and he stares at it with a confused expression.

"What is it?" His eyes carefully examine the phone before looking back at me.

I chuckle to myself. How can I explain something that is so simple to me but probably seems so complicated to Charlie?

"Well, it's a telephone, but also a computer, I suppose."

"A computer?"

"It's kind of hard to explain," I say, laughing.

Charlie tilts his head. "Harder than this already is? Explain it to me. I'll try to keep up."

"Alright. A computer is an electronic device that stores data. In the future, we use them for information, communication, entertainment, just about everything really. Make sense?"

"Hardly, but I trust you." Charlie laughs as he struggles to understand. It's like I'm speaking a completely foreign language to him.

Obviously I won't have any kind of service, but the battery should allow me to access my stored music. I run my finger down to the power button, press, and wait. The screen lights up, and Charlie's eyes follow.

"Remarkable."

"What music would you like?"

He nods his head toward the phone like it might explode if he touches it. "You pick. I doubt I would know anything."

I have a wide mix of music that I listen to during any given mood, but I know much of it isn't suitable right now. I don't think I need to shock him with my music library. I scroll through the options, looking for something slow. Something that would encapsulate this moment. I turn up the volume and make my selection. "And So It Goes" by Billy Joel starts to play.

I set the phone down on the table and turn toward Charlie and extend my arms out to him. "Shall we?"

He suddenly looks nervous. "What do I do?"

"Here, put your hand right here." I take one of his hands and place it around the small of my back. I put my hand on his shoulder. "Give me your other hand." I take it and hold it in mine, and rest my head down onto his chest.

I can feel Charlie unsure of his footwork. His body is stiff and I can tell he's trying to count box steps in his head.

"Hey, don't worry, it's not a waltz. You don't have to step like that. Just relax and sway."

I feel Charlie relax his body against me and move back and forth, calmly swaying to the piano as Billy Joel's tenor voice floods the room.

For a short time, I forget we're aboard a doomed ocean liner. Time stands still and I forget that our time together is quickly running out. It's just us, locked together, in this perfect moment. I hold him tighter and breathe him in. I never want to forget this. I feel his heart beat against my chest and I've never felt more at home than I do in his arms.

It feels as though I'm hearing the song for the first time, or maybe just finally truly understanding it. Billy Joel sings a mournful ballad about a relationship that, although doomed to end, was entirely worth the pain. I have spent my life guarding my heart, hoping to never be hurt again. And I know that within hours, my heart will be broken. But for it to break means it still works. Charlie may be capable of breaking my heart, but he's revived it. He's brought me back to life. And at the end of these magical few days we've spent together, I would do it all again. Even knowing my heart would shatter at the end of the journey, any measure of time with him is worth it. And if the choice were mine to make, I would choose to be with Charlie. I would choose him a thousand times over.

As the song wanes, Charlie looks down at me. His eyes are gentle and adoring, but I can tell he's putting on a brave face for me. He tenderly brushes a curl out of my face and smiles before kissing me deeply. His kiss is tender but desperate, as though he wants to memorize the taste of me before it's too late.

"This isn't fair," I say, my eyes welling up. "We need more time."

Charlie cups my face and gently caresses my cheek, wiping away the tear that's fallen. "I know, love. But we've had more time than I could have dreamed of. And it's been perfect."

I look across the room at the clock on the end table. It's almost eleven. Titanic will hit the iceberg around eleven forty and descend to the ocean floor less than three hours later.

I look back up at Charlie, intent on savoring this moment. I study his face, hoping to etch it into my memory.

"I've spent my life putting up walls, Charlie. I've created armor around myself so no one could hurt me. I didn't let anyone in. I was too afraid. Until I met you."

"Will you promise me something?"

"Anything."

"When this is all over, don't put them back up."

I nod as tears form in the corners of my eyes.

Charlie gently takes my chin between his thumb and pointer finger and tilts my face up toward his.

"Promise me, love."

"I promise, Charlie." I put my head back down on his chest and hold him tighter.

His voice and the comfort I feel looking into his eyes have a calming effect on me. I never want to forget those eyes. I look back over at my phone on the table and have a sudden realization.

I step back and look up at Charlie. "Can I ask for a favor?" He nods, but seems curious about what I could be asking for.

I walk to the table and grab my phone. "Could I take a photo of you?" I don't want to rely only on memories once I'm alone again. Not when I can have something tangible too. Something to remind me this was real and not just a dream.

"With that?" He stares at me, puzzled. "I thought you said it's a telephone."

"And a computer. And also... a camera."

He shrugs his shoulders and shakes his head, impressed at the technology. I open the camera feature and point it toward him. He immediately straightens his posture and folds his hands together, standing still, waiting. He doesn't realize cameras in my time are instantaneous. He doesn't need to hold a stoic pose.

I peer around the side of the phone. "Hey, you can smile, you know. It only takes a second. It's not like your photography."

He laughs, and I immediately tap the button to capture that laugh. I take multiple photos, capturing every candid movement.

"Here, look." I turn the phone toward him so he can see for himself and I swipe through each photo.

"That's incredible. How does it work? Let me take one of you."

I show him how to hold it and what to press. I step back and smile at him.

"I think I did it?" He laughs at himself as he holds the phone up awkwardly.

I take the phone from him and open the photo. It's actually a good picture of me. I'm usually over critical of photos of myself, but I look genuinely happy. I will cherish these photos over any that I've taken of the ship all week. I put the phone back into my lockbox and rejoin Charlie out on the promenade. He's standing at the open window, watching the waves pass by. I feel a dagger of guilt in my chest, wondering what he's thinking about. He hears me approach and slips his arm around my waist, pulling me in close to him. We stand there silently for a moment before I decide to ask a question that's haunted me.

"Can I ask you a question?"

Charlie turns his body toward me. "Of course."

I exhale deeply, part of me not wanting to know the answer to this. "I realize I put you through a lot this week—"

"Alice, you—"

"Yes, I did," I say, cutting in. I appreciate he wants to spare me any more guilt. I know what we've shared this week is special, but I also know that I've caused a lot of damage. "I *have* put you through a lot. I've lied to you. I've hurt you. I've burdened you with the truth of what will happen tonight. Knowing what you know now, do you wish you'd stayed on the Olympic?"

"Not at all," he says effortlessly, as if it took him no thought at all.

"Really? Why?"

"Because it got me you."

"But I'm just..."

"Wonderful." Charlie gently brushes my hair behind my ear. "You're wonderful."

I protest again, fragile. "But you know what's going to happen."

He takes me into his arms, his eyes locked on mine. "And? I'd rather die tomorrow than go a lifetime without finding you."

He kisses me deeply, with one hand around my back and the other on my neck, tracing my jawline with his fingers. I hear the entrance door to our sitting room open, interrupting the passionate moment, and I realize Ben has returned with Sarah and Eric.

There's a soft knock at the adjoining door to my cabin. "Ali? You decent?"

"On the promenade," I call out, giving him the all clear to enter the room.

The door creaks open and Ben steps inside, followed by Sarah and Eric. His eyes sweep the room and he seems surprised at how tidy it is. It's almost as if he expected to find us mid-embrace or tangled in the sheets. As tempting as it is, I just want to spend every moment with Charlie, listening to his voice, memorizing his face and the way he looks at me like I matter.

Ben gestures toward the open windows. "How's it look out there?"

Only now do I realize why Charlie keeps glancing out the window. He's not admiring the night sky. He's looking for the iceberg.

Charlie shifts aside so Ben can look out. "Hard to see anything out there," he responds.

"How was dinner?" I ask Ben.

"You didn't miss much. Just Edward's usual bullshit," Ben replies as he stares out the window before looking back over at me. "He missed you, though."

"Oh, I'm sure he did," I say sarcastically.

Charlie laughs quietly into my neck, his arms still looped around my waist, and the sound sends a warm ripple through me. The five of us laugh together. It's a shared moment of humor that is interrupted by the slightest vibration beneath my feet.

I lock eyes with Ben, and in that instant, we both understand.

Titanic has just struck the iceberg.

Chapter Twenty-Four

HALF OF FOREVER BY HENRIK

April 14th-15th 1912

I grip Charlie's hand tightly. My fingers are cold, but his are colder. We've made contact with the iceberg.

Our eyes lock, and for a moment, the world narrows to just the two of us. It feels as though an invisible hourglass has tipped. The final countdown has begun—for Titanic, and for us. We've made contact with the iceberg. He and I lock eyes and it feels as though the hourglass has tipped to the other side, the final countdown has begun, for the ship and for us.

Somewhere off the icy coast of Newfoundland, Canada, Titanic has sideswiped an iceberg, the result of a last-minute swerving maneuver to avoid impact. The sound of it still rings in my ears. The tremor that moved through the ship wasn't loud or jarring, and most people likely didn't notice it. It was subtle. And somehow, that's worse.

Titanic is mortally wounded.

She had received ice warnings on April 14th, all of which painted a dangerous picture of the northern Atlantic. But she was traveling at a speed of approximately twenty-two knots despite the warnings. When the iceberg was finally spotted, it was too late. Murdoch, trained like every maritime officer to avoid impact, ordered the ship hard to port. There has been a debate for years whether she could have hit the iceberg head on and survived. She likely would only have flooded two to four of the watertight compartments and possibly would have been able to limp to a safe destination.

But that's not what happened.

Instead, the iceberg scraped along her starboard side, slicing open the hull. Six of the sixteen watertight compartments have been compromised. It's a fatal wound—one Titanic was never built to survive.

History asks the age old question: how could it have been avoided?

Was Murdoch wrong to swerve? Should they have heeded the ice warnings and slowed down?

Honestly, who can say?

Anyone can claim clarity with hindsight. That's easy. But if anyone had seconds to make a career altering, life-changing decision, can they honestly say they could choose a different course of action?

History is always hunting for someone to blame. And yes, sometimes there is blame to place. But sometimes, more often than not, tragedies are just that: tragedies. A chain of misjudgements, a cascade of human error, a stroke of terrible luck.

True, things could have been different if they had heeded the ice warnings or if they had seen the iceberg early enough to maneuver. But the moonless sky certainly wouldn't have helped with visibility either, binoculars available or not. A maritime officer trains to maneuver and avoid impact. Perhaps hitting the iceberg head on would not have been as devastating, but that goes against their training.

But now, Titanic is bleeding to death, her fate sealed in ice.

And we stand here, staring at each other, suspended between history and reality, with no clue what to do next.

A thick stillness settles over us. It's not just silence, but something heavier. No one wants to be the first to speak. The first to acknowledge what's just happened, or what it means. Time feels brittle.

Ben finally breaks it.

"Should we... go up to the boat deck?" His voice is quiet and I understand the hesitation. His question isn't really about where to go. It's about whether it's okay to keep moving forward.

I know what he means. Everything we do at this point feels morbid and insensitive.

"I think we should," Sarah says gently. "I know it feels wrong, but... this is why we came. To learn. We can't just look away from the bad parts. It's still going to happen."

She's right, that *was* the purpose of our mission. We came here with full knowledge of what we were walking into, but none of us truly understood what it would feel like to watch it happen. To witness death flood through the ship.

But we're running out of time—literally and figuratively. We have a narrow window left where we can safely move between decks. The ship will take on water quickly and panic will spread just as fast. We need to be able to get back to our cabin before our deck floods.

"Actually," Eric says, stepping forward. "I think Sarah and I should stay here. We need to get the rooms packed up and all our trunks together to make the return quickly if we need to. You three should go and meet us back here."

"Yeah." Ben nods, the tension in his jaw easing. "Good call, Eric."

I move to my trunk and pull out a long green coat. It's heavier than I expected, the wool fabric coarse against my fingers. I slip it on but leave it unbuttoned. The air outside is cold, but I hardly feel it. My body is heated with adrenaline.

Ben glances between us as we regroup in the sitting room. "Okay," he says carefully. "I don't know what it's going to be like up there. If something happens, or we get separated, you all need to hit your buttons, okay? No hesitation. Got it?"

We all nod.

With one last glance behind us at Eric and Sarah, Charlie, Ben, and I head toward the boat deck.

Every step feels heavier than it should. The ship feels darker. Colder. Narrower.

Titanic is dying.

And we are walking straight into the heart of her final hours.

Chapter Twenty-Five

FLESH AND BONE BY CJ STARNES

April 15th, 1912

The boat deck is pandemonium.

People are running in all directions, scared and confused. Some are in search of loved ones, while others are desperately trying to find an open spot in a lifeboat. Every face is the same—twisted in panic.

To my left, a mother clutches two sobbing children to her chest, her face pale with terror. Her husband kneels beside them, whispering assurances that sound more like last rites than comfort.

To my right, a young couple on their honeymoon embrace like they're fused together by fear. He kisses her forehead over and over, pleading with her to step into the boat. She clings to him, reluctant to let go. It's gut-wrenching to watch as her boat is lowered and he jumps into the water after her.

We're on the starboard side of the ship. From here, I watch helplessly as lifeboats are lowering at barely half capacity. Passengers still on board shout, plead, and even jump over the rail in desperation.

This isn't history. It's heartbreak in real time.

I lean over the rail, watching the chaos unfold as I try to steady my breath. I glance behind me at Ben, slowly turning in place as he subtly taps the hidden camera in his walking stick. I wish I could say I envy his ability to compartmentalize and carry on business as usual, but I know he's not immune to the grief that surrounds us.

A sharp tug on my arm spins me around. "Miss Alice!"

Edward.

He's disheveled, his hair slightly out of place and his face flushed, as if he sprinted from the First-Class Smoking Room. He glances at me from head to toe, confused, likely wondering why I'm wearing an evening gown when I wasn't in the dining room. He's still dressed in his evening suit from dinner, but his composure is slipping. His eyes, wide and bloodshot, lock on mine as he grips my wrist with urgency.

"We have a spot in this boat, Miss Alice." He pulls on my arm toward the lifeboat Officer Murdoch is loading.

"No," I say forcefully. I plant my feet, making myself dead weight. His grasp tightens.

"Alice. Now. Come." He pulls again, like I'm his possession to be directed, not a person with a choice. It's not a request, it's a demand. I can feel the anger and tension coursing through his body through his painful grip on my arm. I focus all my energy on getting away from him. He looks down at his hold on my arm, as if surprised I'm not coming along easily for him. He's clearly not used to being rejected or defied. I keep fighting and attempt to pull myself out of his grasp. Pain shoots through my arm, and I twist, trying to break free.

"Don't touch her!" Charlie yells as he steps between us, shoving Edward's hand off mine with force. "Get your hands off her!"

Edward stares at him, stunned by the interruption and the nerve. "Don't speak to me," he growls, finally baring his teeth and showing the monster he truly is.

Charlie ignores him completely, his hands gently resting on my arms as he checks me over. "Are you alright, love?"

I nod, shaken but unharmed.

Out of the corner of my eye, I see Edward step forward, face twisted. He looks between Charlie and I and his expression morphs from confusion to revulsion.

"You? And you?" he snarls. Edward takes another step forward, but before he can get a word out, Ben storms in, eyes blazing. He grabs Edward by the shoulder, and squares up to him, face to face.

"Touch her again," Ben hisses, "and you won't live to tell anyone about this night." His voice is icy and menacing. I've never seen Ben like this. He's always been protective of me, but I've never had to see him under circumstances like this.

Edward freezes. The power dynamic has shifted. I am not worth all this trouble to him. With one last disgusted sneer, he backs away and steps into the lifeboat Murdoch is loading.

"Fools. All of you," he spits, flashing a sly smile. I find it amusing that he only fights back once safely in a lifeboat and a distance away from Ben and Charlie. He's spineless in every sense of the word. I flash him a wicked smile as I take Charlie's hand. Charlie chuckles in amusement, but I also sense a bit of pride from him. I'm glad this is the last sight Edward will have of me as his lifeboat lowers. It's more of a real depiction of me than any he has seen this week. He watches as other passengers attempt to find safe passage off the ship, many jumping to the water or trying to enter the lifeboats by force. There's anger and arrogance in Edward's eyes, but there's fear there, too. It's the first time I've seen anything humanizing in his face. Behind the bravado, he's just a man afraid to die.

Edward survives, of course, because he excels at finding loopholes he doesn't deserve. His lifeboat is safely picked up by the Carpathia. Somehow, he will make it back to New York without a scratch. But he'll use Titanic to his benefit. He'll do interviews and milk the tragedy for every cent it's worth. He marries the twenty-one-year-old daughter of some banking magnate. And they have daughters. *Only* daughters. And while some part of me thinks it's poetic justice—that his precious legacy ends with him, as it should—I also can't help but feel sorry. Not for him, but for those girls. For the father they had. For the gilded cages they must have grown up in. For the coldness in their home that no amount of wealth could warm. But more than that, I hope they stuck it to him. I hope they carved out lives that belonged entirely to them.

Ben leads us to the port side of the ship to collect more data, but each photo feels like the theft of someone's final moments. It's unsettling.

It's almost 1 a.m. Officer Lightoller is shouting orders, supervising the boarding of lifeboat eight. Through the crowd gathered, I spot Violet and John waiting, hoping to board. Violet is trembling, her eyes wide with terror. John is steady, or at least he's pretending to be. He gently cradles her.

Her eyes find mine.

"Alice! Benjamin!" she calls out, desperate.

I push through the crowd and take her hand. She's bundled in a long navy coat, with her life vest over it. Her green eyes are wide, her cheeks streaked with tears.

"My dear, you need to get into the boat." John's voice is smooth as he tenderly tries to coax her toward the lifeboat.

"Not without you," she cries.

"They're calling again. Women and children." John tightens his grip on her. "I'll take the next boat." He gazes into her eyes, silently begging her to be brave. "Darling, please."

She finally sees reason and nods, though it's the most reluctant thing I've ever seen. He kisses her and wipes a tear from her cheek.

She looks back at me, eyes red and puffy. "Alice, are you coming?"

My heart sinks.

"We have a spot in the next boat on the starboard side," I lie. "We were on our way there when we saw you."

She nods, pulling me into a hug. I feel her heartbeat against mine and allow myself to fully feel her embrace. I want to remember everything. With my cheek against hers, I breathe in the scent of roses and warm amber.

"Be brave, Violet," I whisper. It feels as though an invisible baton passes between us, like a plea to continue her work. *I'll take it from here, Violet.*

She pulls away, squeezing my hands. "Godspeed to you, Alice. May we meet again."

Her eyes flick to Charlie, then back to me. Her expression softens with recognition. She knows it's him I was talking about, I can feel it. She understands. Violet flashes me a hint of a knowing smile, as if my great-great-grandmother is granting me her approval. I'm grateful one of my last memories of Violet will be her smile.

John helps her into the lifeboat and kisses her hand. "My love," he says, letting her go.

She cries as she loses his grasp. John stands at the rail and watches the boat lower until he is out of her sight.

Once she disappears, he turns to Ben. "Good luck to you both," he says, shaking Ben's hand. Ben nods, eyes glassy. John fades into the crowd of passengers frantically searching for a lifeline to safety.

I wonder if John knew he wouldn't make it. Was his composure an act for Violet's sake? To get her home to their children? And would things have been different if they had gone to the starboard side instead? Violet boarded lifeboat eight, which was supervised by Officer Lightoller. He was notably stricter than many other officers. Lightoller took the order to mean women and children *only*, while Murdoch interpreted it as women and children *first*. Perhaps if John and Violet had attempted to board one of Murdoch's lifeboats, they would have been able to escape together. I'll never know. But I do know his sacrifice preserved our family.

One step. One choice. That's all it takes to change the course of history. That is both fascinating and tragic.

 Before Titanic's maiden voyage, Charles Lightoller was given the role of second officer, demoting the original appointee, David Blair, who did not board the ship. Blair's exclusion had catastrophic consequences. He held the key to the ship's binoculars, causing the crew not to have access to them, and therefore, a lack of visibility the night of the sinking.

But if Titanic had never sunk, I wouldn't be here. The ship wouldn't be infamous, and there would be no need to study it. I never would have come here. I never would have met Violet or learned the truth of Alice Carney. I never would have found Charlie. I never would have taken a step outside the tiny box I had spent years cramming myself into.

One small choice changed the entire trajectory of my life. I'll never be the same person as the Ali that left Dr. Conrad's lab. A part of me will always be here, with him, and with Violet.

Charlie, Ben, and I huddle together, motionless in the chaos unfolding on deck. It feels bizarre to stand so still while everyone around us is in the midst of madness. Ben checks his pocket watch. We're out of time. I know it from the look on his face. If we want to return to the suite safely, where Sarah and Eric are waiting, we need to do it soon.

The ship has just over an hour before it plummets to its grave at the bottom of the ocean. We have even less time before the upper decks flood. I know that the window of time for a safe journey back to our cabin is dwindling.

But I can't leave Charlie. I don't want to. My heart isn't ready, nor will it ever be.

I know how this story ends, and yet I'd willingly endure the icy waters for another moment with him rather than a lifetime without.

Charlie meets Ben's eyes. The silent exchange is clear: it's time. Charlie knows we need to leave, and he knows I won't make the first move to do it. Like my great-great grandmother, my heart leads me in one direction and logic and reason in another.

Charlie pulls me close. "It's time, Alice." His smile is soft, but the sadness in his eyes undoes me. I can see him trying to be strong for me, but he's anguished.

"No," I whisper. "No, I won't leave you."

I can't let this go. I can't let *him* go.

He clasps his hands over mine. "You have to, love."

I collapse into him, sobbing. Suddenly, the words of Dr. Conrad radiate through my mind, maybe even through my heart.

Anything you're holding will come back with you.

"Anything you're holding will come back with you?" I repeat aloud as a question, almost surprised this idea never occurred to me before now.

Ben's face pales. "Ali, you can't be serious." He knows what I'm suggesting, though Charlie stares at me in confusion.

I turn to Charlie. "Come with me."

"Ali…" Ben warns. "Remember the consequences. We can't change history."

I become frantic. All logic and reason have left my body. I just want him. I want *us*.

"It would work! He doesn't have any family left. It wouldn't change anything. Please!"

Ben looks at Charlie, helpless. He doesn't have the heart to stop me and I think he knows I'm beyond a place he can pull me back from on his own.

Charlie gently pulls me back. "Alice, I can't change my fate. I'm meant to stay here."

"Why can't you? Why can't anyone change their fate? You're *meant* to be with me. Charlie, please, come *home*." I look up at him, my eyes flooded with tears. "I don't want to be without you."

Charlie's hands tremble as he clasps mine. "You never will be, Alice. From the moment…" Charlie's voice breaks. "From the moment I met you, the moment our hands touched on the suitcase, I knew my heart was yours. Wherever I am, wherever you are, it's yours. Keep hold of it and I'll always be with you."

"Charlie," I whisper, broken.

He turns to Ben. "Take care of her."

Ben nods, stepping back.

Charlie gently brushes a wisp of hair from my face. "My Alice," he says, brushing his thumb along my cheek.

We kiss, and for a heartbeat, the world falls silent. My hand wraps around his neck, his hair between my fingers. I memorize the feel of his lips, the taste of salt and grief. His forehead rests against mine and I feel his tears fall on my cheeks.

He pulls back, looks into my eyes, and smiles.

And then he's gone.

Swallowed by the chaos of the panicked crowd.

I feel my entire world crumble around me. I search for a glimpse of him, to no avail. He has disappeared into the crowd as if he never existed at all.

But he was real. And I will never be the same.

I'm almost relieved I couldn't see him walk away, that my last memory of him is the kindness in his smile and the warmth in his eyes. Instead of fear or sadness, his face only conveyed gratitude and affection.

I just can't believe he's really gone.

Chapter Twenty-Six

THE SCIENTIST BY COLDPLAY

April 15th, 1912

Officers are frantically loading passengers into lifeboats as members of the orchestra play somber yet comforting melodies on deck. It's a lullaby for the doomed. The juxtaposition of something so beautiful existing amongst such devastation seems to embody the experience I have had this week perfectly. I've experienced something so beautiful and profound amongst an unimaginable tragedy.

A tug on my arm jolts me back to reality.

"Alice, we've got to move," Ben says, his voice firm but low.

I know he's right. The ship feels unsteady beneath my feet, trembling with each minute that passes, like a wounded creature laboring toward its final breath.

But I feel anchored to the spot in which I stand. I have no momentum or desire to get to safety. I only feel emptiness. I am surrounded by thousands of people screaming, running, and weeping—and yet I feel utterly alone.

Ben catches the look on my face, and without a word, scoops me up in his arms. His strength is astonishing, but what moves me most is the tenderness in it. He pushes through the crowds with me buried in his chest, my hands wrapped around his neck. He shields me from the jostling elbows and frantic bodies, holding me tight like I'm something worth protecting. I feel the thrum of his heartbeat as he forces his way through the crowd, swimming upstream against the current of panic.

We push through a doorway and into the reception area of B-Deck. The floor is slick beneath our feet. Water is rising quickly, like an icy serpent slithering across the decks, climbing higher and higher, swallowing everything in its path.

Ben rests his hands firmly on my shoulders. "Ali, I need you to walk from here. Can you do that for me?"

I nod through my tears. I feel like a ghost of myself. Just an empty shell. But I don't want to do anything that could jeopardize Ben's safety. I would never forgive myself if I let anything happen to him. As much as I don't want to leave, as much as I wish I was back with Charlie, I know it's necessary to go. I may not have the strength to do this for myself, but I *can* do this for Ben. Take a step, put one foot in front of the other, and do the next right thing. I know it's what Charlie would want me to do.

Ben reaches for my hand, and I take it, clinging tightly as we move down the corridor toward our suite.

When we enter through my stateroom, the chaos has already taken root. All the adjoining doors are open, and Sarah and Eric are hustling back and forth, rushing to pack everything they can into the trunks.

Ben leads me toward the sitting room, which has become our departure location. He jumps in to help without missing a beat, heading straight for the luggage cart we used when we first boarded.

I stand in the middle of the chaos, unable to move or feel anything. I watch it unfold like it's someone else's life. The voices around me sound far away, muffled. Like I'm underwater. It's as if the world continues on around me, but I feel unable to stop it. They're all hurrying, and yet to me it feels like slow motion.

Sarah walks toward me and gently takes my hands into hers.

"I've packed all your things, Ali," she says, her voice so gentle I could break.

I can hear her speaking to me, but I somehow can't push words through my tears. All I can do is nod and vacantly stare. She offers a sad, knowing smile, the kind people give when they see someone who's already lost too much. I just don't have anything left in me to give.

Eric pulls the cart full of luggage into the sitting room where I stand. Sarah follows behind him and checks it over, making sure every item is packed and ready. They each check over the staterooms once more to make sure nothing has been forgotten. It feels transactional, like we're hastily checking out of a hotel, minutes before our time is up and we're running around taking every bit of free soap. And yet the weight of what we're leaving behind is immeasurable.

From the promenade windows, I can hear the mayhem on the decks above. People crying out for lost children, for loved ones, for lifeboats that are gone. And yet here I am—safe. Alive. With an easy exit ticket that I don't want.

Out of the corner of my eye, I can see the dinner table on the promenade, still set from my date with Charlie. Our wine glasses sit empty, but the ghost of his laughter lingers there. It feels like just moments ago we were still living in that haze together.

Part of me wants to run right now, while they're all preoccupied, and go find Charlie. Steal one more moment with him. But it's just delaying the inevitable. I'll end up right back here. I'd find him only to lose him again. And I think Ben knows it, too. His eyes stay on me as he moves between the rooms, like he knows I'm on the edge.

As they move around me, I reflect on everything that brought me to this moment. What started as an opportunity to time travel in history has changed the course of my life.

I came here to conduct research on the Titanic, the history of the experience and the story of its demise. Instead, I found something quite different. I found love.

It was not something I intended to find, here or anywhere really, but the moment I saw him, something clicked into place. It was immediate. I tried to deny my feelings, that it was just some kind of intense attraction to forbidden fruit. But I realize now that the moment our eyes locked while grabbing the same suitcase, it was as if something in our souls locked as well.

I was meant to find him, meant to love him. I can lay the blame on fate's doorstep. Fate brought me here to him, and fate is cruelly taking him away.

For the rest of my life, I'll think about what might've been. The life we could have shared if fate had spared us more time. I knew from the start we were doomed. Even before I knew he'd die, I knew this couldn't go anywhere. We are from two different worlds. It's not as if I didn't know how the story would end. I only just avoided it. And yet, knowing all this. I'd do it all over again if given the chance.

I will carry him in my heart for the rest of my life. Even though we have said goodbye, a part of him will always be with me. And for every bit of excruciating pain I feel right now, I also feel grateful. Because loving him—no matter how brief—was worth everything.

And yet, the cruelest irony of it all is that I never even told him I loved him. I believed saying it would make the inevitable goodbye even harder. I thought admitting love for something gives it even more power to break your heart. I thought love was too powerful a word to speak in borrowed time.

But in truth, the goodbye was harder because I didn't say it. I wish I'd had the courage to say it, loudly and often. Because more than anything, he deserved to know. Charlie deserved to know how much I love him. He deserved to be loved out loud, not hidden in the dark shadows of my heart. I never even thought myself capable of love like this.

All my life I've believed that love only brings pain, and I've put up walls to shield myself from that pain. But love brings joy. It also brings pain; I know that. But the joy far outweighs anything else. And the joy gets you through the pain. You can't have one without the other, and that's the beautiful thing about love. It's not about someone shielding you from life's pain, but walking through it with you.

I should have told him a thousand times, every single chance I got. When all is said and done, it matters. When there're no words left to say except the ones that need to be said the most. Those last words are important. They linger, hanging above, long after everyone is gone. Sometimes they're all you have left of someone. And not everyone gets that perfect moment at the end, that closure.

I held my father's hand as he passed, as he left this world for another. In his last few days, he drifted in and out of consciousness as we awaited the inevitable. But in that last moment, he was himself, and it was just us. He lightly squeezed my hand and whispered 'my girl' before taking his last shallow breath and peacefully passing away. And now that it's only a memory I have to look back on, I feel grateful that we had that moment of connection. In the last moment of his life, he knew I was there for him and I knew he loved me. And that is mine to keep.

Ben returns from his final sweep of the stateroom and steps toward me. He takes my hands gently, as if I might shatter.

"It's time, Ali," he says quietly.

His voice is calm, but his eyes betray the sadness he carries for me. He knows I'm not ready, but I don't think any length of time would prepare me for what needs to be done. But time waits for no one, not even for the brokenhearted. I know that for the safety of Ben, Eric, and Sarah, I can't prolong this. I squeeze his hand, not wanting to let go of the one thing I have left.

He leads me gently to the center of the sitting room, where Eric and Sarah are already standing. Eric's hand grips the cart, ready for a sudden surge of water or shift.

Ben opens his palm, revealing his pocket watch.

"Are we all ready?" he asks.

Sarah nods, removing her brooch and clutching it tightly. Eric follows and displays a pocket watch in the palm of his hand.

Ben turns to me, his eyes soft but searching. He nods toward my necklace.

"Ali," he says gently. I'm not sure he has the confidence or trust that I won't back out at the last second as they all leave. Part of me doesn't have the trust in myself either.

"I know," I whisper, my voice a rasp as I reach for my necklace. The ship is creaking and groaning in pain beneath me. With a deep breath, I close my eyes and slide my finger over the button.

It's time.

Chapter Twenty-Seven

FRANCESCA BY HOZIER

April 15th, 1912

The cabin door bursts open, and a surge of seawater sloshes violently into the room. The ship groans beneath us, and yet all four of us are frozen in place. We were seconds from pressing our buttons, and vanishing from Titanic.

But now, we're all staring.

Charlie stands in the doorway, breathless. His jacket is unbuttoned, bowtie missing. His shirt clings to him, soaked. His hair, usually neatly combed, is damp and tousled, like he's run through a hurricane to get here. There's a wildness in his eyes, but it's not panic. It's purpose.

For a long, suspended moment, no one says anything.

I don't trust what I'm seeing. This has to be a cruel joke. My mind scrambles for logic, but all it finds is denial. I'm just imagining him. The grief is fracturing me.

Ben, Sarah, and Eric all gape, their stunned silence make me realize this isn't just in my head. They see him too.

He's real. He's here.

A strangled breath escapes me. "Charlie?"

Without hesitation, he charges forward through the waist-high water, parting through it like it's easy. Like nothing—not sinking ships, not fate, not time—will stop him from getting to me. When he reaches me, he takes my face in both hands.

"Turns out I can't let you go either," he says, voice low, and full of something that sounds like hope.

"What..." I can hardly speak, breath catching in my throat. I never expected to see his face again. "What are you saying?"

My hands shake as I touch him. I half expect my fingers to go right through him, but he's solid. Warm. I feel his heart pounding against my hand like a drum calling me home.

I desperately want to believe this is real. I need to. But I'm terrified. I can't go through another goodbye. It was hard enough on deck. I can't have him watch me leave as the water surrounds him. I don't want my last sight of him to be in the cold, rising water.

He moves in closer, brushing away a tear that spills down my cheek. "I want this. I want *you*."

I have one hand on his chest, and I wrap the other around his neck. I look deep into his eyes and smile in disbelief. Everything falls away—the creaking ship, the icy water, the end bearing down on us. It all disappears when I look into his eyes.

"I love you." My voice is trembling, but I mean every syllable.

Charlie smiles, his eyes glisten with tears in them. His forehead presses to mine, and I feel the soft patter of his tears falling onto my skin.

"I love you, Alice," he says.

"You love me?" I ask, not because I didn't hear him the first time—but because something in me still can't believe it. He's here. He loves *me*. And I want to hear him say those words over and over.

"I do. I knew it the moment I saw you." He smiles, gently tracing my cheek with his thumb. "Take me *home*."

I pull back, just enough to see his face. "Are you sure?" My fingers curl into his hair. "What if it doesn't work?"

"If your face is the last thing I see, Alice Murphy, then I'm the luckiest man in any century." The corners of his mouth twitch upwards, the dazzling optimism in his smile giving me the confidence that maybe, just maybe, luck will be on our side.

I throw my arms around him and bury my face in his shoulder, clinging to him like the lifeline he is. Around us, water churns and groans echo from the bowels of the dying ship, but I've never felt steadier.

Ben steps forward, glancing at his pocket watch. "Al, we're out of time. It's not long before the ship splits. We've gotta go *now*."

I look at him, my eyes searching for understanding. "Ben..."

"Ali, I know better than to stop you when you've made up your mind," Ben says. "Let's go home, shall we?"

He looks to Charlie and gives a nod of acceptance, saying more with silence than he ever could with words.

"All of us," he adds, voice thick with emotion.

I smile and turn back to Charlie. "Are you ready?"

Charlie nods. "With you? Always."

I reach for the chain around my neck, yanking it free. With my finger over the button, I wrap my arms around Charlie. I close my eyes, breathe him in, and hope.

I press the button, and just like days ago, the world is swallowed by a bright light.

Chapter Twenty-Eight

YOU'RE MY HOME BY BILLY JOEL

Everything goes silent.

My eyes are closed, but I know I'm back in the lab.

The smell of Titanic and rising salt water is no longer surrounding me. Gone are the screams of passengers and the sounds of waves crashing against the ship. I stand on solid ground, no water swallowing me. The haunting symphony of Titanic's final moments has been replaced by sterile, humming quiet.

I feel as if I'm in a dream until I feel it. Breath on my neck. A chest rising against mine. Arms holding me.

I open my eyes.

He's here.

Charlie.

Still in his uniform, still in my arms, still alive. The harsh lab lighting washes over him, and for a moment, I don't dare to breathe. I half expect him to vanish, like a figment of my desperation. But he doesn't. He holds me tighter, as if we were always here, always together.

"Charlie!" I whisper, laughing in disbelief.

He pulls back to look at me, his eyes scanning my face like he's trying to memorize every detail. Like he can't believe I'm real either, that this worked. He doesn't even look around the room or take in his new surroundings. His only focus is on me. *Us.* He breaks into a wide, tearful grin.

Before I can speak again, a hand lands on my shoulder.

"Ben!" I turn and throw myself into his arms. Over his shoulder, I see Sarah and Eric, equally stunned but smiling, and I extend an arm to them. "Get over here!"

The four of us fold into each other, laughing and crying all at once. We are forever bonded by this experience, forever changed. Bound by what we saw, what we did, who we met, and who we couldn't save. No one else will ever understand, but the four of us always will.

When I turn back to Charlie, he lifts me right off the floor, spinning me in a burst of sheer joy. I cup his face with my lands, laughing through my tears, and kiss him. I can't believe it worked. When he puts me down, I place my palms on his chest and just stare into his eyes.

It's only us. No time machines. No science. No history books. Just us—two people lost in the same seemingly impossible dream.

Dr. Conrad, from the background we've all been ignoring, breaks the spell with a dry cough. "So... it went well?"

He and Dr. McCoy are standing a few feet away, near the machine that sent us back in time, both grinning. I remember that for them, it's as if we've only just left and come back seconds later. But for us, it's been lifetimes. It's completely wild that we've all experienced so much in the time they took to gulp or blink.

I take hold of Charlie's hand and walk over. I need to apologize. I know I should. I almost destroyed his work for the sake of my heart. I was selfish and acted in my own interests. It worked, which I am grateful for, but I still made a choice that could have been catastrophic.

"James," I begin, guilt heavy in my chest. "I didn't plan it. But I'm—"

"You're not sorry," he finishes for me. And he's right. I'm not. Not for loving Charlie. Not for saving him. I am sorry though for risking everyone's safety and the integrity of their work for my own self interests. I'm sorry for the risk, but not for the choice. He loves over at Ben, then back to me, and smiles. "I'm just glad you're all safe."

Dr. McCoy stares at a screen, scrolling through data. "No major disruptions to the timeline," he mutters, voice caught between shock and relief. "Just a tiny ripple right here." He gestures to a small divergence on the screen.

That ripple is because of me, I know it. Perhaps not even because of Charlie, as he had no living relatives and therefore was the last of his family. Maybe that's Violet. Maybe once she returned to Boston, she looked for me—the kindred spirit she found on the Titanic who vanished without a trace. And maybe she was met with confusion, or even grief. I hope I wasn't just another loss for her to mourn.

Dr. Conrad clears his throat. "At some point, when you're all ready, we'd like to sit and go over this."

Ben raises a brow. "Over what?"

"Everything," Dr. Conrad replies. "The experience. What you saw. What you learned."

They want facts—documents, artifacts, photos. And we collected plenty of it. But what we found wasn't just historical. It was human.

We exchange glances, silently nodding in agreement with each other.

"I think I can speak for all of us," I begin, "when I say this wasn't about data in the end. It wasn't history, or what happened or could have been prevented. It was about *people* and I think each of us got caught up in the human experience of it all more than anything. Maybe I didn't come back with answers about how the ship sank. But speaking for myself, I came back with a deeper understanding of what it means to be alive. I learned how to let go of my pain and my fears and just live. To open myself to not only the possibility of love and happiness, but for the first time, feel like I truly deserve it. I can't thank you enough for giving me the ability to find that. I found something I thought I'd lost forever."

Dr. Conrad watches me with something close to pride. He may never comprehend what we all went through, but he has understanding and empathy for it.

Dr. McCoy leans forward. "I suppose the biggest question we have is: what next? Considering the experience you all had, we're curious to know your opinion on what we should do with this information. This discovery can change the world in more ways than one. We can learn so much. But I realize that each time we open this box, we're taking a risk. Do we shut this down now and pretend we never discovered it, or do we move forward to a new mission to a new historical event?"

"I don't think I should get a vote," I say quietly. "I broke the rules. I put everything at risk for love. I shouldn't get to decide if someone else gets that same chance."

"I want to know what everyone thinks," Dr. McCoy affirms. "Everyone's experience matters, Ali."

I look at Charlie, then back to the team.

"Malcolm, I don't know if I can answer your question unselfishly," I say. "This experience has changed my life. I met people I will carry with me always. We all did. I found a once in a lifetime love that makes me feel like my life has finally really begun, and I could safely bring him home." I squeeze Charlie's hand. I don't want him even for a moment, thinking I regret the decision we made. "But I also realize that I was playing a risky game, and I put everyone in a dangerous position. I know how much could have been destroyed if I took one step out of turn. I don't know if that's something we should do again. What will we truly learn? This was a gift, and I cherish it, but we're playing with fire here. At some point, intentional or not, someone will alter history and then it's game over. I mean, even I almost brought the whole thing down. Can you risk that again? Can you risk your discovery falling into the hands of someone else, someone who perhaps does not have the intention to just learn?"

Dr. McCoy sighs. "I understand that, but to witness history—"

"You're not just witnessing it, Malcolm," I cut in. "That's the thing. You're not *just* witnessing it. You're not invisible. You're part of it. These are real people, this is their real life, and real things will happen to them. Love, loss, all of it. It's real. With all due respect, you weren't there. We got to know these people, learned about their lives, their families, their stories. We heard their screams, saw their fear, watched them say goodbye to their loved ones. I'll never get that out of my head. And I'm telling you, Malcolm, that guilt, of knowing the end and not being able to help them, that will weigh on me for the rest of my life. I don't wish that on anyone. As hypocritical as this sounds, my vote is to shut it down."

Dr. McCoy looks toward Ben, Eric, and Sarah. "And you all share this opinion?"

The three of them exchange a look with each other and nod.

"We do," Sarah says confidently as she speaks for the group. "But in the spirit of compromise, I think we would all be willing to discuss it again if you'd agree to table it for a while. We all just need some time to process this."

Dr. Conrad stands with Dr. McCoy, both looking crestfallen.

"James, please don't be mad," Ben pleads, fearful he has let down his godfather, who hasn't spoken a word for a few minutes now.

Dr. Conrad's frown softens. "I'm not mad, Ben." He pauses a moment, almost as if he can feel his emotions taking over. "What you all went through is something I can never understand. Only you walked that path and only you can speak to what it was like. If you say it's a heavy emotional toll, then I believe you. Do I wish it was different? Of course I do." He gestures over toward Dr. McCoy. "Selfishly, I want the world to know of our discovery. I want us to be recognized. I want to send another group on a time travel mission. But if you all feel so strongly that it's worth putting a pin in the issue and investigating whether it really needs to be done again, then that's what we will do."

I think we all breathe a collective sigh of relief. It's not a win by any means, but it's the closest we'll get to one for now at least. We agree to talk about it again when everyone has had time to digest the experience, letting cooler heads prevail for now. We all recognize that time travel is a monumental discovery. We just want to protect it, and if keeping it out of everyone's hands safeguards it, then so be it. My greatest fear is it somehow becoming a monetized celebrity experience. I don't want to turn on my television one day and find out Elon Musk is at the Battle of Gettysburg or Kim Kardashian is with Neil Armstrong on the moon or Pete Davidson is swooping in on a newly widowed Jackie Kennedy. Money shouldn't be able to buy *everything*.

Ben tugs on Dr. Conrad's sleeve. "James, I need to speak with you," he says, ushering him toward a private room.

I'm not sure what that is about and I hardly have time to worry about it before Dr. McCoy interrupts my thoughts. "Why don't you get changed, Alice? You're soaked."

In all the excitement at the turn of events, I've barely noticed that my dress is drenched. As the adrenaline subsides, I realize how heavy it is and how cold I actually am.

I look over at Charlie and squeeze his hand. "Will you be okay for a moment?"

I have this unfounded fear in my head that if he's out of my sight he may disappear, like this was all in my imagination, simply too good to be true.

He kisses my forehead. "Take all the time you need."

Sarah and I go into a separate room to change, and I am immediately regretting the moto jacket and cropped jeans I wore this morning.

Sarah changes quickly and puts her dress back on the rack. I don't find the task as easy. These clothes hold memories in them. Woven into the threads are the people I'll never see again but have changed me to my very core. I sit down on the bench in the changing room, clutching the emerald gown in my arms. I can't bring myself to let it go. I fix my stare on the trunk and just think about the events that brought me to this moment, and the memories I created in these garments.

Dr. McCoy knocks and enters the room, watching me stare at the collection of dresses. "Ali, are you okay?"

I look up. "Can I keep them?"

Something about being separated from them feels unfathomable to me. I can't imagine I would ever wear them again, but they make me feel closer to Violet.

"Of course," he says gently. He reaches out and takes the dress from my arms. He smiles at me, folds the gown carefully, and places it into the trunk I brought onboard. "I'll have the trunk loaded into your car."

I stare at myself in the mirror, taking a last glance before I return to Charlie. I barely recognize the woman staring back. What if Charlie doesn't either? What if she isn't what he expected or hoped for? What if she's too progressive? What if one day this becomes too much for him? I quickly push those thoughts away. I don't need to think like this anymore, to always assume the worst. Everything Charlie has shown me these past few days makes it clear he fell in love with the real me—every flaw, every sharp edge— and I don't need to be afraid anymore. He loves *me*.

I walk back into the main room. As I enter, I can see Charlie and Ben engaged in a friendly conversation. Ben has already changed, but Charlie remains in his uniform. He stops when he sees me enter and his eyes brighten. I walk up to him nervously. I forget for a moment that he has already seen photos of me in modern clothing. Something about the real thing in person feels unnerving.

He looks me up and down and smiles. "You're still my Alice," he says softly, kissing my forehead. "I suppose I'll need some modern fashions too, yes?"

"Oh!" Ben claps his hands together, except at the prospect of a modern makeover for Charlie. "We are going shopping immediately!"

I laugh. "Baby steps, Ben."

He rolls his eyes playfully.

I know Charlie will need clothes, and I know he will need them soon. But I want to tread carefully with this transition for him and make it as comfortable as possible. I also want him to find his own sense of style in this new world. Right now, I just want to go home.

"Hey, Al. Before you go," Ben says, reaching into his bag. He pulls out a large envelope and hands it to me. "This is for you."

I open the envelope, unsure of its contents and why Ben seems so focused on watching me open it. Inside the envelope is a thick stack of glossy photos, printed as if you went to a kiosk in the grocery store. The first one on the top of the stack is of Violet and I laughing on deck when she initially thought Edward and I were an item. I trace my hand over the photo, over her face, her smile. Something I thought I would have to rely on by memory is now in my hands, to have forever. I flip through the stack to find more photos of Violet and me walking together, talking, and laughing over the last few days. I view photos of Charlie and me, walking together on deck, holding hands, and laughing in the cabin. Moments I thought I'd have to replay in my head can now live forever in my home, to remind me of this experience and the people that have changed my life. The photo of Charlie and I walking on deck is from the night Ben caught us out together, when I gave him some ridiculous astronomy cover story. Ben has been taking these photos longer than I realized.

I gasp. "Ben..." My hands tremble. "This is..."

"Ali, I noticed you changing during this experience. You started acting lighter, more free. I didn't know where it was going, but I knew it mattered. I just started tapping my camera anytime I saw you happy, anytime I saw you being the truest, most free version of you. I didn't expect things to unfold how they have, and I wanted you to have tangible memories to hold on to when we got back. And now, with everything turning out as it has," he nods his head toward Charlie, "I just wanted you to have a reminder that you deserve to be this happy."

I throw my arms around him, crying into his shoulder. For someone who struggles to show emotion in front of others, I sure have broken some walls down over the last week.

"Thank you," I say, voice breaking over each word.

"You? Speechless?" he teases. That's rare for you, Ali."

I laugh through my tears. "Don't get used to it."

Sarah and Eric walk over with their bags and prepare to depart. We share a moment together, just reflecting on what we've collectively been through. I know I, for one, could not have survived this experience without Sarah's support, or Eric's consistent level headed thinking, or Ben's entire existence. I'm sure Ben and Eric bonded, similar to how Sarah and I did. I think we weren't just meant to do this mission; we were meant to do it together.

Before she grabs her suitcase, I pull Sarah aside privately a few feet away from where Ben, Charlie, and Eric are talking.

I lean up against the doorframe with my arms crossed. "Thank you for everything, Sarah. I couldn't have done any of this without you."

Sarah's face curls into a cheeky smile. "You know, I went into this, not liking you at all. I can't even say why," she laughs. "I just think as women, we're sometimes conditioned to see each other as a threat and it makes us want to tear each other down. It's not fair or right, but we do it anyway. But I was wrong and I leave here now with a friend. That doesn't come easy for me. Thank you for making me your friend."

Sarah extends a hand. I pull her into a hug instead. A handshake doesn't seem to capture what we went through these last few days. I can see now that she and I are more alike than I realized, and I didn't recognize the similarities in the armor we've both built around ourselves. We're forever bonded over the transformative experience we both had this week.

"Hey, Sarah?" I ask, just as she's about to leave.

She spins around. "Yeah?"

"Ben and I eat lunch in the quad between Abbott and Whitmer every day if you ever want to join us."

"Are you sure? I don't want to intrude."

I nod. "Of course. You're my friend now. You're stuck with me."

She smiles warmly. "I'll see you next week."

I watch with a smile as Eric and Sarah depart, hand in hand. Ben notices and looks confused, as if he's just putting two and two together. After they leave, he turns his attention over to Charlie and I.

"I guess you'll be going then too, right?" he asks quietly.

We spent all week, the four of us, sharing each other's company. In a world of restrictions and etiquette, we've been a safe zone for each other to let our guards down and be ourselves. I can see in his face he's uncomfortable with going home to an empty apartment while everyone else has paired off.

I smile, holding out a hand.

"Benj, let's go home." I nod my head toward the car waiting for Charlie and I. He looks back at me, almost in tears, realizing that my home is his home and I want him to come with me too.

It's taken me a while to realize that home isn't only a place. It comes in many forms and is different things to different people. It can be a physical place, a literal building you inhabit. But it can also be the people in your life that make you feel safe, and seen, and cherished. The people who hold you through the impossible and bring you back again.

They say home is where your heart is. I used to think that was corny, something that was only embroidered on tapestry and hung on a wall. But it's true. My home is my family, Ben and Charlie.

Wherever they are, that's where my heart is.

Chapter Twenty-Nine

TIMELESS BY TAYLOR SWIFT

The ride back to my house from Dr. Conrad's lab in Concord takes about forty minutes.

Ben has his head in his phone but is chatting away in the car.

Meanwhile, I just sit and watch *him*.

Charlie.

He's gazing out the window, his brown eyes wide, drinking in the modern world with a childlike delight. I tell Charlie all about Boston as the car makes its way alongside the Charles River, with Ben interjecting whenever he looks up. As we make our way toward my house in Beacon Hill, I point out Fenway Park and Chisholm University. I can't help but think about every bit of my life I will get to share with Charlie now. And through his eyes, I'm seeing everything I love for the first time again.

I'm buzzing with anticipation. I can't wait to take him to his first Bruins game. But more than the big things, I'm aching for the small ones. The moments that exist quietly between the milestones: cooking together in the kitchen, Saturday mornings in the park, and summers at the Cape.

Ben once told me, "Ali, you're life is happening without you."

He was right.

But now I get to live it. And not only that, I get to share it with someone.

The car pulls up to my home in Beacon Hill. Ben hops out, hurrying ahead to unlock the front door with his spare key. I open the trunk of the car, and just as this magical journey began days ago, my hand meets Charlie's on the handle of my luggage.

We both pause, laugh under my breath, and let go of the suitcase.

For once, I let someone else carry the weight.

I've spent years taking care of everyone else, shouldering burdens I didn't have the strength to carry. Maybe it's time to learn what it feels like to let someone take care of me.

As I reach the front door, I turn my head back toward Charlie and smile, gesturing to the entrance. "Welcome home."

He steps inside slowly, taking it all in. His eyes widen at the crystal chandelier hanging in the foyer and the large curved staircase.

"Wow. This is... beautiful."

"John had it built for Violet in 1901, right before they married," I explain. "She stayed here until she died, then her grandson—my grandpa—inherited it. Then my dad left it to me." I step toward Charlie and slip my hand around his back. "And now it's *ours*."

His eyes flicker to mine with a smile so full of love that it nearly undoes me. This house has always been full of the echoes of history and family legacy. But now, standing here with Charlie, it doesn't feel haunted. It feels like a beginning. A blank canvas for us, ready to be filled with love, laughter, and possibility.

"I'll save the full tour for later," I say, voice hushed. "But first, there's something downstairs in the basement I want to show you." As much as I'd love to show him all around the house, specifically to our bedroom, there's something else I need him to see.

I lead him down into the basement, flipping on the lights with a soft click. The room glows to life, revealing the rows of polished wooden workbenches and carefully mounted tools. Charlie's eyes widen again as he looks around in amazement.

"My dad was always working on the house," I explain. "He did a lot of woodworking down here. He had every carpentry tool you could imagine."

Charlie runs his hand reverently over the tables of equipment, his fingertips brushing over the tools as if they're relics.

"Alice, this is incredible," he says.

"I want you to have it," I tell him. "All of it."

He turns slowly, eyes glistening, and presses a kiss to my forehead. A teardrop lands on my cheek.

"Thank you," he whispers.

I haven't been down here in years. I couldn't even bring myself to come down and pack everything up after Dad passed away. It was too hard. It felt frozen in grief. But maybe I was just waiting to find Charlie. I was waiting for someone to breathe life back into this space. Into me.

We head back upstairs toward the kitchen and living area. Ben is standing at the counter, opening a bottle of Merlot with theatrical flair.

"I figured we deserved this," he says, sliding the bottle toward me.

I pour three glasses, handing them out as we gather together.

"To new beginnings," I say.

"To new beginnings," they echo as we clink our glasses together.

Ben gently places the cork from the bottle in my hand. "You should keep this one. It's a new chapter. That's special."

My throat tightens. Before I can return a sentimental phrase to him, Ben grins. "I'm starving after all this excitement. What do you say our baby step for today is introducing Charlie to Ray's pizza?"

I laugh at his ability to break an emotional moment with his stomach. "Well, I think that's a great idea." I pull out my phone and quickly order an assortment. It's a Saturday night, so it's going to be at least an hour before it's delivered.

Charlie walks into the living room, exploring quietly. Ben and I lean against the kitchen counter, watching him absorb his new surroundings. He picks up and examines each framed photo on my fireplace mantle and smiles to himself as he watches my life unfold in pictures.

My chest aches with something beautiful.

We'll add to those frames. *We* get to add to them.

"Hey Benj?"

He's staring forward, amused at Charlie. "Yeah?"

"I'm sorry."

He looks at me, surprised. "For what?"

"For everything. For lying to you. For putting you in danger. I should have told you everything sooner. If anything had happened to you, I—"

"Ali," he says, cutting me off gently. "We're good. Always."

I swallow back the guilt. "Are you sure?"

"You're my family," he says. "Always will be."

I can feel my heart swell. *Family.* I haven't had that in a long time.

"Promise?"

He grins. "Trauma bonded, remember?"

I laugh through my tears, though the phrase has a whole new meaning now. "I remember."

"I like you like this, Ali," he says, watching me closely.

"What? How?"

"Happy. Free. In love. It suits you."

I playfully nudge him on the shoulder. "It could suit you too, you know."

He snorts. "Yeah, yeah, yeah, sure. Let's not expect more than one miracle this week, okay?"

But I don't let it go.

"Do you remember what you told me last night, Ben?" He shakes his head. "You said once you realized there was no stopping me, you figured the best thing you could do was to jump with me and hold my hand on the way down. Remember?"

He nods warily. "Yeah."

"Well, I can do the same thing. Whatever journey you go on, whatever path you take, I'll always be there to hold your hand."

Ben slumps his shoulders and looks down at the floor. "But... Ali, I don't want my darkness to become yours, too. Not when you've fought for so long to find the light."

I smirk. "You're forgetting something."

"What's that?"

I lean in close, like I'm about to divulge a secret. "I've been down in that hole. And I know the way out."

We stand in silence for a beat, side by side, sipping our wine as Charlie wanders through the living room.

I let out a small laugh.

Ben glances at me. "What's so funny?"

I smile, tipping my glass toward Charlie. "I had to go to the past to find my future."

The love I have with Charlie is something I never saw coming, and I surely never expected to have to time travel to find it. It didn't come from desperation. It's not a sappy you complete me, I was nothing before I met you, I can never live without you, kind of love.

He didn't save me. I had to do that myself. I had to believe I was worthy of a love like his before I could truly accept it.

It's like in *The Wizard of Oz*, when Glinda tells Dorothy she had the power to go home all along but wouldn't have believed her if she hadn't experienced the journey first. Part of my journey has been finding him and letting him love me so fully. He protects my heart and loves me so completely that I only feel admiration and respect for that love, and not a crippling fear of losing it.

He didn't complete me, but he helped me complete myself. He's the instruction manual to all the pieces I already had. He turned on the light so I could see what I'd been carrying all along.

And I believe that's the best kind of love. I can live without you, but I don't want to. I wasn't nothing before I met you, but I'm even better because of you. It's giving someone the power to break your heart, and trusting that they won't. Because what you've built together is too sacred to shatter.

Ben wraps an arm around my shoulders and pulls me close. I rest my head on him. Charlie looks over at us and smiles.

I can't stop staring at him, wondering if this was all a dream.

Most of all, I just feel incredible gratitude.

For our safety.

For this incredible journey.

For the miracle of *now*.

There will be hard days ahead. Charlie will work through survivor's guilt, as will I. And the acclimation to life in the modern age will surely be full of adjustments for him. I feel grateful to be here at this moment, safe at home with my family, the two people I love most in this world. Right here, right now, I am incandescently happy.

Instead of fear, I am full of hope.

For tomorrow.

And all the tomorrows to come.

I cross the room and wrap my arms around Charlie, holding him tight.

"What now?" I whisper.

He smiles, cupping my jaw in his hand. "We have nothing but time, love."

Time.

It's a curious thing, isn't it?

You can't see it, but you can feel it pass by.

It flies. It waits for no one.

You can't turn it back.

Or can you?

Epilogue

FOREVER BY DROPKICK MURPHYS

One Year Later

The sun shines brightly through the trees, their leaves bursting with vivid hues of orange and red. There's warmth in the air. This may be one of the last mild days lingering from summer before the chilly, brittle autumn takes over.

I sit on my usual bench in Boston Common, now officially known as the Samuel Murphy Memorial Bench. A small plaque bears his name, a tribute to my dad, who once occupied this very seat during his Saturday morning park routine. In a way, it ensures I always get to sit with him. He continues to become a part of my Saturday tradition as I now share it with Charlie.

I sit propped against the rail on one end of the bench, my legs stretched out and crossed at the ankle, with a book open in my lap. Charlie sits at the other end with his legs crossed, reading through the real estate advertisements in the newspaper for commercial space.

The past year has been an adjustment for him, for both of us, really. I've gone from living alone to having a partner in life. Someone by my side every day that pushes me to be the best version of myself that I can. Charlie has been working to adapt to an entirely new century and all that goes with it. But he's done it with grace, humility, and a quiet determination that never ceases to amaze me. Watching him experience things for the first time has made me realize how much I take for granted. But it's also made me appreciate the small things.

Soon after settling in, he began picking up carpentry again, revisiting all the techniques his father taught him. It helped him still feel connected to his family while he settled into a new life. He started with re-furnishing my office at Chisholm, which impressed most of my colleagues, and he had a growing list of clients from there. Eventually his business grew, and now we're looking for a larger retail space for him to showcase his work. He's fortunate to have learned woodworking from his father and bookkeeping from his mother. His shop, *Two Worlds Furniture*, is a nod to the circumstances in which we found each other, and remains a private joke between us.

My phone buzzes in my coat pocket, jolting me slightly. Ben's picture lights up the screen.

Ben: Hey Al, you still picking me up at the airport on Friday?

Me: We'll be there! How's vacation?

Ben: It's been great. Mom and Dad seemed to really like Peter. We stayed with them at the beach house for a few days and then drove up the coast to Napa. It was awesome. I've got lots of wine for you! I'm ready to get home, though.

Me: Just in time for the home opener!

Ben: Hell yeah! Even though I have to fork over a fortune for my own season ticket now that you've got yourself a permanent plus one.

Me: Haha, well I'm not sorry about that. Have a good rest of your trip, Benj. I'll see you Friday.

After we got back, Ben walked straight into the coffee shop and asked Peter out. It was an even bigger deal when, after three dates, they were still seeing each other. Ben was upfront from the beginning and it turns out, Peter doesn't want kids either. They both just enjoy each other's company and the independence they have. They're even talking about moving in together. It makes me happy that Ben found someone who shares his interests and his dreams. The family I've created for myself continues to grow, and I'm endlessly grateful.

I wondered for the longest time what to do with all of my research on the Titanic. From my independent research to the journey we had back in time, there is so much I wanted to say. So much that needed to be said. I could think of no better service to those I've met and lost, those who have forever changed me, than to ensure that they were not forgotten. I can't do much, but I can make sure history hears their story, as they would tell it. I combined all my work and experience aboard Titanic to write a novel. The novel Violet intended to write but never had the chance.

Not long after we returned from 1912, I went to my closet, lifted the loose floorboard, and found her rough drafts. Faded but legible, raw and powerful. I used them to create the foreword for my book.

I sit on the bench reading the first proof of my work. As proud as I am of every word I wrote, it's Violet's foreword that moves me the most. She may have thought that she wasn't the kind of writer suited to author a book, but she was. Her words are bold and assertive, but also relatable and poignant.

> *I am Violet Kelly. I am a wife. A mother. I am proud to be.*
> *I am a suffragette. A feminist. A voice for change. I am proud to be.*
> *I am also Alice Carney. I am proud to be.*

> *Women can be so many things.*
> *There is no limit, no cap, no ceiling.*
> *We have the power to change.*
> *We have the capacity for goodness.*
> *We.*
> *The strength is within us when we act as one.*

> *So, yes, I am Alice Carney.*
> *But the point is:*
> *aren't we all?*

I close the book gently and run my hand over the embossed title.

> *We Are Alice Carney:*
> *The real life of Boston's Suffragette*

I twirl the locket around my neck between my fingers. The familiar etched rose pattern underneath my thumb is grounding. Violet's presence is always with me now—close to my heart.

I look over at the carousel and remember all the Saturdays in the park with Dad. The horses continue to race in circles, moving up and down. A little girl in blonde pigtails and pink overalls rides Duchess. I hope she has fire in her soul. I hope she stands on our shoulders and makes the world even brighter. More than anything, I hope she has someone behind her fanning those flames and telling her she can.

I once thought to myself how life is like a carousel, cyclical and full of ups and downs. Maybe it is. But now I have someone riding alongside me. Someone to share my pain, my triumph, my joy.

Life can be heartbreaking. You keep your head down and just suck in the darkness, inhaling it like heavy smoke. It feels as though the only choice you have is just to endure it, to wait out the storm. It can feel so dark you can't imagine it ever being okay again. But it will. The pain won't hurt forever. One day, when you least expect it, you'll look up and see the sun has come back out. You'll feel it shine on your face and realize you've survived, that you're stronger than you ever thought you could be.

The memory never goes away, but the peace you find weakens its punch. Maybe you find that peace in someone else. Maybe you find it in yourself. Or maybe even both. Wherever you find it, hold on tight. I smile at Charlie with a grateful heart.

My eyes glance down at the book I am so proud of. A book that is mine and tells the story of my family, weaving the past and the future into one. A book that bears the name that I am proud to have.

At the bottom of the cover are the words:

Alice Hughes

Epilogue

THANK YOU AIMEE BY TAYLOR SWIFT

Two Months Later

The doorbell rings.

"I'll get it," I say as I rise from the couch. "Pause the movie, babe."

Part of Charlie's acclimation to the modern world has included us working our way through the American Film Institute's list of the top 100 movies of all time. For obvious reasons, we will skip *Titanic*. This week's selection is *The Godfather*.

"We go to the mattresses," I mumble, quoting the movie in a poor attempt at a Sicilian accent as I walk toward the front door.

I grab the doorknob and quickly open it. A woman stands across from me with a canvas tote bag over her shoulder. Her eyes widen as our gaze meets. She nervously brushes a brown curl behind her ear. I inhale sharply, and she notices my startled expression.

"Hi. I'm sorry to intrude." She takes a deep breath. "My name is—"

"Mom?"

She steps back, as if surprised I recognized her.

"Alice."

"Wh-what are you doing here?"

She looks terrified. "I came to apologize. You can shut the door in my face. I understand if you do. But I'd like to explain myself, if you'll let me."

I wasn't expecting this tonight—or ever. She's right though. I can just shut the door in her face. This is my house. My life. I can move on as if this never happened. I've already put this chapter behind me. I've put *her* behind me. I don't need explanations for why she left. I don't need apologies. I've grown, and I've found peace.

I want to shut the door, and my hand is almost ready to push it, until something in my heart reminds me that while I have found peace, maybe she hasn't. Despite all the anger and resentment I carried against her for years, I just feel pity for her right now.

"Come on in."

Her eyes brighten when I invite her inside, as if she wasn't expecting to make it past the metaphorical front gate. Truthfully, I'm surprised at myself.

She steps into the foyer and looks up at the crystal chandelier. I watch as her eyes sweep over the entryway and into the front den.

That's where you put me when you left me. Do you remember?

Her hands tremble slightly, her breathing shallow, like the house itself is suffocating her.

Good. I hope you're uncomfortable.

I take a deep breath and her perfume hits me. She still smells like lilies. The reminder makes me feel four years old again.

"Can we talk? I thought this might help." She reaches into her tote bag and pulls out a bottle of red wine. Despite not seeing each other in over twenty years, at least that she's aware of, we somehow have the same taste in wine.

"Yeah," I reply stiffly. I'm still unsure what this is about and I'm doing my best to keep a tough exterior. "Kitchen is this way." I motion toward the hall that leads to the kitchen and living room.

"I remember."

Right. This was your house once too. Thanks for the reminder.

The temperature between us is freezing, the silence tighter than a piano wire. I don't want to punish her with harsh words, despite the urge to get a few deserved barbs in. I swallow the sarcastic comment I feel coming up my throat.

She follows behind me silently to the kitchen. Neither of us knows what to say to break the ice.

As we approach the kitchen, Charlie is standing at the counter making himself a cup of tea.

"Who was at the door?" he asks, not looking up.

I clear my throat to get his attention. He looks up and seems surprised that someone is behind me.

"Oh, I'm sorry," Charlie says. He pulls the tea bag from the cup and tosses it into the garbage. "I didn't realize we had company."

"This is my mother, Katherine," I say. Charlie's eyes widen as he tries to keep his jaw from hitting the floor. His eyes immediately search mine, as if he instinctively wants to know I'm okay. "Mom, this is my husband, Charlie."

"It's nice to meet you, Charlie." She smiles as she extends her hand out to him.

"It's nice to meet you as well," he says politely.

She sets the wine down on the counter. I pat Charlie's arm gently. "Could you grab us a couple of glasses?"

He pulls the glasses down from the top shelf of the cupboard while I rummage for the corkscrew. He leans over close to my ear and whispers, "Do you want me to stay with you, love?"

"No, I'll be okay. I need to do this," I whisper back. I love him for wanting to support and protect me, but this is something I need to do alone.

Out of the corner of my eye, I see Mom running her hand down the doorframe of the kitchen, her fingers tracing the notches of my growth over my childhood, as if measuring every year she lost with me.

"Alright. I'm headed downstairs to the workshop," he says in a louder voice. "It was lovely to meet you, Katherine."

"You as well," she says, watching him kindly. He slips his hand around my waist. "You sure you're okay, love?" I smile and nod. He presses his lips gently to my forehead. "I love you," he whispers.

He heads downstairs, and I direct my attention to opening the bottle of wine.

"He seems lovely," Mom offers, settling into the couch.

"He is," I answer quietly, without looking up.

"How did you meet?"

We don't have enough wine to get into that.

"It's a long, complicated story."

I set both glasses of wine down on the coffee table and settle into an armchair across from her.

The silence between us is thick and suffocating. Subconsciously, I run my hand through my hair. When my gaze flicks upward, it's like looking in a mirror, because she is doing it too.

She looks over at the mantle, observing the photos of my life. Alongside my childhood photos of Dad and me, are photos of the family I've created for myself. From Ben, Peter, Charlie, and I at a Bruins game to Charlie's first Thanksgiving. In the center of the mantle are photos from mine and Charlie's wedding at the beach house in Cape Cod, including one of Ben walking me down the aisle.

"I can't believe you're all grown up. You're married. I've missed it all."

"Yeah, that happens when you leave."

No. I'm not gonna let you walk in here and put on a goddamn Mother Teresa martyr act. You missed this because you left. You.

Her face tightens. "I know, Alice. It's my fault. I know that. I wasn't ready." She shakes her head and leans forward before I can respond. "I know that's no excuse. You deserve an explanation."

"I don't need one."

"You still deserve one. I failed you. I wasn't ready to be a mother. I didn't want to be a mother. That doesn't mean I didn't love you. I need you to know that."

"I *do* know that."

Her eyebrows lift with surprise. "You do?"

"I understand why you left. I didn't always, but I do now. I was angry for years, and that anger hardened me. But eventually, I chipped away at it, and I grew. I found love. I found peace. And I moved forward." I take a deep breath. "You don't need my forgiveness. I've already forgiven you."

She stares at me, stunned. "You have?"

"It took me a long time to figure it out, but I eventually realized that you left because you *did* love me. You knew you couldn't be what I needed, so you took yourself out of the equation. Was it brave? Was it cowardly? Was it the right thing to do? I don't know. I can't answer that. But it seems like we both turned out okay."

"I want you to know I loved your father very much," she whispers. "I just couldn't be what he needed me to be."

"I know." I look over at a photo of Dad and me on the mantle.

Her eyes follow mine to the photo. "Did he ever talk about me?"

"After the day you left?" She nods her head. "No." She gulps as she takes that in, as if it was a hard pill to swallow. "He could never find the words. It was too hard for him. He was heartbroken."

Her face looks ashamed, as if pleading guilty to every charge leveled against her. "I hated myself for hurting both of you."

"I hated you for it too."

"I deserve that." Her eyes curve as she looks at me sadly, as if I'm bruised and battered from a lifetime of being tossed aside.

"But Dad... he gave me a great life, okay? Maybe we didn't talk about things we should have, but man, we had fun together. He tried. He did the best he could with what he had. We both did. So don't look at me like I'm a little bird with a broken wing, alright?"

"You're right. I'm sorry."

"Why are you here now?"

She takes a sip of her wine and looks down. "A few weeks ago, I found a lump in my breast." My eyes soften as concern settles into my face. I surprise myself with how quickly the worry comes. She looks up and seems just as surprised. "Oh, it's nothing. It turned out to be a false alarm. But in that period of not knowing if I was dying, not knowing if I was running out of time, I evaluated my life and the decisions I'd made. When you think your life might be ending, that's when you realize the mistakes you made at the beginning." She takes a deep breath. "It took me years to do, but I confronted my feelings about leaving you. I didn't want to be a mother, and I still believe that leaving put you in a better position than if I had stayed. But, I still regret it. I regret hurting you. I regret hurting him. I wish it could have been different. I wish *I* had been different."

I realize if she had shown up on my doorstep a year ago, this conversation would be far more hostile. I would not be nearly as calm or collected. A year ago, I thought I would unleash years of pent up rage on her if I ever saw her again. But now, after everything I've been through, everything I've learned, all I want is for her to let the pain go as I have.

"You can't live life constantly thinking like that. You don't need my forgiveness. You need to forgive yourself. That's the only way you can let the pain go."

"When did you get so wise?" She chuckles through a sniffle. "Last time I saw you, you needed help to tie your shoes."

"That wasn't the last time you saw me."

Her brow creases. "What?"

"There was an art showing. Not long after Dad died."

She gasps. "Oh, my god. I... I remember. That was you?"

"I wanted to confront you. I was going to demand an explanation. I came in with guns blazing. I wanted you to hurt, like you hurt me. But then, the moment I saw you, I froze. I couldn't bring myself to do it. I saw you, and I felt like a child again, unloved and unwanted."

Mom leans over and pulls out a small black wallet from her tote bag. She lifts the gold clasp and pulls out a folded and worn piece of newspaper. She hands it to me.

Riverview Academy senior Alice Murphy with two goals in state championship win

"You kept this?"

"I've always loved you, Alice." She takes a deep breath. "I know you don't need a mother. Look at you. You're incredible. And I know I do *not* deserve the title of mother. But, I'd like to know you. Maybe as adults, we can carve out a small space and make it our own?"

I pause for a moment. "I... I'd like that."

"You would?"

"I would."

A grin extends across her face. I don't know what kind of relationship we will have. The battlefield between us has been fought on for years. But maybe, together, we can pick up the debris and make it something new. Not a typical mother daughter relationship, but something that works for us.

We sit and chat while we finish our wine. She tells me about her life and her art. I tell her about my job and my life with Charlie. It's awkward. But it's a start.

As I walk her back to the front door, she looks around. "It looks the same. And different."

"Dad did a lot of work on it."

Her voice cracks. "He did a great job. With the house... and with you."

"Thank you." I look around at all the renovations he made. It makes it feel like he's here. I hope he can hear her. I hope he has found the peace that I have.

She turns around on the front stoop. "Alice? Thank you for not shutting the door."

I nod. "It's open anytime."

Acknowledgements

It is not lost on me that I am surrounded by people who make me better. I could do none of this without the love and support of people who are far kinder and smarter than I am.

Emily Tudor, my twin mirrorball—You listened to my wild dream and told me to write it down. Thank you. I love you. This is all your fault.

My parents—Thank you for raising me with the belief that the world is mine and that the only person I ever need to be is myself. You have always been supportive of wherever my dreams have taken me. I know we don't do emotions, but I love you both so much. Mom, please let's never talk about chapter nineteen.

Mental illness—This wasn't possible without you. A chemically imbalanced brain is both a blessing and a curse. As Carrie Fisher once said: "Take your broken heart, make it into art." Carrie's words echoed in my heart alongside Alice's story.

My found family—We all have a family by blood, but I've been fortunate to create a family by love. Tristin, you are an infinitely better person than I'll ever be. You have the biggest heart of anyone I know.

Your friendship is one of the things I am most grateful for in life. Josh, I'm glad the darkness in my brain found a friend in yours. If I only had $49 left, I'd give it to you, Mikko San. Roger, thanks for letting me talk to you about Jeff Jeff and for our daily "I hate it here" chats. The world is a better place with you in it, Rubble.

My Lyell Crew—Thank you for embracing me and all my quirks. You let me yap constantly about the stories pouring out of my brain and have constantly supported me along the way.

Taylor Swift—You'll never see this, but your words have taught me that every feeling, big or small, means something. Thank you for writing the soundtrack to my life.

My beta readers—Kathryn, Allyssa, Alison, Lauren, and Emily. Thank you for reading this in every phase of its development, but always seeing Alice's heart.

Scott—Thank you for the most beautiful cover. You are so insanely talented. Your art brought my story to life in a way I never could have imagined. I am forever grateful.

My dog, Bowie—You were no help at all, but I love you.

Daryl—No matter what I may write, our story will always be my favorite. Thank you for always being my home. I love you endlessly.

Me in July 2023—I bet you never imagined a vivid dream would turn into this, huh? You thought your carousel would never stop spinning. Look around and enjoy the ride. "You're on your own, kid. You can face this."

And finally, to you, the reader—I hope you find a little piece of yourself between these pages. Thank you for breathing life into my words.

About the Author

Shannon Carse enjoys writing about love, in all the forms it comes in. She is an avid sports fan and a proud member of Bills Mafia (Go Bills.) She loves true crime, Taylor Swift, and drinking too much coffee. Shannon lives in Rochester, New York with her husband, Daryl, and their dog-baby, Bowie. Between working full time and chasing her dog, who enjoys barking at nothing and stealing socks, she squeezes in a little time for writing.

You can find her on Instagram at:
@authorshannoncarse

www.ingramcontent.com/pod-product-compliance
Lightning Source LLC
Chambersburg PA
CBHW021338150726
47989CB00005B/2031